Kia Lui Media, LLC

LOVE'S AWAKENING

A BILLIONAIRES OF MISSOURI ROMANCE

The Beginning

KIA LUI

This is a work of fiction. Names, characters, places and incidents either are the product of the author's imagination or are used factiously. Any resemblance to actual persons, living or dead, events, or locales is entirely coincidental.

Love's Awakening
Copyright © 2019, Kia Lui
Self-published by Kia Lui Media, LLC
(bluekelela2@kialuimedia.com)

All rights reserved. No part of this publication may be reproduced, stored in a retrieval system, stored in a database and / or published in any form or by any means, electronic, mechanical, photocopying, recording or otherwise, without the prior written permission of the publisher.

ISBN: 978-1-7333198-0-5

Cover design by Creative Chameleon by Design

Cover images by Kia Lui © Kia Lui Media LLC

www.kialuimedia.com

Printed in the United States of America

This novel, my pen name, Kia Lui, and my publishing company, Kia Lui Media LLC, are dedicated to my mom. We took a detour in our lives we never expected. We are still going strong.

ACKNOWLEDGEMENTS

Thanks to all my Angels who walk with me daily, who protect me, who value me and who support me.

Thanks to the WIP group. I was terrified at our first meeting. I had actually rejected attending twice. To this novice writer, your knowledge, advice, critiques and reactions to my writing makes me proud and lucky to be a part of your circle.

Thanks FAS for being my best friend over the years. You are my sounding board, my memory holder, my headache and my shoulders when mine have become broken over the years. Immaturity through maturity, you probably will never understand how valuable our friendship is to me. Trust and believe it has meant a lot over the years.

Thanks AKF. Laughter is your God given gift. Thanks for listening to me and giving me advice. Thanks for allowing me to bend your ear. Daily. Even when you couldn't follow the topic and I had to say "Okay detour". You detoured right along with me. You deserve, earned and needed that place in my book.

I can't list all the names of family and friends. Thanks for putting up with me while I worked to get this, my first book published. You hung in there and listened to me. Thanks for your support. It is very much appreciated.

You end up where you are supposed to be,

when you are supposed to be there--LAD

Introduction

Barcelona, Spain.

Three men are sitting on the balcony of a beach house watching the party going on below. Usually, they would have the party moved; hell, this beach is part of their private land, but none are interested in doing that. Free entertainment.

"Are we seriously considering giving all this up?" LD asks.

"Man, all of what? All this fake ass. Yeah. I'm ready," ZL responds.

"What about you?" LD says as he nods at BM.

"It would be nice not to travel for some ass. Have one at home waiting." BM says staring out at all the nakedness in front of him. "To our home."

"Man, look at them. I can't even get a soft rise out of this. They just displaying it without any discretion at all. I don't want mine, the one I make my wife, out here displaying hers like this," BM muses.

"LD, instead of you wearing a pussy out in a thirty-six-hour marathon, wouldn't you prefer to leisurely enjoy some ass and to have a woman know you and want you and desire you for you and not your money? You can't tell me that isn't something you haven't given some consideration to," ZL asks LD.

"Not often."

"Yes, often. You may be the younger one between all of us but you smart man."

"Look, we not saying bag the next one you meet into marriage. We just saying it's time to stop with all this variety. At some point we all must stop with this variety. At forty-five, I'm getting tired of it," ZL says.

"As we all know, we like what we fucking like. We three stubborn billionaire bachelors considering, and I fucking can't believe I'm saying this, we're considering, ALL OF US, settling down, getting married, and stopping this lifestyle we have put ourselves into," BM says.

"Y'all ready for the possible heartache and headaches. Y'all ready to open y'all selves to emotions, feelings, even love. Sharing, having to think of someone other than your family?" LD asks.

"Shit, why the fuck you gotta point that out?" ZL says laughing.

"Because that's what a relationship, a marriage will involve," LD says.

"I'm ready," BM says.

"I'm ready," ZL says.

"Peer pressure fucking blows," LD says.

"Man, this ain't peer pressure. You don't wanna do it, then don't do it," BM says.

"Oh, he will. He can't stand his life. It will hit him soon enough," ZL says.

"Actually, I'm probably readier than any of you can imagine. I've been in therapy. Yeah, I know. Me in therapy. Yeah, I'm ready," LD says.

"Well, let's drink to love, happiness, and marriage. For us all. Here's to the Billionaires of Missouri Club and their soon to be wives. Agreed?" ZL asks.

"Agreed," BM says.

"Agreed," LD says.

-1-

Today is gonna be a great day. That's my mantra every morning. Today is gonna be a great day, Lea says to herself.

Lea Adams, the head of her department for a technology consulting firm, is running in fifty different directions. Or her mind is at least. She is thinking about the three meetings she has to facilitate; one to a potential client, and two others for client updates whose office technology needs her firm, will be implementing or hoping to implement. Today is leg day with her trainer, something she still wants to get out of after a year of going. And her craving for an Asiago Cheese bagel with cream cheese, apple butter, and a cranberry juice won't go away.

Off to work she goes. Her drive to the office in downtown Clayton takes only twenty minutes. Being centrally located in St. Louis is perfect because practically everything is twenty-thirty minutes away. Anything beyond thirty minutes becomes forty-five minutes because of traffic. With her trusted books on audio, while she is driving, she gets to listen to all those books she can't make time to sit down, sit still, and read. Today it's "What Dreams May Come."

As she arrives at work, speeding into the garage, she checks the car's dashboard clock. Thirty minutes early. Enough time to get to her desk, check emails, adjust her clothing, refresh her makeup and get into her, 'time to socialize zone' for her meetings.

Lea is an introvert, or she considers herself one. The only part she hates about her job is presenting to clients or socializing with people she doesn't know. Her friends and those she are close to would not say she's an introvert. They would say she's open, warm, caring and fun to be around, until you get on her bad side. Before Lea gets to know people and feel them out, she gets tongue-tied and freezes up. Hell, certain situations give her panic attacks and make her sick to her stomach and break out in a cold sweat. She avoids networking events at all costs. If a job depended on her networking, she was not going to get that job.

Lea is also single. Has been single for more years than she wishes to admit to. It's not that she wants to be single. She desires love, marriage, and companionship as everyone else does.

She's around plenty of men on a daily basis, working in a male-dominated field with plenty of available men. None have approached her for dating. Maybe that is stretching it. There was one, but that fell flat. She could have dated him, shown more interest in him than a working relationship but after their first date he backed off. No interest.

Men have been backing off her for years now. Even when she showed interest in them. It got to be so discouraging, she labeled men as weak.

If one isn't moving on her like a Mack truck barreling down a highway, she doesn't give him a second thought. Weak men bore her.

She refocuses her mind on the days schedule ahead of her.

The zone, Lea, get into the zone.

She steps out of her trusty Acura TLX evaluating herself. She is wearing a pencil hip hugging skirt, green and black, a crisp black blouse, tanned heels, practically the color of her legs, minimal jewelry, and her favorite scent from Pure Romance. She checks to be sure she has everything; lunch bag, phone, keys, and purse. Off she goes.

She exits the elevators from the parking garage entering the office building. As she walks toward the lobby, coming out of the door from the garage, she walks through an atrium and past the tables and chairs for the small café. It's empty except for one gentleman sitting in the corner, staring out the window.

She doesn't know why he caught her attention, she can't even see his face, but he did. She shakes off the feeling of wanting to stare and keeps moving.

That there Adonis is so out of my league, she says talking to herself.

Yes, I talk to myself. Some of the best conversations I have are the ones I have with myself.

At five feet, seven inches tall, one-hundred and fifty pounds with caramel brown skin, Lea knows she blends into the background instead of standing out in a crowd, and she likes it that way. She doesn't wear weave, except for the occasional micro-braids hairstyle for traveling, fake eyelashes, fake finger nails or has fake boobs or a fake ass. She now must work with a trainer and be in the gym three to four days a week to keep everything from sagging south. Aging does that to a person. She knows she is slightly overweight, still working to get rid of her sweets and fried foods pooch. Her hair is natural in two-strand twists down to her shoulders today. Some days she doesn't even bother with makeup unless it's a special occasion or she gets in the mood to look and feel unusually sexy. Today, it's a feel unusually sexy day.

Lea has always felt men look through her to get to the real women. Whatever that is.

It doesn't matter how much I smile or look inviting, I still get passed over. As my best friend, Gordon always tells me, 'Your time will come'. Easy for him to say; he's been married for fourteen years. I haven't even had sex in the last two years. At forty-four, I'm aging out of love. I've already aged out for kids. The eggs are dead.

As she rides the elevator alone, Lea, wishes for a hot second the Adonis woulda looked her way, but the ping tells her, she has arrived for work on the twentieth floor and to forget about him. She will never see him again, or if she does, it will be with a fake twenty-something on his arm.

The offices of Golden Technology and Electronics Enterprises. G-TEE, is a mid-size technology and electronics company that works with other companies in testing, upgrading, and deploying technology it wants to invest and implement in its current business structure. When Tom Brasil, her former University of Missouri, instructor, started this business, it took off quickly. Who knew he would remember her as a student from over twenty years ago and find her on LinkedIn to see if she was interested in working for him?

As usual, she blended into class the way she blended into most areas of her life. In his class, she was part of a group, which had to create a database for a real-life company. Lea was the organizer, created documentation, and visual aids, and tested the database. Everyone in the group had to present, and she made sure she was first, doing the group introductions and answering the follow-up questions if there were any. Tom reviewed the project and called it exemplary to put it mildly. He stated, "Lea is always thinking one step ahead of the client to head off problems, and with those skills, she will go far in the technology industry."

She stumbled for a few years, stuck in dead-end jobs, and got her Masters in Information Technology Management. Now, here she is, managing fifteen people and contributing to this company's success.

And I only have to do meet-and-greets with clients when necessary. Absolutely necessary. Like today, or when we have special events to thank them for their business. Reminds me, we're having a wine tasting and a charity event. Oh joy. Yes, I'm being sarcastic. "Just let me sit in the corner and disappear". Ugh. I hate those events. Except for the charity event. I do love dressing up and having a glamour night even if I'm dateless.

The uptick in new clients has been great for G-TEE. More business is always good. Lea talking to strangers and presenting, not so good. She took over this project last week because one of the other Project Leads wife went into early labor and gave birth to their daughter. Carl is now out on a twelve-week leave taking care of them. It was easy for Lea and Carl to switch projects because her latest one wasn't starting for another two months. It's still in the research stage. She had plans to be available for unexpected client meetings when needed. Now she has to step into Project Lead mode earlier than expected.

I hope this one is simple, please let this one be simple, please don't let me be working with a clueless CEO.

Lea walks into the office making sure the meeting room is set up and ready to go for the day. The office manager, Crystal, has everything in place. This woman thinks further ahead than Lea. Lea never met a woman who enjoyed being a receptionist/office manager/drill sergeant the way Crystal does.

Tom told Lea that when he interviewed Crystal, she stated, "I love talking to people, planning events, keeping a household running and organized. You are a small company right now and you are going to need an all-around person with skills like that and that's me. I want to stay with a company for a long time. I have no interest in being in management. I have kids and a husband I love dearly at home, but I can't sit on my behind all day."

"Can we begin with part-time, work our way into full-time, fluctuate the hours, days and time I work as needed based on your business growth. All I ask is that I'm not treated like a lowly peon with nothing to offer."

Tom hired Crystal on the spot and she has been running this office, him, and everyone he hires since. She is a mother hen and cupid rolled into one. To her everyone needs to be coupled up and black love is a wonderful love to behold. She wants Lea married off and can't understand why she is single.

Unlucky in love, that's me.

So, when getting off the elevator, Lea see's that Crystal is on the war path with a delivery gone wrong. Lea looks at the meeting room, and scurries off to her office knowing things will be on point for the first appointment at nine-thirty this morning.

-2-

Zion tries not to yawn and attempts to get himself into business mode for this nine-thirty appointment. It's been a long week of meetings and more meetings. This is his last one before the weekend, and after, he can find a piece of ass to release some tension.

His buddy, Tom, has been on his case for a couple of years to upgrade his office technology "the correct way", as Tom puts it, and with the relocation here to St. Louis into an old warehouse, now was as good a time as there ever will be. Landon Enterprises has made Zion Landon a lot of money by being a financial counselor/consultant to the famous and not so famous, the rich and not so rich. His clientele consists of next-door neighbors to people in the sports, music, and entertainment industries.

They have one thing in common. They didn't have a clue about the correlation among working, living, saving and retiring. Zion's biggest goal was to get these up-and-coming young knuckleheads who sign with these lucrative contracts to be focused on a financial plan before they spent that five-figure check before the ink was even dry.

Who knew counseling these young non-know-it-alls could still be so lucrative after all these years? No matter how Zion has tried, he has never been able to understand how these wanna-be famous people can't write a damn money order let alone understand not to cash a check at these instant loan places. At twenty-two he made it his business to catch prospective clientele at the onset of their careers and sit them down with some real talk about spending, saving, and retiring.

His team of counselors, accountants, financial planners, and insurance brokers know their shit and understand they can make bank when working for Landon Enterprises. They also understand if they were to cross him or rip off his clients, he will bury their ass in financial hell and leave them working multiple minimum wage jobs trying to make ends meet.

In his years of business, only two former employees attempted to rip off Landon Enterprises and his clients. Before any damage could be done, he had them barred from working in the financial industry for life. One is in jail for attempting to run a Ponzi scheme, started prior to joining Landon Enterprises.

That fool was the one who taught Zion that basic background checks and low-level financial investigations were insufficient when hiring financial professionals. Anyone who applies to work at Landon Enterprises is subjected to FBI-level security background checks. When working with money, the last people you want to hire are those in debt, with low credit scores or living beyond their means. That's like opening the door to the Federal Reserve bank and giving them plastic bags to fill with cash.

The final building design presented to him by Elivations Architecture Designs is ready to implement. Now he has to decided on the upgrade of the company's technology. Tom has been bugging Zion for weeks to pin down a meeting so here he is. Zion prefers working with small to mid-size black owned and operated companies and pushing their business their way.

Give back to those who look like you, give them respect and respect their business and you get loyalty every time. But don't fuck with my money and the respect I give you, because Zion Landon has no problem going someplace else, whether in my personal and professional worlds.

Landon Enterprises employees are eighty percent minority with a large percentage of minority clients. It covers old and young. Not one client has lost money doing business with Zion. He doesn't like his money fucked with and therefore no one is going to fuck with his client's money.

Being who Zion is, some call him money hungry. No, he just doesn't like seeing those who make money lose it because of dumb decisions. He is frank and to the point. This attitude allows him to enjoy life, living, sexing and dabbling in a piece of non-committed ass every once in a while, and tonight he has plans to hit up an old standby.

As he sits in this atrium waiting for Tom to come back with their coffees, he stares out the window looking at the traffic speed by in downtown Clayton. Tom likes to meet in the atrium when he is not in business mode.

When Tom Brasil is in his office, he is all business. He is a straight shooter, making money, business man on the twentieth floor behind the doors of G-TEE. When relaxing and taking a coffee break, they catch up talking of old days.

As Zion stares out the window, he adjusts his focus from the outside world and onto the reflection of the sexy ass that comes into view.

My dick swells to attention. Down man. Later.

Taking in the view, he see's a nice behind and strong calves in a pair of sexy heels, a tight skirt and black silk blouse. He quickly glances up and sees a beautiful head of spiral curls he imagines his fingers twirling through. His fingers clench and unclench in his hand mimicking the movement as if they are in her hair right now. She looks his way, pauses for a heartbeat then keeps moving.

What the fuck. She kept moving and I sit here like a stunned deer caught in the headlights. And her headlights weren't big but damn they looked nice.

He turns around getting up to go after her but Tom unknowingly blocks his path.

"Here you go, man," Tom says, "told you I had this."

Zion responds in kind saying thanks to the cup of coffee and sits back down adjusting his dick and mind, thinking of ways to find that ass.

Tom tells Zion about his wife, kids, and grandkids and how proud of them he is. Zion has never fathered any kids, never been married. He has been too busy making a living and worrying less about a family.

Besides who would want a man who couldn't give them children.

This six-feet, four-inch tall, two-hundred and thirty-pound football looking player is shooting blanks. A bad case of mumps left him sterile when he was a kid.

It was never a bother until those witches in college told me I wasn't the type of man they could marry because I couldn't give them kids. So, I became the guy to fuck, to hang out with but never the guy to have a future with because I couldn't give them a child. Or a guaranteed financial dependent. Friend zoned every time.

From there, he became the wealthy billionaire. No, black billionaire. No, single break their hearts, leave them wanting more, black billionaire. Women became fucks, eye candy, someone to hang with but always staying in the not-gonna-snag-him-into-something-permanent zone.

Oh, he made sure to feel them out about how they felt about kids and what they would do if they never had any, and the answer was always the same. If they couldn't have any biological kids, they would always be unfulfilled. His answer was to introduce them to friends who could give them exactly that. Amazing how they forgot he existed when they found a dick who could give them a baby.

He sips his coffee.

Did a woman attempt to trap me by claiming a child was mine? Fuck yeah, plenty of times. And always that DNA came back that I was not the father. Broke my spirit so many times that my motto became if you ain't fixed you ain't gettin this dick. Especially without a condom. Hell, I should take stock out in a condom company. My dick hasn't touched a raw pussy in decades. And oral only with a condom, with the condom going with me to be disposed of. There was a time I was an expert at sucking and licking on a clit. Ain't licked one of them since college and that was almost thirty years ago.

As Tom continues to talk, Zion concentrates on keeping up his side of the conversation. He tells Tom about his latest travels and the events he attended, but he can't get his mind off that ass hugging green and black skirt and those tan heels.

How do I find this woman? Will I find myself hanging out in this damn atrium waiting for her to walk pass? No. Oh, hell no. Time to pump Tom for some information. Later, after our meeting. It's time to go upstairs and talk business and watch a damn demo. Another boring presentation.

Zion and Tom exit the elevator, walking in the reception area of Golden Technology and Electronic Enterprises. The offices take up the entire floor with demo and meeting rooms on one side and offices and cubicles spaced closely to the rooms with others lining the opposite side of the floor.

The man has done well I must say.

Tom looks after hiring people with ideas and not just those looking for a job. He believes those with ideas will go further than job hoppers. The idea individuals need an outlet for their minds and creativity, and they have come up with some major new ones for Landon Enterprises.

They are greeted by the office manager Crystal. Although Zion learned years ago that she doesn't use the manager title, she runs this place like the best of managers could.

He greets her as he always does, with a kiss on the cheek and a pout for a peach pie. She says, "It's in the fridge and do not forget it before you leave."

Other than the women in his family, he loves this woman dearly. She has seen him through some bad years and has always been a shining star in his eyes.

"So how you been Bear?" she asks, calling him by his college nickname.

Ugh, that name. Crystal and my mother are the only ones who can get away with calling me that. It's a name I earned in college from women who liked my hugs. They always stated I gave such great bear hugs. When I escaped college, no one ever got those hugs out of me ever again. I saw that side hug shit on TV. Shit it has worked well for me. Side hugs, and the kisses became side mouth kisses or quick pecks. Don't get me wrong; I respect women with the utmost regard, especially my black Nubian queens, but when it comes to all that love, and affection, and touchy-feely stuff, it gets in the way of dick meets pussy. Just let me fuck you, release some tension, and move on.

"I've been great and it's Zion," I whisper, "I'm in business mode, remember?"

"Oh, okay, Zion," she smirks, "how are Star, Garrett and the twins?"

She always asks me about my sister and her family. My sister Star has twin girls, two years old, named Cam and Denise and they have me wrapped around their fingers. Even Star's husband, Garrett has become an old softy. He is the toughest college football coach around, but those three females bring him to putty each and every time I see them together.

"They are wonderful," Zion responds in kind.

They hurriedly finish their conversation and he is escorted to the meeting room with Tom. Zion sits down across the table from him. At his place setting is a nice pen, coaster, and documentation he assumes are the presentation and contract to sign.

Tom should know he has the contract. We just have to hammer out a few details, see some prototypes, and we're set. Thirty minutes to an hour tops, and I'm done and on my way to some ass. Even this early in the day someone is available. Or will make herself available.

After about thirty seconds, the door to the conference room opens and Zion looks toward it. In walks the green and black skirt and killer calves in tan heels and an ass that makes his dick stand up and say "Hello That's Her".

He looks up into a smile that warms his soul.

Her. You. It's her. My conscience is screaming. Hold it together Zion.

As Tom walks over to her, Zion gets a grip on his raging hormones, adjusts his pants and stands for introductions.

"Zion," Tom says, "this is Lea Adams. She is the Technology and Implementation Manager for G-TEE, will be the lead on your project, and is here to walk us through the technical side of things."

"Lea, this is Zion Landon of Landon Enterprises."

Kia Lui

-3-

Lea looks up at who she's being introduced to and freezes.

Holly fucking lord in heaven. It's Adonis. My groin and the resident Sex Diva on my shoulder wake up at the same time and scream.

WE FUCKING HIM, RIGHT?

"Hello, nice to meet you Mr. Landon."

I manage to get those words out while thinking, fuck me now why don't you.

On the surface, Lea is pure professional, presenting a proper business woman persona. Mentally, she has just swooned and fainted into a heap of sexually aroused woman, wanting to be taken.

SEE YOU AGREE, WE FUCKING HIM, RIGHT? RIGHT? DAMMIT DON'T GO BRAIN SILENT ON ME NOW.

"The pleasure is all mine," Zion says as they shake hands.

Okay, some men voices are so sexy that you can't listen to them. The former President of the United States has that voice. That black man's voice makes women, well this woman at least, hot, wet, and tingly. Lea can't listen to any of his speeches. She has to put the TV on mute and read the closed captions. Mr. Landon, this sexy specimen of the male species, has the same kinda voice as the President's.

Only Mr. Landon's voice, has my clit throbbing and my nipples rock, fucking, hard.

Okay yes, Lea cusses. She can cuss like a sailor working on the docks. But back to this voice. It touched her lips and slid up and down her spine like wet hot kisses.

The Sex Diva is yelling and jumping, YES, YES, YES, WE FUCKING HIM.

And I'm saying no. We not. I think.

"And please, call me Zion," he says as Lea puts the Sex Diva on the back burner. His grip is strong and soft. Her hand feels as if it was meant to be there. She can't let him go. No, she can't let his hand go. And those eyes. Lea doesn't often stare too long into a man's eyes, but Mr. Landon's won't let her turn away.

Tom clears his throat and she releases his hand pulling away, looking down at it, running her thumb across her palm, wanting his back. She forces distance between them, purposely moving over to the side bar offering both men something to drink, trying to busy herself. Crystal rushes to her side, shooing her into the head chair and instructing the men to have a seat.

Okay, where the hell did she come from? Dammit, I needed that distraction. Suddenly, my shirt and bra feel too damn tight. Oh, Lord, what bra do I have on?

I glance down sneakily and check that my nipples aren't perky and visible. Padded. Yes.

I adjust my top and look up and catch Mr. Landon staring at me. He probably saw every move I made. If I was pale enough, he could probably see me blush. But nope. All I feel is a hot flash and a cold sweat coming on.

I need a touch-me break.

Lea looks away from Mr. Landon and takes her seat at the conference room table getting as comfortable as she can. They are sitting at a table that has a glass top in the middle surround by polished mahogany wood on the edges. With the glass portion in the middle you can see the occupant's legs and Lea is doing everything she can to keep hers still. She crosses them at the ankles and tucks her feet under the chair out of view so she can at least, on the sly jiggle her feet every few minutes. One of her coping methods she uses when she is around strangers.

Damn this glass top table.

She curses its open visibility.

Adonis, I mean Mr. Landon, keeps glancing at me. He needs to stop looking at me.

UH NO, HE DON'T. YOU NEED TO LOOK AT HIM. ON SECOND THOUGHT, PEEP OUT HIS CROUCH. CAN YOU SEE IT? AND YOU KNOW WHAT I MEAN BY IT.

I won't make eye contact, I won't make eye contact, don't look up. Lea, don't look up. But glance at the crouch. Shit. That part of the table top is blocking it.

AW, DAMN.

Tom goes over the proposal and the general ideas G-TEE has for Landon Enterprises.

"Zion. Since we have been informally meeting and discussing the plans for this project, there will be no need for me go over the basics of what G-TEE does and give you a background on our company. What I'd like to make sure you understand is that even though we are friends, that will not change how we handle your contract."

"Tom, it never crossed my mind you would treat me any differently. Thanks for the reassurance," Zion says.

And thanks for bringing Lea into my bed. I want to touch her. Caress her legs. Spread them open. It's hard keeping my work face on when I want to smile and seduce her. But ima get through this.

Lea is concentrating extremely hard on not biting her lip, playing with her necklace, caressing her legs and adjusting her neck. All the things she would normally be doing when attempting to hide how aroused, or how nervous she is.

This man has me on overload. And the smell of him. It's time for a walk through the men's cologne department to find that scent so I can use it as an air freshener in my bedroom.

Lea turns her focus to listening to Tom discuss G-TEE's proposal. It's for upgrading Landon Enterprises with tablets, smart phones, infrastructure wiring, voice over internet protocol, security, and programs for his business structure.

"Per the documentation Carl gathered in his initial meeting with Landon Enterprises, G-TEE will be working with vendors and suppliers to get this implemented during the move into your new loft-style headquarters. Landon Enterprises has purchased an old eight-story warehouse in Chesterfield, which is being remodeled to accommodate the company's financial specialists. The top five floors will be exclusively Landon Enterprises headquarters. Each floor will have a top-of-the-line secure area to meet with famous and multi-million-dollar clients. With this new space, Landon Enterprises can go above and beyond to maintain client confidentially, ensuring privacy and safety."

"The second floor will be rented out as offices to other companies and the first floor will house a restaurant, eating area, and building reception."

"G-TEE will be working with vendors for the installation of phones, the setup and programming of smartphones and tablets, working with Landon Enterprises personal IT and security teams to transfer data to the new systems and dispose of old equipment and systems, implement procedures to maintain, service, and order new equipment, and to be a second line of defense to backup and maintain his company data, working with the IT department when necessary."

"Lea will now discuss the equipment recommended, time frames for implementation and cost savings to Landon Enterprises."

Lea goes over all of this, pausing to clarify and answer any questions Zion has. And he has a lot.

He looks and listens intently, asking questions she never thought a client would think of. He has left Lea impressed, stunned, and mesmerized.

"Lea, tell me about the decision to use the smartphones and tablets you selected?" Zion asks her.

Lea hesitates a fraction of a second on hearing her first name from his lips not expecting such an informality from him. "Well, you want your technology to fluidly communicate with each other. Not just through having to upload and download files to save to each device. With all your equipment being able to communicate this way, it saves you money on having to purchase different programs for different equipment, and it saves you time. As in any business, time is money," she responds to Zion's question.

"And does the equipment you are recommending do all this?" Zion imagines himself propping his head on the palm of his hand watching Lea as she speaks with an awe-struck look on his face. It takes every muscle in his face not to break out in a silly grin from the thought of it. The corners of his mouth slightly twitch though and Lea catches the movement.

Another man who thinks I'm some silly, little girl who doesn't know anything. Screw you Mr. Landon.

"Yes, it does. And we also have made sure your current IT department and security team are comfortable with working with this equipment. Actually, when I spoke, with them they indicated a preference for this equipment over two other setups. The majority of your staff currently has this equipment or was thinking about moving to this equipment for personal use."

"You have talked with my staff?" Zion asks shocked.

"Yes sir," Lea responds with a panicked look. "We always like to talk with those who will be using the technology and programs to determine their needs. It's not an affront to management or yourself.

When Tom told me about your requirements, he specifically gave me details on what you are currently using and how much of a hands-on CEO you are. Sometimes, executives make decisions without understanding how their employees use the available technology or programs," Lea quickly adds, not wanting to offend Mr. Landon for the sake of Tom and this contract but sneakily being a smart ass. If this were any other situation, she wouldn't care about his offense. But this is business.

"No affront taken. I'm impressed. None of my staff ever mentioned these discussions."

Tom speaks up quickly, "Lea is adamant about talking with the users of technology. You were out of town when we set up the meetings with your staff. Remember, you had to go put out a fire regarding a spending spree. You were supposed to be there, but left explicit instructions with your staff to be honest and open with us."

"Oh yeah, right, I remember now. Biggest waste of money on bling I had ever seen," Zion says glancing at Lea.

Let's get this over with shall we gentlemen? I'm horny and aroused and horny and my bra feels like it has shrunk three sizes. I need to escape to my office.

YOU'RE REPEATING YOURSELF.

Oh, Shut. Up.

Lea plays with the charm on her necklace, taking shallow breaths, calming her body down.

"Lea, I wasn't questioning your interacting with my staff. I forgot, that's all. I'm glad you guys took that extra step," Zion attempts to reassure her.

"Thank you. Sir."

"Please. Stop calling me Sir. There's no need to be so formal."

"Sorry. It's a habit and a sign of respect," Lea says peering at him for a pace longer than usual, then looking away.

AND SOMETIMES IT'S A WAY TO SAY YES SIR, THAT FEELS NICE. YES SIR, DO THAT AGAIN. YES SIR, SPANK ME. YES SIR, HARDER PLEASE.

Diva down, Sex Diva, sit down, Lea admonishes her.

Lea smiles and slightly adjusts her neck moving it to the left and right, looking away from Mr. Landon and down at her paperwork.

Damn, I can't stop imagining his lips on the sweet spot on the back of my—.

Tom interrupts the silence. "Well, now that we have discussed all the written stuff, how about Lea giving you a tour and a demonstration of what we have in mind."

At Tom's suggestion, Lea looks at him stunned.

Me? Tour? What? No. I have to run to my office and unbutton my blouse, unsnap my bra and breathe. My tits have doubled in size. Or it feels like it.

HEY, WHAT DO YOU THINK ABOUT ADONIS' HANDS MASSAGING OUR TITS? HIS LIPS AND TONGUE, NIBBLING THEM. YOU THINK HE A TIT, ASS, OR LEG MAN?

Uggggghhhh. SHUT, UP.

"Sure, Tom. No problem. Shall we go, Mr. Landon?" I respond back wanting to punch Tom.

Really, me give the man a tour? Ughhhh.

Lea imagines herself stomping across the room, mouth pouting chanting, 'No I don't wanna give the sexy Adonis a tour'. She slowly pushes the chair away from the table, places one hand on the edge, making sure her legs are closed, and gracefully stands.

GLAD YOU DIDN'T POP OUT THE CHAIR LIKE A JACK IN THE BOX.

I'm moving like this to try and catch a look at the dick. I kinda see a print.

NICE MOVE. NICE BODY. WE FUCKING HIM.

"I'd love to take a tour, Lea," Zion says ignoring her using his formal name and purposely continuing to address her by her first name.

As they move to leave the conference room, Lea steps past him, breathing deeply, glancing at Crystal who is waiting to get into the room and straighten up. She is staring at Lea strangely.

What I do now? I'll get with her later. On with the tour.

As Lea and Zion leave the conference room, Crystal and Tom turn toward each other grinning.

"I told you this hookup would work," Crystal says to him, confident in her cupid skills.

"Hold your horses. I sense sexual attraction, I agree with you on that, but we want more for the both of them than sex," Tom says.

They whisper, not wanting to get caught discussing Lea and Zion.

"Tom. Whatever."

Crystal finishes straightening the room for the next meeting.

-4-

Where in the hell has Tom been hiding this sexy goddess at? He has never mentioned her, introduced her, or brought her around to any events. I would have spotted her from a mile away. Hell, I can't stop wanting to be near her, hear her talk, watch her fidget. Watch her arousal ebb and flow. Because home girl is clearly fucking aroused.

Zion's mind is all over the place with thoughts of Lea.

When she came into the room and he realized she was the woman from the lobby, he silently thanked the Lord for giving him this lottery win. He thought he would to have to break into security cameras, scan for her face, and hunt her down. But no, she is the lovely Lea Adams working with his friend Tom on a technology contract that if he hadn't had before meeting her, he sure as hell has now.

This woman truly knows this business.

She was able to answer all my questions beyond my expectations and thought of things I never would have considered. Yes, G-TEE will be doing a great job with getting my company up and running with its upgrade.

And Lea? Well, let's just say Lea and I will be getting to know each other better. Much better. Indeed.

During the meeting, he glanced at her every now and then, wanting eye contact, but she kept her eyes focused on the documentation in front of her. He could see her legs through the glass table top and her thighs were slightly parted with her legs crossed at the ankles. Every few minutes, her legs would do a little shake and she would glide her hands down to stop them.

Damn, her lower legs looked muscular. I had to tell myself to concentrate on the meeting instead of them golden limbs wrapped around my waist.

The initial briefing went as expected, but it was better with Lea there. And now, the tour. As she stood up, he got a whiff of her scent.

Dammit, I can't place it. Kinda fruity, flowery, intense yet haunting. Geez. What is that?

As Lea walks out the door, Zion follows her noticing her heels are not those overly high heels that bend back a woman's feet into an ungodly image of being straight. He is noticing a lot of things about Lea. Things he can't recall even caring about. High heels, flats, tennis. He never cared. With Lea, he even notices her jewelry. A multi-colored bracelet of green, black, and gray marble swirls.

Oh, my fuck, she is not even wearing stockings. All that smoothness from the tip of her toes to the juncture of her—. Man stop, just stop this. This is business.

"Lea, again, I'm impressed with the steps you have taken for this proposal. You have thought of everything," Zion says, wanting to hear her voice.

"Thanks. Our goal is to make sure things run as smoothly as possible with as little down-time for your company and yourself."

Zion attempted to draw her in with his impenetrable gaze but she looked away quickly.

Man, you supposed to be in business mode and you can't stop trying to flirt. But this woman here. Got me in sex mode.

They go into the Idea Room and Lea introduces Zion to some of their programmers and electronic personal, the wizards as she affectionately calls them, almost like a mother hen. Zion laughs at the plaque on the wall. 'No idea is too small or can't be accomplished. Your ideas set you apart. So, what we thinking about breaking today?'

"What's so funny?" Lea asks him, feeling self-conscious.

"The plaque. 'What are we thinking about breaking today?' How is that a positive?"

"Oh that. My crazy attempt at keeping up the humor and fun. Ideas are fixing what is broken, even if you didn't know if it was broken. Shall we continue with the tour?"

"Please do."

Yes, please do, so I can watch you move. Zion, man, concentrate. Business mode. Focus. I may be in business mode, but I ain't dead nor am I blind.

He sees groups of individuals working on phones, laptops, and tablets. Zion looks around and approaches the individual groups, standing to the side watching them work.

He asks Lea to explain what two of the techs are doing.

"They are giving the tablets and laptops viruses and attempting to do a remote cleanup and even a security hack. The best way to learn is to break and fix," Lea says, watching him intently.

"Ahhh, the Idea Room's motto coming into play," he comments, staring at a smartphone in pieces. He takes out his phone looking at it, shaking his head.

"Exactly."

Lea turns away, moving to exit the Idea Room and wanting to quickly finish up. He stalks her, keeping close. "Everyone here thinks outside the box. They work to make what they are thinking about, happen. We have staff from as old as those who can retire to those as young as high school interns. We keep staff because they are encouraged to keep thinking and trying. We don't hover as a management style, but they understand they must meet our client's deadlines and must document everything, with credit given where credit is due and discipline administered when necessary. We do what it takes to complete the job."

"The way I think about business myself. Of course, Tom and I are friends first and business associates second, so I guess our business practices would mirror our thinking," Zion states.

Instead of following Lea to the door, Zion walks over to another group of techs standing over a laptop in pieces. Lea steps in and explains. "Over here is the test equipment we have that will be a setup for your employees at your office. As you can see on this screen the VoIP phone—."

"VoIP? Oh right, Voice over Internet Protocol. Never mind."

"Yes, so the VoIP phone, smart phone, and tablet are all talking with each other. A call comes in, and it can be answered by all three. Files are being uploaded and downloaded among the smart phone, tablet, a mock server setup, and a laptop. Simultaneously, employee's can use the tablet outside the office, and whatever they are doing is uploaded to your office servers. Once a tablet is closed or a smartphone is locked, without the secure way to unlock the device, the device will look like a broken device. Something that can't be fixed," Lea explains demonstrating what a locked device looks like to Zion.

He watchers her intently, not wanting to interrupt for fear she will stop talking and he won't hear her voice again.

What the hell is with me? This is a woman, a possible working colleague. It's not as if I haven't worked closely with women before. Just not one I want to—. Naw, man, don't even finish that thought. Let it go. Let that thought go. For now. Until you get out of here.

Zion gives himself a mental shake and refocuses on what Lea is saying.

"Only you and your security team will know fully how this works. Once our testing phase is done, all we will know is that it's locked and we can't unlock it. Even our programmers will be unable to access it," she says.

"Wow, what happens if someone on my security detail gets compromised?" he asks her.

"That is between you and your security staff on how you want to take steps to getting devices unlocked. In speaking with your head IT and security personnel, they have ideas about all extenuating circumstances."

"I must meet with Sam and Saul to see what they have in mind," he tells her.

"I'm sure you will be impressed."

"I'm pretty impressed with you, Lea. And your ideas."

Shit, man take it easy. Don't blow this. Business, remember. Business. But it doesn't mean you can't feel her out to see if she could be interested.

Earlier, when Lea turned her back on Tom and him in the conference room looking down, Zion thought she was one of those demure shy types attempting to be coy. Then he realized she was checking out her own tits.

I perked up then.

He watched her adjust her shirt and skirt before she sat down, from the corner of his eye.

Baby girl is wearing a padded bra. That means she gets perky and has to hide those budding nipples. Betcha they stand at attention with a cold breeze. Winter in St. Louis can't get here fast enough.

Yeah, like you will be seeing her during the winter time. It's a year or longer project and she is project lead. Oh, I'll be seeing more of Ms. Lea Adams.

I argue with my conscience.

Or, oh shit. Shit, Shit, Shit. She could be married or engaged or dating. Let me back my ass up. I don't do taken and I don't do ass on the side. We gotta be free and clear of entanglements to enjoy each other before I get involved.

Lea and Zion continue with the office tour. Everyone would speak up and offer suggestions and advice, some arguing with each other in front of Zion and Lea about what would work.

Zion noticed no name calling, no petty bickering, just all-around no, yes, how, I don't understand, clue me in, make it make sense, okay let's try it out. The seasoned programmers guided the less seasoned ones into understanding and the younger ones would respectfully absorb the information while offering ideas and suggestions.

Yes, Tom has done a damn good job with this company and hired the right people. Zion muses.

Lea leads Zion back to the reception area and are greeted by Tom and Crystal.

Tom is waiting to take Zion to his office to discuss more business and Zion is ready to sign the papers and get on the topic of Lea.

Lea turns to Zion, "Well, it was nice meeting you Mr. Landon, and I hope we get to work with you and your company to implement all our ideas."

"Lea, again, it was my pleasure, and once more please call me Zion. I hope to talk with you soon. May I get a business card?"

"Sure." She grabs a card off the front desk and hands it to Zion.

I look down, her office number, email address, and cell number. All the information instantly seared in my memory.

"Thanks again Lea." Zion takes out his wallet and provides Lea with one of his business cards.

I reach out to shake her hand once again, wanting to touch her. When she places hers in mine, I try not to react to the jolt that goes straight to my gut. Damn it's just a hand shake.

"No problem Mr. Landon. Tom, let me know if you need anything from me, I'll be in my office preparing for our next meeting." She looks up at Zion and withdraws her hand while talking to Tom then turns to leave without saying another word.

As she walks off, I watch her, her ass, nice and firm, not one of those jiggly kind. Buns of steel I bet.

Zion notices the total silence behind him.

He turns around and catches Tom and Crystal staring at him.

"Tom, in your office. Now. Right now," Zion growls.

I need to find out if Ms. Lea Adams is available to entertain my way.

"Sure, follow me," Tom says grinning and walking toward his office.

Crystal makes a beeline to Lea's office.

-5-

"Man, where the hell have you been stashing that beauty away? I mean fuck, damn," Zion suddenly lowers his voice, "Wait, can anyone hear me?"

"No, all the walls next to the demo rooms are sound proof. It gets loud in there. I haven't been hiding her from you," Tom says quietly.

"Yes, you have. Shit man, she is sexy as hell. Damn. I haven't been this worked up about a woman like this in hell, in forever."

"I noticed."

"What do you mean?"

Tom says, smiling, "Well, I have seen you do business; you normally talk little. You ask questions, but they are curt, terse and to the point. With Lea, you hung on her every word. You could not take your eyes off her whenever she made a move or noise."

"Was I that obvious?"

"Only to me because I know you. It was like you were tuned into her."

"Man, tell me, where have you been hiding her?" Zion asks.

"I've never hidden her. This is the first time you and I have ever done business with each other. I've invited you both to many events I've had. You didn't show up, sent a representative, or gave the tickets to clients. Don't get me wrong, with your schedule and workload, I have completely understood. You only came to my house when you didn't want to be bothered with business. Again, I understand. Lea would stop by, but hang out with the wife and grandkids. You guys just never managed to run into each other, and I never discussed you or your business. I know you are a dickem-and-leavem kinda guy. I had no reason to introduce you to Lea."

Until my office manager and wife suggested we do a behind the scenes connection, Tom reminds himself silently.

Tom has tried to get Lea married, but none of the men would get past his protective father/daughter opinion he has of Lea. Each time he thought he had one, he would maneuver an introduction, but as soon as he saw them together, he would change his mind. Finally, he left it alone. Then his wife and Crystal suggested Lea meets Zion. Shit, Zion was the farthest idea of a love interest he would have for Lea. The man avoids commitment like a disease. After being bombarded by the two ladies for the last six months he gave in and here they are.

"Shit. Am I really a dickem-and-leavem guy? Never mind, don't answer that. I get it. Okay, so she is off limits to me?"

"If you looking to dick her and leave her, yes. I really don't know much about her personal life like that," Tom says lying through his teeth. "She has dated, was even in a long-term relationship for several years. But that was over ten years ago. I see that look. She is not angry, damaged or is focused on career. Her motto has been live and enjoy life. That's all I know," again, lying as best I can.

"Man, I just—. Where the paperwork at? I need to sign so we can get started."

"Wait, we got the contract. And get started on what?" Tom asks him wondering where Zion's mind is headed.

"Duh, hell yeah, you got the contract. You knew that the day you brought this up to me months ago. Fuck, don't play with me. I needed to hear ideas. And start working on getting things with my company implemented."

"Wonderful. My staff, my wife, and our bank accounts adore you. And one more thing. Lea is not like your dickem-and-leavem woman. If, and I say this with all the fatherly and brotherly love I have for the both of you, if you decide to move along with getting to know her, your typical methods won't work."

Zion stares at Tom, and Tom knows what he is thinking. "Don't give me that look. I saw the sexual heat and tension between the two of you. Your regular shit ain't gonna work with her. If you looking for some temporary shit or if you're unsure, bring your dick in check, and move along. She is not the one."

"You used the word ain't. Shit. I gotcha bro, I gotcha. So, she's single then?" Zion asks getting kinda excited about a new chase.

"Yes, she's single. I don't want to have to kick your ass if something happens between you two, and you end up hurting her," Tom says.

"Kick my ass?" Zion looks at Tom on the other side of his desk. He is not completely out of shape, but he could lose a few pounds.

"Yes, kick your ass. Or find someone to do it. Two hundred and forty pounds and all muscle. Geez don't you have any fat on you anywhere? I'm tired of my wife telling me I need to get in the gym more."

"Two-hundred and thirty-pounds. I told you to come train with me. You will be muscle bound like me in six weeks, tops. Let's wrap this up," Zion says sitting across from him.

Tom and Zion sign all the paperwork, and Zion calls for his driver to meet him in front of the building. They have ten minutes to finish discussing Lea.

Sexy ass Lea. Shit. Time to grow up Zion. Or walk away. And walking away would be against the goal I talked about with the guys years ago. I can't embrace, accept love and settle down if I keep running away. I knew it wasn't going to be one of my temporaries, so it has to be someone new.

"I have one more thing to say about a Lea and Zion possibility," Tom says.

"And that is?"

"The next time I invite you to an event, maybe you will show up," Tom says as he hands Zion an invitation to G-TEE's wine tasting event at his winery.

Reading the invitation, Zion says, "RSVP me for two."

"Two. Who you bringing?"

"Sam, my driver."

"Oh, yeah right. I'll make a note of it."

"Where is my pie? I need to get outta here. I have things to do."

Tom laughs at Zion as they walk to the kitchen to get his pie. Lea is coming out of the kitchen as Tom and Zion are walking in. Lea bumps into Zion, and he catches her before she falls. She stares at his chest saying, "Sorry," and moves out of his embrace as fast as she can. Zion looks down at her and says "No problem. Lea," and steps aside to let her pass.

Zion leans out the kitchen watching her walk down the hallway. He looks at Tom after she disappears and says, "Don't say a word, not one word."

Tom smiles, riding down in the elevator with Zion.

On his way back up, Tom thinks how easy it was after all to make this cupid connection.

Crystal and my wife were right. Lea and Zion are perfect for each other. Poor Zion, his single days are dwindling. And watching this is gonna be fun.

-6-

Lea escapes to her office catching her breath thinking. *Ice, I need ice. Ice on my neck and tits will calm me down.*

She heads back toward the office kitchen praying the whole time she doesn't run into anyone because even in the padded bra she can feel the perkiness of her nipples. She manages to grab a cup of ice and turns around to leave but runs into a solid, soft, I wanna fuck this man, brick wall. A brick wall that smells heavenly and feels as delightful. A pair of arms encircle her. She says, "Sorry", without even looking up. When he says "No problem. Lea.", it takes every bit of concentration she has not to look up at him like a kitten wanting to be stroked.

Oh, his voice. Yep I'm gonna need a marker and white-board for this man. I won't be able to focus on the topic at hand, when he speaks.

LOOK, AS LONG AS HE IS SAYING HOW WONDERFUL WE MAKING HIM FEEL, HE CAN RECITE THE FRICKING ALPHABET TO THE TUNE OF 'FREAK ME BABY' FOR ALL I CARE.

She pulls away and power walks to her office closing the door.

Lord that man's arms felt so damned inviting.

The Sex Diva on Lea's shoulder is pacing back and forth chanting, NEW DICK, NEW DICK, WE GETTING' SOME NEW DICK.

Not more than a minute later there is a knock at Lea's door. She gathers her emotions and says 'Come in'. Crystal stands in the doorway.

"Will you get in here?" Lea hisses pulling Crystal into her office. "What took you so long? You knew I needed to vent. I coulda sent you for the ice but, no, I had to go get it and who I bump into? Mr. Landon."

"Yes ma'am," Crystal asks and smiles, "How the hell am I supposed to know you needed ice? I'm not a mind reader. Well not this time anyway. I got waylaid walking past the Idea Room. The guys wanted to give me their opinions of Zion. Are you okay?"

"Uh no. Do I look okay?"

Crystal continues smiling.

"I just met a Greek God. The sexiest, tastiest, lickable, fuckable, one I could ever imagine that existed. I haven't been this turned on in months. I can run up and down this hall screaming."

YOU NEED TO RUN AFTER ADONIS.

"Who? Where? What? I mean why? Why, have I never met this man if he's a friend of Tom's? I've been to numerous events he's held. I've met numerous single men he's attempted to hook me up with."

Crystal looks away quickly. She kinda knew Lea had an idea she and Tom have been trying to get her married off but she doesn't want to blow this hookup by giving anything away.

"Yes, I've known for years about you guys 'introducing me' to men. But this one, no. Never knew he even existed. Why not this one? Okay. I get it. He's rich and can have any piece of ass on this earth with the snap of his finger. Hell, I get I'm out of his league. But I coulda got an introduction for the heck of it to see. Right? No, maybe not, maybe so. Maybe it was a good idea I've never met this man. I mean there is no way I could grab his attention. Look at me. My tits are too small, my ass is starting to sag, and I got this gut that I need to starve myself to make it go away. But dammit, I betcha a fuck or two outta him would've been satisfying. Don't just sit there, say something."

"Will you take a breath and sit down."

Lea hasn't realized she has been pacing this whole time. So, she sits.

"First of all, stop calling him Mr. Landon. Second, stop putting yourself down like that. You know I hate it." Lea opens her mouth to respond, but Crystal halts her. "Shut up and don't interrupt me, it's my turn to talk. Bear has been focused on building his business."

"Bear, who is Bear?" Lea asks.

I thought we were talking about Adonis, I mean Mr. Landon. Shit Zion. What kinda name is Zion.

UNIQUE. KINDA RHYMES WITH LION. LION, TIGER AND A BEAR. ALL ROLLED INTO A BLACK TALL POWERFUL—.

Crystal brings Lea back to the conversation and away from the Sex Diva's musings.

"Oh sorry. Zion. I keep forgetting not to use that nickname. Anyway, Zion has a reputation of sex-them and leave-them wanting. He doesn't attend company events or things like that when he isn't doing business deals. The events or get-togethers he has attended with Tom have been family events, hanging out. Zion knows his money gets him attention, and he does everything to avoid that. Those close to him are lucky to be in his inner circle, and they know this and respect his privacy. The guy is a black billionaire. That's right. Billionaire. But you don't see him in the tabloids, news, or anything like that and he likes it that way. Women do chase him and he gives them a play, but it's for sex. As for being out of his league, you are never out of anyone's league. I'm sure glad you're turned on."

"Thanks for the reality check." Lea slumps in the chair in front of her desk across from Crystal.

"Wait, what reality check? This is not a reality check. After I saw the way he looked at you, this is a wake-the-hell-up-that-man-wants-to-sex-you check, so let's-make-it-happen check."

"What?" Lea asks her stunned.

No way is this man interested in me beyond a fuck. Dammit, I've given up on temporary fucks. Even for a billionaire, I'm not sure I want to go back to those kinds of men. But getting a taste of that dick. Just may have to dip back into temporary mode for a bit.

IT HAS BEEN WAY TO LONG SINCE WE HAVE BEEN PENETRATED BY A NICE THICK LONG ONE.

Sex Diva back off, Lea tells her.

"I believe you would be a good woman for Zion," Crystal says, bringing Lea back to reality again. "You guys think a lot alike. Even with you being an introvert to his extrovert, you guys can make a powerful combination. No, hear me out. I'm not going to play cupid," she lies, "I don't know where Zion's head is at right now. I don't know if he is still the playa getting ass on the fly or if he wants something permanent and solid. All I'll say is be yourself. Don't play these female games to get his attention. Like you have told me so many times, if a man wants you, he will move heaven and earth to be with you and accept you as you are because that is what you're ready for. Just remember that, please?" she tells Lea getting up from behind her desk.

"Do you really think he was attracted to me?" Lea asks her with the sound of hope in her voice.

In the kitchen bumping into him and having him embrace me felt so good. But that could be because I haven't been in a man's embrace in two years.

HEY, DON'T TAKE THAT EMBRACE AWAY FROM ME, Sex Diva is admonishing her, WE NEED ALL WE CAN GET RIGHT NOW.

"Girl, that man could not take his eyes off you. I've never seen so much sexual tension between two people on a good level like that before. If things move to something between you guys, enjoy it. Have fun. You haven't enjoyed a dating life for the last few years. It's time to date a little. Just don't lose what you've accomplished. That self-confidence on you looks damned good. I love the skirt by the way."

Crystal leaves and I return to earth with a thud. Zion is sexy and handsome and exudes a carnal sexuality that speaks to my Sex Diva and I did feel an attraction between us. But him being attracted to me and doing anything about it, well that ain't gonna happen. Me and a billionaire. Yeah right. Back to work Lea. Back to your boring life.

Kia Lui

-7-

Tom, Crystal and Lea meet at the end of the day for their daily review. The last two meetings went without a hitch. They closed out one contract with a happy and satisfied client and the promise of pushing more business G-TEE's way. They provided a three-month status update regarding changes another client had requested. The client agreed, with a check for an additional six figures.

"Well, ladies, we've done great. Landon Enterprises' contracts are signed and sealed. With the other contracts signed as well, we're set for the next year to run the business. After today any additional contracts or new clients are going to bonuses, raises, and hiring," Tom boasts.

"Good job to us all," Crystal adds.

Lea is feeling relaxed and back to herself. "Wonderful. Can I schedule some vacation time? I need a break," she laughs and stretches her legs flexing her calf muscles. Walking in heels all day makes them cramp up.

IF WE WERE DATING ADONIS, HE COULD BE MASSAGING OUR LEGS TONIGHT.

You're on a roll today, Sex Diva. Anyway, we just met the man. It's pretty presumptuous of you to be talking about dating and what he could be doing to us while we're dating. I mean seriously. Get a grip. We truly don't even know if the man is even interested in us. It's hearsay from—.

Lea notices the quiet in the room and looks up and sees that Tom and Crystal are watching her.

"You wanna clue us in on the conversation you are having with your inner self?" Tom asks. The first time Tom noticed Lea talking to herself, they were working on a client's computer issue. Her hands and head were moving all over the place. Every now and then, he would catch a word. He would ask if she was talking to him. He got yelled at with her saying, "When I'm talking to you, you will know it. Now leave me alone." He cracked up after the retort and has learned to enjoy and watch her silently until she returns back to the living.

"No, not particularly. I'm done. What were you saying?" Lea looks away sheepishly.

"I was saying, no, not yet, you can't take a vacation. None of us can. We have the wine tasting event and don't forget about the charity ball next month. Crystal, add an RSVP for Zion with a plus-one for the wine tasting. How are things going with that?"

Crystal, looking at her to do list, provides Tom an update, "Great. All the wine gift bags are ready, the menu is finalized. Wine glasses arrive two weeks before the event. Lea and all the staff will be there working and socializing." Crystal stares at her pointedly.

"Yes ma'am. I'll be there with my happy thoughts, a smile, and my camera."

Oh, great. Zion will be there and he's bringing someone. Well, at least I get to see what kinda woman is in his league.

Crystal continues, "Things are set to go without any issues as usual. And Lea, you don't get to run off and take pictures with your camera for at least the first two hours. Wait until after sixty percent of our guests have arrived. Got it?"

"Yes ma'am. Got it."

"Good," Tom says, "Lea, keep me in the loop on all of Landon Enterprises' implementations. I see a problem with an outside contractor for the wiring in his new building. Make sure we have at least three other contractors we can recommend if things don't work out."

"Sure, will do. Did the current contractor not agree to the dates of completion as laid out in the proposal?"

"He agreed, but he was hesitant about doing so. Just have our backups ready. Okay ladies I think we're done here. Anything else?"

Crystal and Lea say no.

Lea gets up to leave so she can change clothes for her workout. As she leaves the office she notices that everyone is gone. G-TEE has a firm policy: go enjoy your Fridays after five o'clock. You never know when you may get called in on a project. Idea people need time to wind down and relax.

As she gets to her car, she notices Crystal's, Tom's and his wife's cars are here. Even Crystal's husband's car is here.

They must be having dinner tonight.

Lea smiles.

They party harder than any other couples I know.

Up in the office, the four cupids are talking. And scheming. Tom comes back into his office from walking around checking to see if anyone is still here and closes his door. "Okay, she's gone. Today was rough. I thought I was going to have a heart attack."

Tom's wife Linda, "Well? Did they click?"

"Like you would not believe. Shit, the sexual tension was off the fricking chain. Those two are meant for each other. Why wasn't I pushed to do this sooner?" Tom asks.

"I'm so happy we decided to hook them up. Carl's wife going into labor was perfect. That placed Lea right in line to head this project," Crystal chirps, smugly ignoring Tom's question.

Crystal's husband Stanley is pouring everyone wine, "And you guys are sure they aren't suspicious? I don't want to see either of them get hurt. If Zion is still a player, this could be hard for Lea. She has been through enough."

"Hun, you're right, but she needs to live a little. I'll keep telling her to be herself and don't lose who she is," Crystal says taking a glass from him.

"Okay, well, here is to another happy and loving couple. To Lea and Zion," Stanley says handing the others a glass.

They all clink glasses, drink, and leave for dinner.

-8-

As Zion steps out of Tom's building, Sam, his driver gets out to open the door of his BMW 750i. He takes the peach pie from Zion and places it on the back seat.

Sam has been with Zion for almost thirty years. They met in a gym talking while lifting weights. When he and Zion first met, Sam was just getting out of the Air Force transitioning into the corporate world. He has remained a burly man since those days. He could break a man in two.

Zion discovered Sam's special skills at the gym one day when a cocky dumb ass kid was looking for a fight. That day the kid chose Zion. The guy was determined to fight him, but Zion always walked away from fights. A man in his position, even almost thirty years ago, couldn't afford to get caught fighting, even if it was justified. It's amazing how steroids can make wimps think they are the Terminator with something to prove.

So, one evening as Zion was leaving the gym, here comes the cocky kid looking for that fight. It was dark and deserted in the garage and normally Zion is aware of his surroundings. But that night he was slacking. The kid came out of nowhere with a blow to his side that knocked the wind out of him.

In the few seconds, it took for Zion to re-group and prepare to rip the guy's spleen out, Sam was on him subduing him in a choke hold. The guy was losing conscience.

"Let him go. Hey Man. I said, 'Let him go.'". Zion feared for the wimps life.

Sam looked at him with a hard look that said, "'I got this'".

The cocky kid sank to the floor in a heap, snoring. The dude was snoring. Zion burst out laughing.

Sam apologized to Zion for not getting to him fast enough before the kid hit him. "Don't worry about the kid. My chokehold was only to slow him down. Amazing. He fell asleep. Never seen that before, have you?"

"Uh no, never. I'm Zion," Zion says introducing himself, leaving off his last name.

"Sam.", Sam responds following Zion's lead with skipping his last name.

They shake hands and right then Zion knew he needed a second, third, and fourth pair of eyes. He made Sam an offer he couldn't refuse to head his security detail and Sam accepted. Zion's motto was simple: pay individuals for their skills and for what they can do handsomely, and you'll have loyal employees for life.

Years later, Zion asked what happened to the kid.

"Cancelled his gym membership. Got off the juice." Sam is a man of few words.

Neither never mentioned the incident again. They have been working together ever since. Twenty-eight years and counting.

"Sam, how did your meetings go with Lea Adams? Will her ideas work with what we have in mind?" Zion asks him.

"She's good. She knows her stuff. I liked the idea of once they write the program or finish the security setup, we take it from there. All they would be doing was maintaining equipment or letting us know when to make tweaks based on our schedules. All the other companies wanted their hands into everything. When I asked her why G-TEE didn't want that, she said two words while looking me straight in the eye. Plausible Deniability. I was sold."

"When did you meet?"

"Saul and I met her when you went away with your sister and family for the week. I had finished early with my son dropping him off at college and decided to do that meeting. I hope that was okay? Saul was all for it."

"No, that was perfect. I'm glad. Uhm, what do you think of her? Personally."

Sam glances at Zion. He has never asked him about any female he has "entertained". They know his usual type is for temporary release.

"Sir, if I can be frank?"

"I think I like the name Sam better but go ahead. Be Frank. For now." They laugh.

"She is much understated. Doesn't seem the type to need the flashy trappings most of the women you get, uh, involved with. She's no bull shitter, if I can describe a woman that way. She presents herself as one who, if you put in the time and effort, will blow your mind."

As I listen to Sam, I kinda agree with his assessment. Yes, there is something underneath the quiet, shy demeanor of Ms. Lea Adams.

"I signed the contract with them today. Until I say otherwise, she has all access to me when she needs it."

They arrive in the garage where he lives and park near the private elevators that take owners up to the top-level apartments.

"Yes sir, duly noted," Sam says staring at Zion.

"Oh, don't look at me like that."

"Like what?"

"I won't be needing you tonight. I don't know my plans right now. If I leave, I'll let you know."

"Goodnight, Sir."

"Goodnight, Sam."

Zion enters his apartment and the lights come on automatically. His apartment is on the top floor of the newly constructed Warehouse Lofts in downtown St. Louis.

Although I live down here, I neither have nor want my offices down here. My clients deserve privacy and confidentiality. The buildings in downtown St. Louis don't provide that. Ergo, that is why I have offices near the Chesterfield Airport and am renovating the warehouse near that location.

Maybe I'll look at a house out that way. Maybe.

At night, downtown is perfect. Zion has a view of Busch Stadium on one side and the Gateway Arch and Riverfront on the other. He can even catch events at the stadium sitting out on his deck when he's home. Since the redevelopment of downtown, it is always popping with social activities.

It may not be a Times Square or a Hollywood Boulevard, where someone is always hoping to run into someone famous, but a nondescript billionaire like himself can go any place around here and enjoy a meal and music alone or with a group of friends.

Man, I love my hometown.

Walking into his kitchen for a drink he sees that his housekeeper Mrs. Vance has left him a note.

"Mr. Landon, a light dinner is in the refrigerator should you elect to stay in this evening. I'll be spending the weekend with the grandkids before my son goes out of town. Should you need me for anything, please do not hesitate to call. The boys would love to see you."

It amazes me how good I am with everyone else's kids. I would have been a great father. She is a wonder. Think I'll survive on my own this weekend. I may do something new. Like stay home and think about Ms. Lea Adams.

Zion pours a drink and stands looking out the window.

It's only two o'clock in the afternoon. Time for a slice of pie and to get some work done.

-9-

Lea is finishing off her evening with a session with her trainer. She hates working out. She does it to keep from going crazy with loneliness, to control the stress of taking care of her mom, to get out of the house, and to get off the couch.

Okay and the fricking health benefits also.

Lea misses the days when she could eat and enjoy food without gaining weight. Her trainer keeps her in line forcing her through workouts that when done, her energy, mind, and body are drained and ready for sleep. Usually. Tonight, her mind and body are focused on Mr. Zion Landon.

Over the last few years Lea has changed. She decided to really look inward and figure out what she wants and needs compared to what she has been settling for and accepting. She had been falling in line with what she now calls the peanut gallery of advice givers, in living life their way and not her way. She accepted the if- game, the waiting- game, the just-living-life-keeping-it-simple- game, the I-don't-do-titles- game, and all that other bull crap excuses men give.

Geez. All that time wasted when I think back on it. Let's not get it twisted. There was a time when I would have considered a fast, quick, in a hurry sexual night of gratification. But with those you never allow yourself to experience the joy of being with the person. Enjoying the moment. I always found myself uptight and holding back.

Lea has wanted to take her sex life to another level, to step out of her comfort zone and see what else is out there. With the flirtationships, constantly flirting with men knowing neither of them were going to take it any further for reasons neither of them understood, she had over the years, found herself on the path to wanting the committed, monogamous, with lots of sex relationship.

One day, she decided to do an Internet search of the word "submission", adding the key word "sexual". For years she has heard this word mentioned in relationships, but it would always turn her off. Talk about a mind-blowing discovery. She discovered much of the research was about a woman submitting to a dominant man. A dominant alpha male. The kind of man she imagined she could allow herself to trust without being hampered by what is or isn't the norm.

Bondage, Discipline, Domination, Submission, Sadism, Masochism. BDSM. She had to be careful discussing this topic. Lea thought she would like some aspects of bondage, being restrained during sex, to be disciplined and dominated and to submit to a man she could trust. All this was a desire she didn't even know she had. Sadism and masochism, however, will never come into play in her relationships. Ever. Lea wants to be man-handled, she desires some hard-carnal sex. When she looked into submission and began to understand it, she found it wasn't just the biblical version where a woman submits to the man of the household or head of the marriage. Or at least not all of it. In a relationship, it's about fully being able to trust someone without hesitation knowing they will, in turn, trust you. For both the male and female. Few people get or deserve that trust, so they don't get that kind of submission.

She learned to explore her freaky side with her first boyfriend but never took it as far as she would have liked. They were young and only knew the basics. Her other boyfriends were into plain old boring sex, but she didn't realize how boring it was until she opened her mind to other possibilities. She gets hot thinking about all the things she wants to explore. She just needs the right man for that.

Lea wants to be spanked, tied down, lustfully made love to and fucked hard. She realized these soft, oh-let-me-be-gentle with you lovers bore the hell out of her.

A bunch of gutless wimps who think man-handling is brutally beating a woman. Uh no. If a man tried to beat me, I would put a bullet in his brain.

This woman, does not do abuse. Oh, hell no, not gonna happen.

She has been aroused all day, needing to get off because of Mr. Zion Landon, Adonis, Bear, let-me-worship-your-dick-you-Greek-looking-God kinda man, but could never get away. Yes, to get away, to her car or even go home for lunch for a quick touch-me feel-me session is always an option for Lea. Like now. She can't get home fast enough. She rushes through the door dropping everything in the middle of the living room and disarming the alarm. She grabs the candles from the bedroom and places them in the bathroom along with her Bluetooth speaker. She lights the candles and runs bath water adding oil and bubble bath.

She goes back to the bedroom pulling out her "blue box of entertainment", as she calls it. Over the years she has purchased a number of vibrators, instructional books, arousal oils and books of erotic short stories. She has added a few BDSM items, feathers, blindfolds, Ben Wa balls, and a leather whip/tickler. She always thought, in any relationship, she would need to know how to pleasure her man as well as pleasuring herself, knowing what she likes and doesn't like. It has been a wonderful discovery. Now, if she can only get a man that can help her take that knowledge further.

Adonis, maybe? I get tingly thinking about him.

Lea learned when purchasing vibrators that most women go for penetration items, penises, the bigger the better. Not her. When Lea wants to be penetrated, she does not want a fake dick. She desires the real deal. For her, masturbating is a release of built-up sexual tension. She enjoys clitoral stimulation and her vibrators are all specifically designed for that. Sometimes she wants a fast, quick and explosive orgasm. Sometimes, she likes to draw out her pleasure.

Tonight, she wants explosive. Tonight's vibrator selection, the We Vibe Touch, fits into the palm of her hand and is gently curved at the tip, very soft with eight vibration modes. She spent a hundred dollars on this vibrator. Some investments are worth the money. She hopes someday to retire, i.e. trash them all, for the right man, or at least hopes to be with a man who is not intimated by one and would join in on the fun.

Shit my tits are swelling and my clit is already throbbing.

She strips down and goes into the bathroom turning off all the lights and making sure the playlist from the Bluetooth is a sensual one. Nineties and Eighties old school R&B. She steps into the tub enjoying the hot water, sliding down all the way to her shoulders, spreading the bubbles around her, covering up.

As the music plays, she relaxes and thinks about Zion. From the top of his head down to his soft hands and his upper body, so powerful.

I wonder if his chest is bare or has hair.

She caresses her lips, slowly trailing her fingers down to her breasts, pinching her nipples, imagining Zion licking and sucking them.

Lord, his lips looked so soft. Not at all chapped or dry.

Her thumbs have a mind of their own, moving to her nipples, circling them, her palms squeezing and gripping her breasts.

They feel so heavy.

She is a small 'B' cup but when aroused they feel like a full 'C' cup. She glides her hands down to her stomach, fluttering her fingers pretending Zion is kissing her, licking her. Her fingers reach for her woman-hood, and she touches her swollen clit.

Geez, it is so tender to the touch. Hell, it has been months since I've masturbated. I need this, I need to cum. Explosively, over and over and over.

She slips her fingers between the folds of her woman-hood and glides them up and down. Even under the water, she is lubed and slick.

Shit. Oooohhhh, Zion. Finger fuck me. Play with my clit.

Moaning, she uses one hand to hold open the walls of her woman-hood rubbing and squeezing her clit.

Oh Zion, squeeze harder, yes harder.

She adds her fingers, gliding up and down and back and forth and in circular movements.

Shit Lea you feel so good, so wet, I imagine Zion saying. *Cum for me, that's it, cum for me.*

She glides her fingers to her clit tapping it, causing her to jump. The bath water sloshes over the top of the tub. She can feel the orgasm, wanting to cum, to reach that release, to feel the orgasm Zion can give her. She uses her fingers, vigorously rubbing her clit.

Oh, please don't stop, more, more.

She keeps moving faster and applying pressure to her clit, circling it, rubbing it and squeezing it. With one final squeeze and flick, she cums.

Oh, fuck yes Ziiiioooooonnnnnnnn.

Wishing he was here to fuck her, she comes back to earth out of the throes of her orgasm, sated, for the moment. Looking over at the toilet, her eyes focus on the vibrator still sitting there. Lea busts out laughing.

OH YES, WE ARE SOOOOOO FUCKING HIM.

Kia Lui

-10-

Zion spends the rest of the afternoon checking emails, responding to urgent correspondence and planning out the next week. He informs his assistant, Morgan, to add Lea Adams to the list of people who has availability to him at all times on the premise that she is the lead on the construction project with G-TEE.

He feels like a school boy, with a silly grin on his face thinking about liking a girl and wondering if she likes him. He also has Morgan add the wine tasting to his calendar. Zion is looking forward to this event.

During the drive back to his apartment, Zion gave Saul a call to have him run a personal background check on Lea. Just because she comes highly recommended and favorable doesn't mean he should slack on the basic background and relationship check. Especially if he plans on getting to know her better.

Getting to know her better; what the hell does that actually mean to you Zion?

He checks his email and sees the response from Saul.

"Mr. Landon:

Following is the information I have obtained regarding Ms. Lea Grace Adams.

- Single never married, no kids
- Social media accounts: six. Only active on one daily, all others she has few followers, fewer than fifty, following fewer than twenty-five.
- Minimal personal details found on these accounts, none involving relationships
- Homeowner

- Has three degrees: Associates, Bachelor's and Master's
- Hobby: photography. Some pictures have won local contests
- No siblings
- No pets
- Debt: student loans and credit cards
- Mother: living
- Father: unknown, no information found
- No criminal record or legal issues

Should you need anything else, please let me know. Saul"

Saul's thorough background checks on staff, clients, and potential associations have steered Landon Enterprises away from many of the financial issues other similar companies have experienced. His background checks have even steered Zion away from troublesome women. It will be interesting getting to know more about Lea and seeing if she truthfully fills in the blanks or lies about anything.

Zion's latest sexual standby texted him while Sam was driving him home, and he hadn't responded back. Wendy is always willing to sex when he needs sex. Most people would say he is leading her on. They don't know, but Wendy is 'dating' her way to marriage and Zion is a pit stop for her.

She wants that family life. When they met, she was looking for temporary. It has worked out just fine with him. No strings, no expectations, no demands. He considers going to her place for a quickie and as soon as he gets the thought, he feels a twang of guilt.

Guilt. What the hell do I have to feel guilty about? Before the meeting at G-TEE this morning, I was looking to release some sexual tension. Why not her? Because you can't stop thinking about Lea and how you want to bury your dick inside her and let it sit and throb in her warmth. I haven't even dated the woman, and I'm feeling guilty thinking about sexing another woman. This lady has me acting crazy, thinking crazy thoughts, and I don't even know her. Wendy it is.

>Zion texts Wendy back:
>>*You up for a visit tonight?*
>Wendy responds instantly:
>>*Sure, I guess.*
>Zion: *Why do you say 'I guess'?*
>Wendy: *Going to the movies, wanna join me?*

The only hanging out Zion has ever done with a woman is a movie with Wendy out of pure boredom. Movie then sex. Even with a fuck, you must lay the groundwork.

>Zion: *Sure, I'll meet you there in twenty minutes.*
>Wendy: *See you then.*

Wendy always goes to the same theater in the Chase Park Plaza Hotel. To her, it is classy, expensive, yet semi-normal. Considering what kind of man she wants, she figures going to upscale places that come off as normal gives her a better chance at finding The One.

Yeah. Okay. Whatever. I like it 'cause I can get a drink and dinner if I want.

He informs Sam he is going out after all by sending him a text. Arriving at the theater, Zion checks the time: nine-thirty. Wendy is waiting at the entrance. He suggests getting something to eat instead and she agrees. They wander into the restaurant being seated immediately.

My patience tonight can't handle a ninety-minute movie in silence.

They begin the evening with some basic small talk, Zion asking her about work and her latest dating endeavors. He learned early on with Wendy to do this to keep their understanding clear, that she should keep looking for The One and it's not him.

Not gonna happen.

"So, how's work?"

"It pays the bills or barely."

Here we go, the push for a hand out.

Wendy works as a hostess at one of St. Louis' high-end private smoking clubs. Zion doesn't smoke, but a client wanted to go, so they went. That was a night to remember. Tits, ass, and legs were everywhere, serving drinks, being nice and allowing squeezes and pats. Wendy caught his eye because she stayed out of the smoking lounge as much as she could but made sure all the guests were happy. He made a pass at her the second she greeted him, and she took the bait. After a few wining and dining dates and finding out her STD status, they became fuck buddies.

Why fuck buddies? She wants marriage and kids.

Zion told her not him. She suggested a plan. They fuck every once in a while, that way she could get her sex fix while looking for Mr. Husband. No strings attached, no problems, no headaches.

I informed her no drama because I don't do drama and anything that goes on between us stays between us and our personal lives stay separate at all times.

Wendy agreed. They would fuck every couple of months. She was even willing to try some things she thought was freaky, most would consider normal. She never complained about Zion not giving her oral or his using condoms even after they confirmed they were clean.

She is soft in her love-making skills.

Love-making skills, yeah right. Skills my ass.

Wendy wants to be made love to, is silent for the most part, and as freaky as she thinks she is, her skills are tame. Especially compared to what Zion desires.

This tame sex is boring the hell out of me. Over the years, I have become a boring lover even by my own standards. I want to jungle fuck, but you can't do that with women who want to be made love to. As we talk more, I come to the realization I don't want this tame, soft love making anymore. Hell, my dick is not even semi-hard. This morning seeing and meeting Lea, I was brick hard with a third leg. Now I'm limp as a noodle. Oh man, I need to cut this shit short and off.

Zion asks the waiter for the check and looks at his phone. Making up an excuse, he tells Wendy he needs to take off. She looks disappointed but doesn't ask why or say a word.

She better not asking me anything. You got a meal and leftovers out of tonight.

He escorts her to her car.

"I'll text you when I get home. Okay Zion?"

Zion responds back distractedly his mind already away from Wendy and on business. "Yeah okay. Drive safely."

Getting back to his car, he decides to take a drive through the Central West End before heading home. As he is cruising the streets, a head of spiral curls catches his eye.

Damn, I think I saw Lea.

-11-

Zion couldn't have seen Lea in this throng of people walking up and down the street. No way. He swings around and slowly drives, scrutinizing the crowd.

Nothing. Maybe I got Lea on the brain and I'm hallucinating.

He makes a right turn toward Kingshighway Boulevard to head home.

Zion go home and get your mind off the vision stuck in your head, man.

He gets to the water fountain, and she's standing there taking pictures. She is flicking away, circling it and snapping at different angles really fast.

Is she alone? What the hell is this woman doing out alone taking pictures this late at night? It's almost eleven. She is so damned engrossed that anything could happen to her. Fuck, I'm pissed. Why am I pissed? I have no control over what she does. But I think I want to.

Zion hasn't realized he's been sitting too long in the street blocking traffic until he hears a horn blowing. The noise attracts Lea's attention and she snaps a picture of his car.

The little minx.

He pulls over and parks. His windows are tinted dark. The Acura NSX he's driving is black, has a matte finish with slim silver trim detailing. Zion gets out glancing around, hoping he hasn't lost her again.

She couldn't have seen me.

He spots her on the other side of the fountain, sitting on a bench people-watching and blowing bubbles from the gum she is chewing.

A grown woman chewing bubble gum. How fascinating and kiddy like. Not sure how I feel about that. Hope it isn't a nasty habit.

He stares hard, wanting her to look his way, then she does. She freezes, and he thinks she curses under her breath.

So, she cusses. Oh my.

He smiles devilishly walking Lea's way, not taking his eyes off her. She is fidgeting with her necklace, brushing her arm across her breasts. He stops in front of her, and his presence forces her to look up at him.

I see innocence and heat mixed in that look.

She hastily takes out a bubble gum wrapper and puts her gum in it, putting the old gum in her pocket.

"Hello Mr. Landon. I mean Zion. Can I call you Zion outside of business?"

"Lea, I insist on you always calling me Zion." I smile. "May I join you?"

"Sure."

She scoots over to the far end of the bench and allows him to sit.

"You have yet to address me as Ms. Adams. Why do you use my first name?"

"I like the sound of your first name. I like saying your first name. Ms. Adams seems rather formal, and I feel relaxed with you. Do I offend you by addressing you by your first name?"

'Cause I won't stop using your first name.

"No, it just seems odd that you never addressed me as Ms. Adams. Different. Unexpected." Lea says, looking into the water and not at him.

"I'm a different kinda man. Did I see you taking pictures of the water fountain?" I don't see her camera anymore.

"Yes. Photography is my hobby."

"Where did the camera go?"

"Oh." She opens her jacket and shows me the camera. For a March evening, it is kinda cool.

"Nice camera."

"Thanks. Um, nice car. A rather simple nice car for a man of your stature and status."

"Thanks. It may look like a simple, nice car but what's under the hood is completely out of the ordinary."

"Out for a late-night drive?"

She looks at me intently like she wants me to tell her exactly what I'm doing out tonight and probably with whom. "I just finished dinner with a friend and was about to go home when I saw you."

"Saw me. You saw me in this crowd?"

"Yes. You stand out."

Lea bursts out laughing. "Really. I have never had anyone say that to me before."

"Well you do. Believe me."

I like the sound of her laughter. An actual laugh and not that coy hee-hee type.

"Thanks. In what way do I stand out? Or did stand out?"

"I noticed your hair, and well, I noticed your—," Zion pauses for effect, "shapely ass."

Lea drums her fingers on the bench.

"My ass isn't that shapely."

"It's shapely enough that I noticed it."

This woman is some kinda fun. We are having a simple conversation about her ass, and she is not even offended.

"I guess the squats are kinda working then."

"I'd say they're working perfectly. Are you alone or waiting on someone?" Zion looks around hoping not to see someone walking toward them to join them.

"Alone. I was bored at home and decided to come out and take some pictures."

"This late, sorta dangerous, don't you think?"

"Please, don't you chastise me, too."

"Too? Who else is chastising you?"

If it's another man, I may go ballistic. What is with me?

"My best friend. I'm fully aware I should not be out alone at night taking pictures, and I need to take precautions or maybe stay at home locked away."

Zion mutters under his breath "'locked away, stripped naked, pinned down and fucked'".

"Pardon."

"Nothing, go on."

"I thought heard the word 'fucked'."

"I may have said the word 'fucked'."

Lea stares at me waiting for me to respond, so I change the subject. "Why are you not out clubbing with your girls, partying, and dancing, meeting men?"

"I don't do much clubbing and most of my girls are in relationships, booed up in some way or doing other things."

"You don't go out?"

"Oh, I do, but it's never an every weekend kinda thing. Sometimes, it could be four weekends in a row or sometimes we won't hang out for months. I enjoy my own company. What about you? Why aren't you out on a date with some sexy piece of—? Sorry, never mind. Not my business."

Lea turns her head, staring at the fountain.

So, I do affect her. I can see the pulse in her neck throbbing. Well, I think I'll be honest with her.

"I did have dinner with someone tonight but got bored and sent her home. I wasn't feeling her tonight."

Lea looks at him with a stunned look.

"What?"

"I don't know what I'm shocked at more. The fact that you sent her home or that you just told me you sent her home. Isn't that like giving away too much of your personal life or something?"

"Maybe. You asked. I saw no point in lying."

Lea looks away from Zion and glances at his car again. "Nice car."

"You said that already. Boys need their toys. Will you send me a copy of the picture you took?"

"How do you know I took a picture?"

"I was watching you before I pulled over."

"Watching me?"

"You were extremely engrossed while taking pictures. Do you always lose yourself that way? That could be dangerous. I see why your best friend would chastise you. You need a pair of eyes to watch your back."

"I wasn't as engrossed as you think. But, yes, sometimes I do need a pair of eyes to watch my—," Lea thinks about her next word, "back."

This time, Zion looks away.

"Do you always chew bubble gum?"

"Nope. Yes. Maybe. Only when I am alone and only when I remember to buy a pack when I happen to be in the store that sells the brand I can get really great bubbles from."

"Never knew answering a question about bubble gum could be so educational."

"I never expected to be asked about bubble gum. By a man. Usually he dismisses it as a bad habit, and he tells me to stop doing it."

"I did think it was a bad habit. After hearing you talk about it, it doesn't sound like a bad habit."

"Mr. Lan—. Zion. Why are we talking about bubble gum?"

"I like hearing your voice. I also like hearing you say my name."

"Oh. I'll be more than happy to send you the picture. Of your car that is. Text or email?"

"Text would be great. Would you like to have a drink?"

"Coffee Cartel?"

Zion smiles. No alcohol for the lady, and a coffee shop is right behind them.

"Coffee Cartel it is."

They stand. She has on jeans, purple running shoes, and a powder blue zip hoody with a college name emblazoned on it. Zion laughs.

"What's so funny?"

"Your clothes. You look extremely comfortable. Where is your purse, keys, and phone?"

"Ah. Never a purse when I'm out taking pictures. Keys are in my pocket. Phone, ID and money are in my workout belt around my waist and I'm wearing a Bluetooth headset. And lip gloss in my back pocket. Never leave home without lip gloss. Dry lips are a sin." She stares at his lips a moment too long, then licks hers and looks away.

Zion notices she isn't wearing makeup. She looks just as fresh as she did this morning. She is as sexy now as she was then. He's so glad he spotted her.

And maybe I'll get a taste of those lips and tongue.

Neither Lea nor Zion notice the two individuals watching them from separate cars.

One is wondering who the fuck the guy is. Some random dick I need to scare off as usual. Naw man, that pussy you ain't getting. That pussy taken.

The other is wondering why they let this opportunity pass to tell the big exciting news. Did the chance just slip though their fingers? Of course not. There's plenty of time.

-12-

Of all the people for Lea to run into in the Central West End, it would have to be Adonis. Mr. Zion Landon, the subject of her wet fantasies. How could this be happening? They walk over to the Coffee Cartel in silence. He opens the door for her, and they walk toward the counter.

"What would you like?" Zion asks her.

"A bottle of water."

"Water? Are you sure?"

"Yes, please. Thank you." *Last thing I want is a cup of coffee keeping me up all night*, Lea thinks to herself. She will have her dreams of Adonis for that.

He purchases two bottles of water, and they sit down at a small table across from each other.

"So, tell me about yourself?" Zion asks.

"You don't want to talk business? Or bubble gum? I don't mind if you want to," Lea says.

Zion laughs. "It's late Friday evening or early Saturday morning, depending on how you look at it. The last thing I want to discuss is business. I think we have exhausted the bubble gum topic. I want to hear about you. Tell me about you. Unless you don't want to."

"Oh, we could never exhaust the bubble gum topic. I can tell you horror stories about finding the wrong bubble gum. But talking about myself, I guess I can make it sound as interesting. Talking about me makes me feel like I'm interviewing for a job. Since this is not business, I need to adjust from business mode and think about what position I'm interviewing for. Friend, associate, buddy, or lover?"

I look at him and he is smirking at me. The guy is smirking at me. Good. That means he is not stuffy and may have a sense of humor.

"Well, all of the above sounds great. Pick one and go for it. No bubble gum."

"Okay, let's go with friend. Okay, an interview to be your friend. Here goes. I consider myself to be an introvert. Most of my friends wouldn't say that, but they don't remember how I was before I met them. I'm quiet but love to have fun and laugh. I'm learning to enjoy life now more than ever. I have no kids, never been married, nor engaged. I avoid drama, pettiness, and behavior unbecoming an adult with common sense. But I can get angry and check people when pushed. Once we become friends, and you treat me right, I'll treat you right, and we'll be friends for the rest of our lives. No matter where or with whom we end up with."

"You have impressive friend qualifications."

I'm not going to even question her state of singleness. Hell, at our age, she could have had multiple kids with multiple baby daddies.

"And what are your friend qualifications?" she asks him.

"Okay, well, I'm a private person. I keep my circle of friends small. I'm driven and will help friends and family without a second thought because they respect me, and I love and respect them. My business has allowed me to enjoy the finer things in life but I never forget where I was before I ever had anything. I don't make friends easily, but when I do, I keep them. I'm also single, never been married, no kids. So, I say to you, 'Welcome friend'."

Zion extends his hand for a shake. Lea shakes his, and he squeezes and caresses hers upon letting it go. Normally, this move would freak her out, but with him she wants more, she wants it to linger. His hand is as soft as she remembers from their handshake earlier in the day.

"Thank you for the warm welcome," Lea says as she stares at his hands wanting them on her breasts. She grasps her water bottle sliding her fingers up and down it. She moves her hand to her lap when she notices Zion watching the hand movement. He adjusts his body in the chair.

They talk for another hour about a whole lot of nothing. His car, her photography, their love of music, and travel. Lea is feeling extremely comfortable with him. She can talk with him without that nervousness she usually feels around men. She tries to hide the yawn building, behind her hands, but he catches her.

"I think it is time we call it a night. Even though we did not discuss business, I'm looking forward to working with you on this project. And keeping a lifelong friend."

"So am I. You are so down to earth. No offense that is. It's just that with someone in your position, I would never think you would relax and enjoy something as simple as having a conversation with a woman over a bottle of water."

"No offense taken. Usually I'm in business mode twenty-four/seven. I'm even amazed at myself. Today has been a strange and good day. May I walk you to your car?"

"I couldn't allow you to do that. It's actually a mile away in the opposite direction of your car."

"What? A mile away? I'll drive you to your car. No, I don't want to hear of it. A mile away. Lady, that being locked away is sounding better every minute."

"I needed the exercise. In all honesty, if I hadn't run into you, I would have been back at my car and safely on my way home before midnight."

Zion stares at Lea intently. The tone of her voice is something I have never experienced from a woman before. I like it. That set-me-in-my-place tone, shit, I have never heard from a woman before and directed at me. They usually are sweet, accommodating. This from Lea. It gives me pause.

"What?" Lea asks him.

"Nothing. Let's go," he says holding the door open.

"No. What's wrong?"

"The tone of your voice. It just— It— A woman has never talked to me with that tone of voice before."

"Oh. Sorry. I was terse? I'm sorry."

"Stop apologizing. It's odd hearing a woman talk to me that way. A woman who isn't my mother or sister that is."

"Oh."

They walk to his car in silence. He opens the door for Lea.

Shit, there goes my smartass mouth. Hope he doesn't take this out on Tom and the project by cancelling it. Oh well at least I'll get a friend and a great business partner out of this. Maybe.

He gets in and starts the car. Soft R&B music is playing through the speakers.

Lea gives him directions to her car.

"It's the Acura on the right."

He pulls up behind it.

"So, you drive an Acura. You have nice tastes. I like the Gold. Sunroof, tinted windows. Yes, you have nice tastes, Lea, real nice tastes."

"Your Acura NSX is nice, too, but I have already said that. Twice. Sorry."

"No problem. I would like to ask you something."

I pray this woman doesn't get offended, but this is my chance and as a money man you never pass up a chance when you see it.

"Ask away," she says, thinking she can salvage at least a working relationship with this man.

"Have you ever mixed business with pleasure?"

Please, don't slap me or cuss me out.

"No," she says calmly.

Okay, where the hell this conversation going? Never expected that question.

"Why not?"

I'm going for broke and see what happens. Maybe she can be my next temporary fuck. Taming that smartass mouth could be fun in itself.

"Never been tempted to take that kinda risk, never met anyone I was attracted to like that. Don't get me wrong. Men have tried, but walking away was easier. Why do you ask?"

Lea is thinking, so let's play this game. I'm all in.

"What about you. Ever mix business with pleasure?"

"No, I have never mixed business with pleasure, or wanted to that is. Until today," he says staring directly at her waiting to see if she gets offended before he continues. She sits, expressionless. "I have never met a working female colleague that I want to bend over my car and feverishly fuck as I want with you at this very moment. I know you feel the sexual tension between us in addition to feeling comfortable and relaxed with me as I do you," Zion rushes out before she can object.

Some women get upset at the word fuck. Lea takes in a deep breath and smiles.

"I'm feeling something, I'm just not sure I want to give into it."

So, a man that talks dirty. I wonder if he fucks or makes love. Will he man-handle me? Would he be willing to try out some BDSM? Hhhmmmm, let's stoke the fires and see.

"Why not?" he asks.

"I'm not a temporary piece of ass. I don't want a temporary fuck. You're a career bachelor. I've done my research. You haven't been in a steady relationship since college, you're extremely private, and you don't have any personal social media pages. Don't look so surprised. An Internet search is a girl's best friend. What I need and what I desire can't be obtained by fucking every now and then."

Let that shock his ass away. Men be wanting a temporary freak in the bedroom and a lady they refuse to claim out in public. Sorry, I'm not doing this temp shit.

"You aren't offended at what I said? You don't want to slap me?" Zion asks incredulously.

And she said the word fuck. Rolled off her tongue like she was saying water. And it quenched my appetite just like a shot of Patron would about now.

"No, you were honest. A tad blunter than I would have thought being as we just met today in a business capacity, but a man as you are would be blunt to see where things would go. Have other women slapped you when you were blunt, or did they say your place or mine? Or was I supposed to be offended at the word fuck. That is what a playa does. Fuck."

I can't stop myself from saying that word. Every time I say it, he stares at my mouth. Lea stop playing. Heeheeheehee. I can't help but laugh inwardly.

KEEP UP WITH THE WORD FUCK. WE GOTTA VERBALLY CONVINCE HIM TO GIVE UP A LOT OF FUCK SESSIONS.

Zion adjusts himself in his seat.

She keeps saying fuck and I will fuck her. Now.

"It was always them suggesting my place," Zion says, "but we would end up at a hotel eventually. Now that I think of it, maybe we should keep this as business."

AW DAMN. MAKE SOME KINDA MOVE ON HIM. DO IT.

He gets out and comes around opening the door. Lea takes his offered hand getting out. In tennis shoes, the top of her forehead comes at his chin. He stands aside and closes the door walking her to the driver side of her car.

Lea turns around prepared for a business-like goodbye. Before she can say anything, he puts his hand on the back of her neck, draws her mouth close to his, and kisses her.

Damn his lips are so soft.

GLAD ONE OF YOU MADE A MOVE. GEEZ

She leans into the kiss gripping the front of his jacket kissing him as hard as he is kissing her. He puts his hand on her waist in an attempt to draw her close, to press his body into hers but her camera stops him. He pulls back and looks at her.

"I needed to taste you. I want to be inside you. I don't know how to do anything but temporary, but I know I want you," he whispers in her ear.

Lea pulls back.

Nope, I'm not doing this temporary bullshit. He can go fuck one of his usual string of waiting pussies. Nope, no sir, I'm not that girl anymore.

"Good night Zion. I'll send you the picture of your car. Talk to you soon."

I smile up at him, staring at his lips instead of his eyes and lick my lips. His lips would feel nice on my clit I bet.

She kisses him one last time, nibbles on his bottom lip, then pulls away, and steps back from him.

Lea, that was wrong. So wrong. Business colleagues don't kiss each other like that.

BUT TWO PEOPLE WHO WANNA FUCK DO.

Zion looks at Lea closely. Wanting to see judgment, denial or rejection. But all he sees is desire. Complete sexual desire.

Her licking her lips like that and nibbling mine sure as hell don't help the situation.

He lets her go, opening her car door for her to step in. "Drive safely, Lea," he says looking down at her.

"You, too, Zion," she gives him a wicked smile, looking at the front of his pants.

DICK PRINT.

As Lea drives off, she stops at the Stop sign watching Zion in her rearview mirror. He starts his car and just sits there.

WE FUCKING HIM. I DON'T KNOW WHEN, HOW, WHY OR WHERE, BUT WE FUCKING HIM. HE WON'T BE LEAVING THAT KINDA KISS, OH HELL TO THE DAMN NAW. NO SIR, WE GETTIN THAT DICK.

Lea drives home thinking maybe she should be agreeing with the Sex Diva.

-13-

During the next few weeks, Lea can't get Zion out of her head. Day in and day out, he is on her mind. His hand on her neck drawing her in for a kiss over and over and over.

This is not good. I must get this man out of my mind.

She spends her weeks going over all the details for the Landon Enterprises project. She has ordered the equipment. All the contractor deadline dates are set and have been agreed upon except for one. She has little to do, but is available to keep things moving smoothly.

She has to buy a dress for the Humane Society Charity Ball event coming up in a week. G-TEE always gets tickets and this year, she has been ordered to attend. Crystal and her husband, Stanley, will be there, and so will Tom and his wife, Linda. They're all riding together in the limo Tom has rented for the evening.

Lea heads out to West County Mall on Friday after work in search of THE dress. She hasn't heard from Zion, not that she had expected to. After that kiss, it would have been nice, but he wants temporary.

She goes in and out of too many stores to count having no clue what she wants to wear, only knowing that it has to be a formal dress. She hasn't even decided on a color yet.

All these stores selling formals and not one catches my eye.

She walks into the last store she plans on shopping in tonight and heads straight for the sale and clearance rack. She spots a cobalt blue dress peeking out of all the other purple, red, and green dresses.

Blue, oh yes, let's go with blue. Please let this be in my size.

She pulls the dress off the rack. This is a one-shoulder strap dress, form fitting down to the waist and flares out as you walk. Its material is light-weight and will catch the breeze and move with her curves.

I am so loving this dress. Please let it be in my size.

She tries it on and it fits perfectly.

Yay. Now I need jewelry.

Lea finds a crystal necklace, chandelier earrings, and a crystal bracelet.

Perfect. Now shoes. What color shoes?

As she goes through multiple shoe stores, she doesn't find any blue ones to match the blue of the dress, but she does find a pair of silver strappy heel sandals.

Dang it. That means I have to paint my toenails. Oh well, glamour night it is.

Crystal has been hounding her all week about what she is going to wear. Lea says nothing. She wants it to be a surprise. Saturday arrives. She is excited. Even being dateless, she can't wait to wear this dress and walk into a room feeling sexy.

Her hair is in loose twisted curls pulled to one side. Because she had to polish her toes, she goes all out and paints them cobalt blue, the same color as the dress. They are only visible if she raises her hem. Her fingernails are painted clear with an iridescent overlay that catches the light and sometimes look blue or purple.

At six-thirty, Tom is knocking on her door. She opens it, steps outside, and he whistles. Crystal, her husband and Tom's wife all step out the limo and stare, clapping for Lea as she walks to the car.

"Geez, will you guys stop it? Please. Enough," she begs but grins from ear to ear, "this is going to be a hilarious night, I can see that already."

They climb into the car and enjoy the luxury ride. The event is being held at the Stonelight Athletic and Dining Club. Everyone decides to have a drink in the car before they arrive. Lea takes one for some courage. She is walking into the party alone after all, and refuses to allow herself to freak out. She is going to enjoy this night as best as she can, being single and the fifth wheel.

They arrive at the club and queue in the line of cars. At their turn to exit the car, the men get out, assisting their wives. Tom and Crystal's husband stand on each side of the door, helping Lea out, each gripping a hand. She looks at them, shaking her head. They are acting out too much tonight, and their wives are letting them. Tom crooks his arm for his wife first and then Lea.

"Come on Lea, you are not walking in here alone," he says. "Two beautiful women on my arm. I'll be the talk of the town tonight. Make sure we are smiling for the cameras, ladies. This won't happen for me again. I look fire. It's all about me. I thank ya'll for looking cute, but I must be the center of attention," he laughs.

She puts her arm in the crook of his offered arm, and they walk into the club. Guests are everywhere. The Humane Society has rented the entire club, with dinner and dancing being up a grand staircase in the Grand Ballroom. The second Lea steps into the club she feels exposed, as if someone is staring at her, but when she looks around she doesn't catch anyone.

Oh, well, must be her own nervousness.

She shakes it off and squares her shoulders to enjoy herself tonight. She greets people she knows and allows herself to be introduced to new ones.

Everyone in Lea's group walks toward the stairs. She releases Tom's arm and lifts her dress so she can walk comfortably without tripping. Upon reaching the top of the stairs, she stops, seeing a woman coming out the ballroom and making a direct path toward her. Lea is barely able to step out of the way to keep from getting knocked over. She watches where the woman is walking and looks directly into the eyes of Zion Landon of Landon Enterprises. He gives her a sly smile, ignoring the woman approaching him, who glues her breasts to his arm. Lea now understands the staring she was feeling.

He is here with a piece of arm candy. Well, well, well. So, this is the kinda woman he uses for his temporary fucks. She could be someone he is settling down with. Maybe she is the one he was out with in the Central West End.

Either way, Lea nods an acknowledgement and follows the others to their table.

I should have known. He is a dream, and I will never be his type. Tits and ass too small. The Sex Diva is sitting on my shoulder pouting. I feel ya girlfriend. I feel ya.

Lea points out to everyone at the table that Zion is here and with another woman. They look around for him, spotting him walking to a table with his sister Star, her husband Garrett and the arm candy.

"Dammit," Crystal and Tom say looking at each other.

"Who the hell is she, and why the hell is he here?" Crystal hisses to Tom while Lea is being distracted by a client's wife of G-TEE.

"This was not the plan tonight. Zion was not supposed to be here with another woman or be here at all. Now we have to re-think this and somehow get them together. Shit," Tom whispers.

Tom places his jacket on the chair next to Lea and all the ladies put their purses on the seat effectively blocking anyone from sitting down for long. Oddly enough it works. Men come over to speak and then wander off.

All through dinner, they keep up the chatter making sure Lea stays relaxed and upbeat, knowing that when she realizes she is alone, she will get nervous and want to bolt out the door. That dress is giving her confidence tonight, but at any second, that confidence could blow away in the wind.

After dinner is over and the plates are cleared, Lea excuses herself and goes to the bathroom. She purposely walks as far away from Zion's table as possible, not looking his way. She is constantly stopped and greeted by men, exchanging business cards and even hugs.

I have no claims on him. It was a kiss. We have a right to our own lives.

And she has enough business cards in her clutch, so at least one of them could be a tentative replacement for Mr. Zion Landon, Adonis, and Greek God in a black tux.

I wanna rip it off and fuck him into next week.
HELL YEAH NOW WE TALKING.

-14-

Zion has been thinking about Lea and that kiss. He has picked up the phone numerous times to call her. He had the perfect excuse: he hasn't received the picture of his car yet. But he didn't call, email, or text and he knows she won't be a temporary piece of ass. During the next couple of weeks, he is in and out of town handling business. He signed four, multimillion-dollar clients and had meetings with existing clients to discuss future investing needs. Making money is a wonderful thing. Especially for his company.

He checks his schedule and notices he is scheduled to attend this Saturday's Humane Society Charity Ball. One of his sister's projects she feels he needs to support. And she has even set him up with a piece of arm candy.

Must be one of her silly ass friends wanting to be seen. I could have gone to this thing alone and had a piece of ass lined up for later. Shit, now I gotta put on a gentleman face and play the interested role.

For the night of the event, he rents a stretch limo and uses Sam as the driver. He needs his own personal security detail. They arrive at his sister's house and she introduces him to his 'date' for the evening.

My sister, my sister, my sister. My date she has arranged for me is a double 'D' babe with a big ass. I may be fucking tonight after all, or at least rubbing my dick between some nice lips. Her name is Kelly something. Who gives a damn about her last name? I'll turn up the charm to get my dick into her.

They all get into the car and Kelly becomes really chatty telling Zion about her job, her social life, her friends, her everything.

He looks at his sister with a look of, *"Really, Star? You really think I could be interested in her on a regular basis?"*

She grins at him and turns her head to talk to Garrett. Zion focuses as best he can on Kelly.

They arrive at the club before the smothering crowd gets there. Zion walks everyone over to the bar and orders drinks. They ascend the stairs to the dining room to find their table. He greets people and socializes as instructed by Star and gives Kelly enough attention to make her think he's interested in her as she presses her tits up against him.

Yeah, I'm fucking this ass tonight. Probably in the car after I drop off Star and Garrett.

Kelly and Zion are standing outside the dining room at the top of the stairs in a corner. He looks toward the entrance of the club and sees Crystal and her husband, Stanley, walking in. And right behind them are Tom and his wife, Linda on one arm and Lea on his other arm.

My dick gets hard. Kelly thinks it's for her rubbing up against me, but hell no, it's saluting Ms. Lea Adams.

She is smiling and bubbly, greeting and hugging people.

Crystal is introducing Lea to multiple men, and she is shaking their hands, listening to what they have to say as they lean in to talk to her. Some are even brushing up too damn close and Zion wants to rip their guts out. Kelly is leaning against him, wanting his attention but he can't take his eyes off Lea.

"Zion, who are you looking at?" Kelly asks.

I am thinking on the fly, planning how I'm going to get rid of Kelly and get her attention onto someone else.

"Oh sorry. I saw a client of mine. He made it, and I thought he was going to be sitting at home tonight. He's single, and, well he needs some happiness in his life."

"Oh, who is he?" she perks up looking around. Kelly knows a lot of rich men are here tonight. She only came with Zion because

Star said he needed arm candy, warning her he is single and will stay single, and there is no way she will get her clutches into him.

"Oh, he vanished into the ballroom," Zion says. Kelly takes off, not realizing he hasn't even told her who the hell the guy is.

Thirsty much?

Tom's group ascends the stairs. Lea releases Tom's arm and grabs her cobalt blue dress so she doesn't trip over it. Blue toe nails peek out from under the dress. The curve of her breasts is tantalizing. The cheap costume jewelry she is wearing sparkles in the light as if it is the real thing.

I want to rip it off her and make sure she is only wearing the real thing. Costume jewelry is not good enough for this woman.

Zion steps farther into the shadows and watches them. No, watching Lea.

She looks beautiful. There is nothing fake about this woman, other than her jewelry.

Her hair pushed to one side makes him want to kiss the area between her shoulder and neck.

To bite it and make her moan. Dammit, I have to get through this dinner tonight with Kelly. And Lea will see me with Kelly, and here she comes gliding my way. Fuck and she walks right in front of Lea almost knocking her over.

Lea steps back out of Kelly's way. She looks over directly in the direction Kelly is walking. When she reaches Zion, she presses her tits into his arm saying something.

I don't know what.

Lea makes eye contact with him, nods her head, turns and walks into the dining room.

Did I just get a damn fucking head nod from this woman? Oh, fuck she is good. She just dismissed me. I'm not having that tonight.

87

The dinner bell chimes and everyone moves into the ballroom to their tables. Tom and his guests are sitting at a table in the middle of the room and Zion's sister's table is off to the right of Tom's and toward the back. In the correct seat, he can sit and watch Lea's every move.

And I plan on it.

Lea sits down next to Tom with his wife on his other side. Tom does the old trick of putting his tux jacket on the seat next to Lea, allowing people to think the seat is saved for another male guest.

Ha, yes, she is alone.

Man upon man stops at Lea's table and sits down next to her and talks. It looks as if she knows some of them, and some look to be complete strangers leaving their business cards with her and taking one of hers. This is the professional's way of exchanging phone numbers, and tonight Zion hates it. He's counted ten so far pulling this shit with Lea.

Kelly is sitting on Zion's right chatting up a stranger. He catches bits and pieces of their conversation. The guy she is chatting up is single, in town for the ball, and pretty lonely as his date had to cancel on him.

Man, yeah right, I know that damn line. Keep it up, go ahead flash that expensive jewelry, and smooth-talk Kelly. Please.

Star takes Zion away from his staring of Lea.

"Zion, who the hell are you staring at? Yes, I know you and you are staring at the woman in the blue dress. Who is she? Is that Tom, and Crystal, and their spouses?"

"Yes, that's them. The lady with them is Lea Adams. She is the Project Lead on the technology upgrade for the new office," I say.

"Oh. So why are you staring at her then? Is she supposed to be working or something?"

"I didn't know she would be here tonight, and no, she is not supposed to be working."

"Then what's the deal?" Star stops and looks at Zion closely. "Holy fuck. You like her. Uh-uh, don't turn away and go cold on me. You do, don't you?"

"Star, will you shut up." Zion looks over at Kelly and sees she is engrossed in conversation with the other guy.

"Oh, screw Kelly. She is going home with ole boy instead of you tonight anyway," Star points out. "I'm sorry I set you up with her. So this Lea Adams. Is she a fuck?"

"I don't know. She wants long term. I don't do long term, you know that," he whispers.

"Ooooooo, here's a thought, why not give it a shot for a change. You never know. You may enjoy it," she smiles, looking at him and squeezing his thigh. He puts his hand over hers and squeezes.

"You know I love you, baby sister," Zion says and eats the dinner placed in front of him the whole time keeping his eye on Lea.

Zion watches man after man approach Lea, talking with her, touching her. With most of them, she is standoffish, not allowing them to get close to her, yet with one or two of them, she not only allows a closeness but also leans into them as if she is showing interest.

These fools need to stop touching my Lea. My Lea? Where in the hell that shit come from? Hell, man, you know you want her. Go ahead and make her yours. Stop with the fucking denial game. She could be the one, your queen.

Zion's gaze follows Lea's every move and gesture.

Fuck no. This has got to stop. Too many men approaching her, too many business cards exchanged. Nope, uh-uh, can't be having this.

As soon as the plates are cleared, Kelly and ole boy get up and disappear out the door. Star gets a text from Kelly saying not to worry about her, she isn't feeling well, something with the food made her sick, she's going home. She will take a taxi and please, thank Zion for a lovely evening.

Zion looks at his sister, and they say at the same time. "Sick, my ass. Jinx."

"Well, Zion, go get your girl. Garrett and I'll sit back, watch, and enjoy this immensely."

Zion watches as Lea leaves the ballroom. He gets up and storms out the door in search of her.

If she is standing out here talking to a man, I will go nuts.

He sees her go into the bathroom and decides to hover close by looking out the window. He wants to give this long term a go. He won't lose much. She may consider a temporary fuck after he drops the no-child bomb. Either way, he is determined to get to know Ms. Lea Adams. He watches her exit the bathroom from the reflection in the window. She instantly stops when she notices the back of him.

Yes, baby. You are as aware of me as I'm aware of you.

"Good evening, Lea," Zion says, turning around to look at her.

-15-

Lea takes a deep breath before answering Zion, the movement lifting the swell of her breasts in her dress.

Delectable, suckable breasts, Zion is thinking.

"Good evening, Zion. How are you?"

Damn, a black man in a tux is fucking nice. On Zion it exudes pure sex.

"I'm good. You look beautiful." Zion cannot take his eyes off her.

I don't want to take my eyes off her. I want to hold her. Kiss her. Fuck her. Make love to her.

"You dress up nicely. You dress down nicely also."

Get a grip Lea. He's a Greek God in an exquisitely tailored tux made for every fucking inch of his body. No big deal.

UH YES, VERY BIG DICK. I MEAN DEAL.

"Thanks, I have been thinking about you and what you said. May we sit down and talk?"

Okay here goes. Let's make this deal.

"Here? Are you sure?" Lea asks.

Talk about getting straight to the point and skipping all the small talk. Geez man, seriously. Let me shut this down quickly, 'cause he is looking for a piece of ass and I'm not it. Even if my clit and the Sex Diva is screaming.

WE *COULD* BE.

"Yes. The music is starting, and people are moving to the dance floor. I'm sure we'll have some privacy."

"Okay, sure." They walk back into the dining room.

I want to touch her but hold off. Not yet man, not yet.

Zion's sister and Garrett are on the dance floor. He looks over at them and shakes his head motioning for them not to come back for a while.

They sit down and Zion turns to Lea and without hesitation or second thought asks, "Tell me what you want. You said you won't do temporary, but what does that mean exactly."

Lea decides to be upfront and go with it. She leans into him making sure he smells her.

It's fun playing the seduction game.

"I want to date, I want to have someone I can talk to, and I want to be with someone I can be seen with in public, someone I can really get to know. You are the poster boy for temporary fucks. Oh, don't look at me like that. You are sexy, rich beyond all riches and can have any woman you want with the snap of your fingers. You can do things most people only dream about. I'm sure you have a number of women you can hit up for a fuck anytime you want, and they will drop everything they're doing to be in your presence or be the chosen one for the night. For me, at this point in my life, temporary is not going to cut it. I'm looking for long term. By the way where is tonight's fuck at?"

I never thought I would ever be able to say all that to a man, but once the door was opened, I barged right on in. Zion is sitting there staring at me like I have grown two heads.

"Are you okay?" I ask him. He is stunned speechless.

Run or stay baby, run or stay, but you are not wasting my time.

AND YOU CAN GIVE ME ONE TRY OF THE DICK IF YOU UP TO IT.

Dammit Sex Diva. No.

NO MY ASS. TEMPORARY OR NOT WE GETTING A RIDE OF THAT DICK.

"Yes, I'm amazed at what I just heard. I've never had a woman say anything like that or remotely close to that to me. It has always been 'let's try it out'. Let's have some fun. Let's fuck. I've had so much temporary ass thrown at me, like you said, that I haven't bothered to consider anything long term for decades. When you walked into G-TEE's boardroom, all I could think was I wanna sex you on a daily basis, in numerous ways, on numerous surfaces, making you cum multiple times.

After seeing you in the Central West End, a part of me was considering I could really get into having you sexually and not holding back. I haven't been with a woman and allowed myself to let go since college. Back then, I was a kid getting ass. With you, I wanna do more. And tonight's temporary fuck has found another dick. Thank goodness."

Lea watches him while he talks and all she can think about is getting away to a room or car and sucking on his lips. But mixing business and pleasure may not be a good idea with him. He hasn't said he wants permeance, just that he wants more.

Whatever. Let me back this up and let him off the hook. Give him some peace of mind so he can get back to the normal things in life. I'll have to live with my dreams and fantasies for now.

Sex Diva screams, NO, NO, NO, NO, OH HELL TO THE MF NO.

"Zion, I understand. Don't worry. I get it. I'm not your type. No hard feelings. We can keep it as a business relationship. You have plenty of other options. Don't stress yourself out over one woman." I glance down looking at his crotch and look away toward the dance floor.

SEE YOU WANT THE DICK TOO. LOOK AT IT AGAIN.

Shit, can I cop a feel to see what you working with, I think silently.

FINALLY, WE'RE ON THE SAME PAGE, Sex Diva screams.

Zion brings Lea's attention back to him by placing his hand under her chin and turning her face to look at him and not at the dance floor.

Lea looks him in the eye, then down at his crotch. Again.

YES.

"What stresses me out is the idea of another man with you. I want more than a business relationship with you," Zion says. "I don't want to do temporary with you. I see all these other men looking at you, talking to you, hugging you, and I want to rip them to shreds. I don't like seeing another man touch you and I've just met you. How crazy is that? I want you. Long term. I want to do this. I want to date, to talk, to be seen, to know you are mine and I'm yours. Keeping it as business is not going to work when I'm alone with you, I want to devour you. And if you keep looking at my dick like that, we'll end up fucking tonight."

She turns her head away grinning.

What a total switch, Zion is thinking.

Here he was ready to give up a quick no-attachment fuck to Kelly and this woman sitting in front of him has just blown his mind making him rethink the temporary liaisons he's had over the years.

He can't recall any of those stating they wanted more. Whatever time, attention or lack of attention he gave, they accepted. Lea tells him that she not having any of it, and he liked it. She put her cards on the table, dealt her hand, and the play became his.

Zion is hesitant. He doesn't know how to do long term. He has avoided it, keeping himself from rejection. With Wendy, some would say they have long term. That is nothing compared to what the taste of Lea's lips offered him.

Oh, those lips and that kiss. My mind is on our first kiss in the Central West End. Her neck fit perfectly in my hand as I grabbed her, inviting, and before she could consider a 'no' and step back away from me. I was kissing her. And if it wasn't for her camera, I would have had full body contact with my dick pressed against her, letting her feel exactly what she was doing to me. Then she kissed me, nibbling my bottom lip. That nibble made a beeline straight to my dick and stayed there. I've been walking around with a semi-hard-on dreaming about releasing inside of her.

Kissing is intimate. Not every woman gets a kiss out of me. Wendy only got them infrequently when I thought it would turn her on. Sometimes kissing her was like kissing a wall, so I kept it at fucking. With Lea, I wanna French kiss her clit.

Zion notices the wolves are hovering. He needs to stake his claim and fast.

Lea is looking out at the dance floor, people watching and ignoring me. Nope we can't have that. Zion Landon is not about to be denied this beauty.

"Lea, will you dance with me?" I ask.

"Uhm. Sure," she responds hesitantly.

It's the only chance I'll get to find out what he is packing in them pants. Do I really want to know?
SHIT YEAH.
Hell, why shouldn't I get at least a farewell body rub.
FAREWELL MY ASS. WE GETTIN' IT.

"Why do you say it like that?" Zion asks as he stands and holds out his hand for her. They walk to the dance floor and a slow jazz song is playing. He gets to hold her close. Well, he has no way of controlling his dick and he doesn't want to.

"Maybe it's not a good idea we should be dancing," Lea says, confusing her own damn self.

First, she wants to dance to cop a feel of the dick and now she is thinking not to dance.

Zion pulls her close as she walks into his embrace. She places her hands on his chest in the lapel of his jacket. She presses up against his hard-on, freezes, and looks up at him.

"I'm not apologizing for it either," he says looking her in the eye. She slides one hand up to his shoulder and slides the other hand down to his chest.

His hard, muscle bound, flexing, pectoral chest muscles I wanna kiss and caress and lick and—. Shit Lea, get a grip.

"I wouldn't expect you to. That's not your style, and that's why I didn't think it was a good idea for us to dance. At least, now I know what you're working with. What you will be giving up to another woman. What I won't be getting." She looks away from him and moves in tune with his movements. Staying pressed against him.

"Holy shit. Woman keep talking like that and I'll gladly show you. Tonight. You'll be getting it. I promise you that. I want to kiss your neck, but I won't because too many people are watching us. Why, I don't know. Don't turn your head, I don't want to distract you from me. I want to scream for them to turn down the damn lights so we can make out," he whispers into her ear, brushing her earlobe with his lips.

Lea trembles from the sensation. "Will you shut up, Zion, and dance? What makes you think I wanna make out with you?"

"Dang, okay. 'Cause you know you do. Anytime you want to go sneak off into a corner, I see about four of them that will do just fine. Say the word. Kiss, kiss."

She looks up at him and licks her lips.

Dammit that tongue. Shit woman.

Zion leans in to kiss her but gets interrupted by his sister. He hadn't noticed the music had stopped and they are standing in the middle of the dance floor.

Dammit, Star. Dammit, no music. Dammit, missed my chance.

Lea steps away nervously. Out of the corner of her eye she saw the woman approaching them.

"Hi Zion, don't I get an introduction?" Star asks.

"Lea Adams, my sister Star Landon Leon. Star, this is Lea," Zion says.

Lea relaxes, slightly.

She must have been worried about some woman walking up to me and claiming me.

She shakes my sister's hand.

"Nice to meet you," Lea says.

Zion puts his hand on Lea's waist, possessively keeping her at his side. Lea puts her hand behind her back, clasping his trying to move it but he keeps it in place where it is. They are having a hand war behind her back. Star catches the movement and smiles.

"It's nice to meet you also. This is my husband, Garrett." Lea shakes Garrett's hand and they exchange pleasantries. Next thing she knows, they are surround by Crystal, her husband, Tom, and his wife, and everyone is exchanging greetings.

Will these people go away? Please. This being the center of attention is working my last nerve, and all I want to do is fucking scream.

The introvert has kicked in, and too many people are around Lea right now.

Zion releases Lea's hand from his grasp, ending the hand fight and glides it up her back caressing her neck. He feels the need to keep touching her, and this one curl sitting there is drawing his attention. He grabs the curl and slowly twists it around his finger. Lea quickly moves away and excuses herself

"I'm sorry. Could you excuse me; I need the ladies room. I'll be right back." She doesn't look at the others but looks at Zion with a glance of pure fuck me sex.

Zion moves to go after her, but Crystal catches his eye. He glares at her questioningly.

Okay, what just happened?

She grins at him and excuses herself, following Lea, grabbing their purses off the table on the way. In the bathroom, Lea is standing in front of the mirror.

"Don't roll your head off that pretty neck of yours, young lady," Crystal says.

"Oh, shut up, why don't you. Crap, he was driving me up the wall. I could handle the hand on the back and even the playing with the hair, but as soon as he brushed up against the back of my collar bone, I almost jumped like a startled cat. Damn it felt so fucking good. I had to get away so I could re-group. What is with all you people standing around us anyway. Geez. Crystal, I could rip his clothes off and screw him right now. In the middle of the fucking dining room," Lea tells her.

"I know. I like watching you two together. Well, let's go, Missy. It's time to go home anyway." Crystal hands Lea her clutch grinning.

Another successful Cupid match. A good one, thinks Crystal.

They leave the bathroom and walk toward the ballroom. People are meandering around the doors, stairs, and bar, talking and having a good time. Before Lea can get back to the group, one of the men she was talking to earlier approaches her. His name is Patrick.

"Hi Lea. Patrick," he re-introduces himself, "I was wondering, could we talk? I would like to get your number and maybe take you out sometime."

Before Lea can even answer Patrick, Zion is at her side with his hand on her ass, of all places.

Loves Awakening

Zion sees Lea and Crystal coming out of the bathroom. He watches some guy approach her, talking with her.

Oh. Fuck. No.

He cuts off his conversation with Garrett in mid-syllable and beelines for Lea and the guy.

Not another one. Shit, where the hell all these wolves come from?

"Hey baby, I missed you. My arms are pretty damned empty when you are gone for too long," Zion says grabbing Lea by the waist, pulling her into him, kissing her. Lea, unquestioningly, leans into the kiss sliding her leg between his attempting to rub against his dick without giving it a second thought, not caring that she was just talking to a man named Patrick. When she pulls away, Patrick is gone.

"Really Zion, really?" she asks grinning at him, wanting to control her aroused emotions and the embarrassment she is feeling.

"Yes, really. No way in hell you are walking out of here tonight with another man interested in dating you. Fuck that. And you can tear up all those business cards you got tonight." Lea jumps at the word fuck. "Yes, baby we will be fucking. Let's get you home. Nice leg movement by the way. Firm. When you ready to feel it, skin to skin, let me know," he says kissing her on her cheek then twirling her around toward the exit where everyone is waiting.

"You caught that, did you?" She asks him.

"Hell, yeah baby. And I'll be more than happy to give you a look if you really want one."

He puts her arm in the crook of his, enjoying the feel of her warm smooth skin.

The entire group of couples walk down the steps to the entrance. Zion's limo, with Sam standing waiting to open the door, is parked in front of the limo Lea arrived in with Tom. She walks toward it, but Zion stops her.

"Let me take you home. Ride with us. We can drop my sister and Garrett off, then we can make out. How about it?"

"Uh-uh, no way, I'm not getting in that car with you. Good night Zion. Nope, no sir, I'm not. Bye Zion," Lea sprints to the other limo and gets in before the others do. Zion follows her and gets in, slamming the door on the others. He takes Lea in his arms and kisses her, nibbling on her bottom lip, mimicking the move she did to him. Lea puts her hands on his cock and squeezes. He places his hand over hers and groans breaking away from the kiss staring at her.

"I believe we're going to be good for each other in so many ways. Goodnight beautiful. Talk to you soon." He caresses her cheek for one last touch.

Zion gets out of the car making a display of adjusting his clothes and wiping lipstick off his mouth. "Tom, Crystal, everyone. It was great seeing you this evening. Take care." He strolls to his car and gets in, and it drives off.

The others look inside the car. Lea is sitting there trying not to laugh. They get in and bust out laughing.

"Tom, aren't you supposed to be telling me how I'm not allowed to fraternize with your business clients and how this is wrong and to stop it, now?" I ask him.

"Oh, hell no, I ain't saying a damn word. I ain't seen nothing. I don't know nothing. I'm just out with my wife and friends enjoying a fun-filled evening and when we get home my wife and I gonna make out. Yes sir, I'm getting' me some kissing tonight. And Lea done got her a man."

They kid and tease her all the way home. She takes it in stride and enjoys the fun. In her mind, she is thinking Zion is not ready for long term. He simply having a little fun right now.

On the drive home in Zion's limo, his sister hands him a tissue.

"Burgundy is not your color lip tint," she says, teasing him.

Zion takes it and wipes his mouth staring at it in awe.

"Star, your brother is love-struck. Never thought I would see that," Garrett says.

"It's amazing, isn't it. Check out that grin on his face. Lea Adams has put a silly love-struck grin on the face of Zion Landon. Finally, someone has."

"You two need to shut up," Zion says, unable to stop grinning.

-16-

Zion spends his Sunday in the office trying to get away from his thoughts of Lea and their kisses. He could kiss her all day long. Is he willing to try long term for Lea? With Lea, does he want her that much? Maybe he can change her mind about things being long term and still get to enjoy those warm folds. Or it may be time to grow the hell up.

It would be nice to have a female to talk to about things, to truly date, share my world with. It could be real nice. It will be real nice.

He needs to feel her out more about that baby/child issue.

Zion has more than caught up on his client files, and he is now checking on the accounts and processes of his staff's clients. He's the boss and has access to look at everything they do. They are fully aware of this. When ten of them get in Monday, they will have a long list of items to address and fix.

He notices Saul is online, which means he is in the office. Zion decides to head down and find out why. When he arrives, he see's him working on the prototype equipment Lea has suggested for the upgrade.

"Saul, what's up? Why are you here today?" He asks, entering and taking a seat across from him at his desk.

"Because you said we're going to be working with G-TEE on the new office technology upgrades, I decided to get a head start on cleaning up data on the servers and tweaking the programs for the additional security you requested. In the next few months, equipment for the server rooms will arrive and I want it installed and programs working the same week."

"Good. Have you been to the site lately?"

"Yes, sir. Outer walls are going up, then the structural walls. You have an appointment to stop by there this week to take a look."

"Yes. Wednesday. Anything you need from me this week?"

"No sir," Saul says, staring at his boss and waiting. Watching Zion, he can tell his mind is working a million miles a minute in many directions. He can request near anything now, and this conversation and visit can go in any direction.

Zion realizes he hasn't said anything and Saul is sitting there waiting.

Saul asks him. "Was the report on Ms. Adams thorough enough? Do I need to dig deeper? I didn't add any information on addresses as that was done earlier in the project paperwork, but I can get more for you if you need it."

Zion glares at him and cracks a smile. All pretense of business gone. "Sexy. Isn't she?"

"Yes, she is very sexy and has a lot to offer a man on paper and in person. I hated you asking for a background check on her. Knew I waited too long."

"You never had a chance."

"Man, give me a break. See, all I needed to do was—. Shit never mind. I didn't have a chance. She is old enough to be my mother. But dammit that cougar coulda tamed this cub."

"Hey, cool it."

"Sorry, sorry. I figured she would rattle you. Replacing Wendy, are you?"

"Would you believe I'm considering getting rid of all of them? Wendy is boring. Or shall I say too boring for me. She could be perfect for someone else."

"Burning the proverbial black book, are we? Yeah, Lea Adams has you rattled. This will be fun to watch. Yes, indeed."

"Don't provide me any more information on her. It's time I learned on my own to trust what I'm feeling and not what's on paper."

"Duly noted boss."

"And go home, Saul."

"Eventually. I could say the same thing about you, but I won't as you are the boss."

The rest of Sunday brings sports, sports, more sports, and more thoughts of Lea. Zion prowls around considering what to do. Instead of sitting around the apartment he decides to head over to Jazz at the Bistro for some dinner and entertainment.

As is his norm, he arrives and asks for the top level of the Bistro for some peace and quiet. It's not open for business tonight, so the manager is more than okay to have Zion sitting up there.

Money does bring its perks.

Zion gets to enjoy the music and people-watch in peace. Tonight's group is boring him until he sees Lea walk in with a group of three women. They are seated and from the way they are looking around the place, this may be their first time there. From his vantage point, he can see them clearly but they cannot see him.

She is a beautiful sight, laughing and chatting with her friends. This must be one of those rare nights when she gets out.

A guy sits at the table behind her but places himself close enough to Lea and the women at her table so he can speak with them. He talks to them all but especially to Lea. They seem to know each other, but Lea isn't giving dude much play. Then a woman comes in and sits down at the guy's table. He becomes attentive to her, and ignores Lea and her friends.

In my business, I'm skilled at reading body language, and Lea's saying she is slightly pissed, a little hurt, and about to flee.

Between the band's sets, the guy turns to Lea and her friends and introduces the woman to her table, looking at Lea as if he wants

Lea, and is apologetic he is with the other woman. They greet each other and Lea turns back to the band.

I continue watching them. Lea was up and bubbly with her friends, and this guy had to walk in, sit down, and her demeanor changes. I wanna destroy this jerk for ruining her evening.

Lea gets up and excuses herself. Zion and the guy watch her walking out the door.

I don't know about him, but my dick is on alert. Her ass in that dress-skirt-whatever the fuck it is, is hugging her behind where I would like my hands.

She returns to her seat looking in control, in command, and wearing red lipstick.

My dick just waved hello, 'cause damn I need them lips on it sucking away leaving me groaning her name. Shit, man she is beautiful and all she did was put on lipstick. But I can see ole boy adjust his body in the chair. I wonder if that is a desire or a memory adjustment?

Zion attempts to focus on the band but looks at Lea more. She looks around at the venue checking out the place even glancing up to where he is. The manager keeps the lights dimmed when he doesn't open it for regular business. Lea looks away and turns back to the band enjoying the music.

As they play their last song, Zion gets up, going downstairs to exit the place while people are focused on the stage. This way he can get out unnoticed without women trying to holla or gaggle at him and get into his car. Tonight, he is parked to the right of the front door in the parking lot. He decides to sit in it hoping to get a glimpse of Lea walking past. Zion noticed her car is parked on the street a few spaces down from the entrance of the parking lot. Turns out he has great luck. He is in the Acura. The parking lot is dimly lit. The matte color of his car practically disappears in the dark.

She comes out of the door way ahead of her friends and stands, waiting near the side of the gate entrance. Out comes ole boy, heading directly for her. She moves away from him and stands leaning against the iron fence, close enough to the car where if Zion slightly lowers the window, he can hear the conversation, which he does.

"You mad at me?" the guy asks her.

"Why would I be mad at you? You made your choice. You told me you were seeing someone else. It's not like we had anything going on, life moves on," she says, not looking at him.

"Lea come on, I can tell you kinda pissed. You don't need to keep ignoring me like you do. We still friends, we still good," he tells her.

Lea turns, facing him. She glances toward the parking lot in the direction of Zion's car then looks quickly away, shaking her head.

"Look, let's get something straight, we fucked a few times and it didn't go anywhere. You made the choice of being with someone else. You claim it was because you had more in common with her, but the truth is you never even allowed me to get close enough to you to find out what I had to offer. We made it about sex, and it stayed about sex and even that didn't go as far as it could have. Go, be happy. Have the boring ass sex life you are destined to have. I wish you the best. She looks to be more your speed anyway. Oh, sorry was that bitchy of me? Oh well, go figure," she says and turns to walk off, hesitates, and looks at the black Acura. She shakes her head again, walking off with her friends leaving ole boy stunned.

Damn, I wonder did his dick deflate. And looking at the woman he is with, Lea pegged her correctly. Boring, infrequent, lackluster sex. She is a mirror image of Wendy. She can give him plenty outside of the bedroom and just enough to call it sex in the bedroom. Lea looks like she can give it all over the damn house and still have you wanting more. Lea is not a temporary fuck indeed. She is a bury yourself deep and stay there forever woman.

-17-

After Lea's and Zion's kiss on Saturday, her decision to keep things as business with him is turning out to be a bad idea. He is sexy as hell and knows how to lay a kiss on a woman. And she wants more of those kisses. She knows she needs to hold strong to what she wants. She is un-interested in temporary dick. She wants her own monogamous relationship where she doesn't need to hold back, hesitate or wonder where she stands with a man.

Running into Jake Sunday night at Jazz at the Bistro proved it. Seeing in the flesh the woman her ex decided to be with instead of her almost deflated her that night. She had to sit there with him and his new girlfriend behind her trying to enjoy the music. After a few minutes, her mind drifted off, thinking about Zion. In the few times she has been around him her body has been on fire. Being around Jake, she couldn't even get a hot flash.

When she was talking with her ex, Lea couldn't take the pity and apologetic crap from him and reverted back to the old dick meets pussy, with Lea setting him straight before he could get with that oh I miss you, I wish it could have been you, let's still be friends line.

No, no, no. Not having that bullshit anymore.

So she, told him off and walked away. When she was done, for some reason she thought she saw Zion's Acura. She shook it off as wishful thinking and headed home, dreaming about Adonis and having an orgasm in her sleep, waking up frustrated and arguing with herself again, convinced a Lea and Zion relationship will never be.

Me being with a billionaire is totally crazy. Even if I could seriously grab and hold his attention, how long would that last? He can have any woman he wants. Any woman. Okay, although it may seem like I'm putting myself down, I'm not. I'm just accepting of the truth. Well, there is another way to look at it. I can be his friend and business colleague and hopefully meet a cute available 'friend' who wants to get married. And not have kids or is done with having kids.

On Tuesday, Lea finally downloads the pictures she took in the Central West End. She stares at the picture of Zion's car. Nice car indeed. Was this his car she saw Sunday night? She racks her brain, trying to remember details about it. She scrolls through the other pictures and she realizes she was snapping away while he was standing on the other side of the water fountain and while he was walking toward her. She has evidence of the hunger in his kisses she experienced right here in still images. He may be unsure of wanting a relationship, but sexually he wants her.

Lea knows a man wanting you means nothing if he has the need to run away from that want, ignoring it and electing to be with someone else. The fight to stay rarely beats out the flight to flee with some men. Facts prove it daily with all the broken hearts. No matter how much you love someone, no matter what you think you have to offer them, no matter how good of a catch you know you are, if they don't see it and want it, you can do nothing when they walk away. It has happened to her twice. She has done some hard chasing in her time by bending over backward and wanting to be what a man said he needed at that moment, ignoring all kinds of red flags. It got so bad that she no longer had any idea what she wanted and needed. All she knew was she wanted that man and she would change one-hundred eighty degrees to become what he was saying he wanted. Then he would walk away and be with someone else, leaving her questioning herself, doubting what she was doing or not doing to keep his attention.

With the last one, she was fed up. She didn't bother with why he left or why he chose another woman. She accepted she wasn't the one, and would never be the one. Fuck him. Her self-analysis brought her to the person she is today. Stating what she won't put up with from the moment a man shows any interest in her beyond friendship or business is now her plan.

The way she figured it, don't let a date go further if at all avoidable or stop it right after the first time. It's amazing how men shut down and lose interest after they realized she wanted long term and not temporary. She'd rather be alone and stress free with her battery-operated-boyfriends, her B.O.B.s, than waiting on a man to get his shit together hoping he will see her and want her.

So, keeping it business with Mr. Zion Landon is my goal.

She sends him the picture of his car via text, keeping it short and apologizing for the delay in getting it to him. He responds back immediately.

> Zion: *It was fun talking with you also. I love the picture of my car. You are more than welcomed to use it as a photography subject anytime. Enjoy your week.*
> *Zion.*

Yep, he has written me off as a no go.

The Sex Diva is throwing a tantrum screaming NO, NO, NO, NOT THIS ONE. NO, NO, NO.

Moving on and getting back into work mode after sending Zion the picture is a letdown. She loves her job, and she gets to meet plenty of men. You would think by now one of them would have caught her interest. Somedays, she thinks she's blind to the male species. Then she meets Adonis. Nice, sexy, packing a pair of lips and nice sized dick, Adonis. Can't-get-him-out-of-my-mind-and-away-from-thoughts-of-pressing-up-against-her-groin, Adonis. She shakes her head attempting to shake out thoughts of him.

On Wednesday, she received a call from one of the contractors to meet him out at the Landon Enterprises construction site. Martin Jones, the winning contractor that Tom stated she would need to keep a close eye on.

She changes into her worksite boots, grabs her hard hat, camera, and purse. She informs Tom and Crystal she will be out for the rest of the afternoon as it is one-thirty and she has no need to return to the office after this meeting.

Tom asks. "What's up? There shouldn't be much to do out there right now for us."

"Martin Jones, the contractor on the wiring detail wants to meet. Maybe I'll get a handle on your doubts and find out what's up with him."

"Good, send me an update."

Lea arrives at the site thirty minutes later. Grabbing her hard hat, she gets out the car, waving and yelling greetings. A lot of the workers know her because G-TEE tends to use the same contractors and crew. They wave greetings in return, some joke around, a few show her pictures of the new additions to their families. She always brings her camera to sites because these guys love hamming it up and posing for pictures when they have breaks. Today, they look busy, so she'll find Martin and get this over with.

Lea finds him on the north side of the building site staring into space. She approaches him.

"Hi Martin. What's going on?" I ask, getting to the point of this meeting he asked for.

Martin turns to Lea with a lost look on his face. His look changes into one of recognition and it clicks that he asked to meet with her.

"Lea, hi. How are you? It's so good to see you," Martin has been dreading the reason for this meeting but has been looking forward to seeing Lea all day. When he found out about G-TEE getting the business for Landon Enterprises new headquarters build, he knew he had to be working on this project somehow.

G-TEE only allows bids on their projects via blind submission. He bid for everything, underpricing on projects he knew he should not be low bidding on but making up for those low bids by overcharging other clients. Being on a G-TEE project is every contractor's dream, and not just because of the money and prestige.

"Fine, what's up? Everything on schedule?" Lea asks.

"Yes, well, kinda. I'm running into some supply issues, and I wanted to talk to you about re-arranging some things." Martin used some of G-TEE, hell not some, most of the materials on another project and now he can't get payment from the other client in time to start G-TEE's project.

"Re-arrange what?" Lea asks him flatly pining him in place with her voice and look.

Oh, I'm panicking. I brace myself knowing what is coming but praying a silent prayer I'm wrong.

"Martin, before you mention delivery dates of needed deliverables, understand I have no leeway with those dates considering we suggested you purchase items before G-TEE had signed the contract. You were paid for those purchases and you stated you had ninety percent of the items available when asked about it last week. What happened to what you purchased?"

"I had to use it for another quick job that came up. They promised me they were going to pay me before I needed it back for this project, but I'm still waiting. I only have about twenty percent of what is needed to even begin this job."

There. Martin said it. He has been sitting on this information for weeks now, not wanting to tell her, hoping he did not have to tell her.

"What do you mean you HAD TO USE it for another job? That money was not given to you to purchase items to use for another job. Martin, your first walk through and plan layout were scheduled seven days ago, and NOW you are mentioning this. What happened to calling Tom and telling him?" she yells.

"I've been dodging him," Martin said, avoiding making eye contact with Lea.

"Dammit. Martin, what are you expecting me to do, 'cause whatever it is, you can forget it? I can tell you what is going to happen, and you won't like it."

"What?" *Just please don't fire me. I can fix this*, he tells himself.

"Let me explain how important this job is in a language you can get with."

Lea. Hold it together and get this out before the tears of frustration flow.

"This client is Tom's good friend. He doesn't bullshit around. Once a contract is signed, it gets done. Period. That is why every company working on this project signed its own contract with its own terms. We gave you leeway by giving you money up front to stay ahead of the game, and you took it and screwed it over."

I'm pissed and ready to rip Martin to shreds.

"This job is top priority for all the companies here. Read your contract, get a lawyer, and pray Landon Enterprises doesn't come for you. G-TEE will work with you on you refunding our money."

As much as I would like to keep Martin, my hands are tied. I can't jeopardize this project because of one contractor not doing his job.

"Are you saying you are firing me?" Martin asked incredulously, snapping at Lea.

Lea takes offense at his tone. She wasn't the one that stole money to use for another client.

"Martin, listen to me. READ the fucking contract you signed. You fired yourself by not having a deliverable. Tom is not giving any second chances on this project, and I am making sure everyone keeps to the schedule. You are not going to derail this project. G-TEE is not going to bail your ass out of this so you can keep going. We're going to Plan B."

Martin looks stunned. He knew something major was going to happen, but this? Fired. He hadn't explicitly read the contract terms like he was told to and have a lawyer review them.

Now I can forget about ever working with G-TEE.

"Look there has to be something I can do to salvage this?" Martin says.

"Did you try anything before calling me? Anything at all?"

Please have something, so I can keep you on this job, I hate firing people, especially the small black business owners.

Martin runs his business as a small business but with his resources and contacts he can do any size job in the state. He is good at keeping focused and on schedule. Give him what he needs to do and when and he does it.

But this, dammit, is putting me in a bind, and I have to fire him and get someone else.

"Only trying to get my money the other company owes me." *And take out loans, and beg, borrow or steal*, Martin thinks.

"I can't believe this. We tell you guys to keep us informed, and we'll work with you. But this? I can't help you this late in the game," Lea says in frustration.

Whenever someone does something this stupid, Lea gets frustrated and wants to lose control, scream, and cry all at the same time. But she has to hold it together. No one has ever seen that side of her. Well, Gordon did once and it was ugly.

"Late? How is it late when the inner walls are not even up?" Martin asks.

"Check your damn deliverable dates. Your wiring and your guys are due onsite, and you don't have squat to install before the walls even go up. Someone will be at your warehouse on Friday to pick up everything you have left. Email me what is missing and how much you have spent. Martin, be there and get me my information. Do you understand?"

"This is a bunch of bullshit. Working with a damn independent strong ass woman who doesn't know her fucking place." *Especially this one.*

Lea clenches her hands in fists wanting to punch Martin. For that stupid comment, she could push him off the ledge of this building and have concrete poured over his body. She instead uses her words to cut him to shreds.

"Are you fucking kidding me? Did you just fucking go there? This independent strong ass woman was the one who was willing to trust your ass when you were working out of your damn basement. Now you having an issue with working with a damn independent strong ass woman because you fucked up? You need to work on your fucked-up ass attitude and give me an apology and fast. Personally Martin, you can kiss my black ass. Professionally, we're done. And just so you understand where my fucking place is, it's to get you the fuck out of my sight."

Someone behind them clears their throat and steps into view. Lea turns toward the noise and freezes.

Oh, fucking great. Zion.

Kia Lui

-18-

Zion's week goes as expected. At the meeting, his staff addressed and fixed the issues he pointed out and answered all his in-depth questions. No one got fired today. He managed to stop a number of potential client fires and make money for everyone.

And I continue to think about Lea, her soft lips.

He had to travel out of town to stop a young client from spending money on women he has no business even talking to.

Dreaming about Lea, her red lips wrapped around my cock. Her getting ole boy told off. Her ass in that skirt, my hands wrapped around her ass while she is riding my cock. Why haven't I received the picture of my car from her yet? She did say they could keep this as business. Maybe this is her way of doing so.

Any other woman would have blown up his phone the next day after a date with him. Even Wendy sent him a couple of text messages asking how he was doing and wishing him a good week. He didn't respond. Wendy wasn't the one he wanted to hear from. As he picks up his phone to call Lea about the picture, he gets a text from her. Perfect timing.

> Lea: *Zion, I'm so sorry I haven't sent this to you until today. I didn't get a chance to download them until last night. I hope you like the picture. It came out nice with the water fountain as a backdrop. Very nice car. It's haunting me around St. Louis. Lol. Maybe someday I can do some sunset pictures. Take care, Lea.*

I can feel the ginormous grin on my face. The picture does look good. I realize I can't wait to see her again. It's time for a change Zion.

Arriving back in town, he instructs Sam to go straight to the build site. He is on schedule and stops by, to take a walk-through with the foreman and get an update. When they arrive, he sees Lea's car parked next to the building manager's trailer. He gets out, gets the manager, and with hard hats in place, they walk around the site.

I wonder why Lea is here.

When they get to the north side of the building, he finally sees Lea, and she is talking to a man.

Who the hell is this?

As they move in closer and he is ready to announce his presence, he catches the conversation. Something about missing deliverables, missed deadline dates, and contract standards.

Lea is laying into this man as, well, hell, as he would. He recognizes this terse tone as the one she used on him in the Central West End. Zion places his hand on Neil's arm, silencing him, hanging back to listen.

Shit girl, yes. Set his ass straight. I silently cheer her on.

He never would have imagined this quiet unassuming woman in their first meeting would be the type to let loose like this. She is cussing, her stance is aggressive, she is flushed, and her words are firm. She looks like she wants to punch this guy.

And right now, I want to fuck her into submission. Shit submission. I haven't thought about a woman submitting, being submissive or submission in the bedroom in years.

Zion brings himself back to the conversation when he hears the man say something about 'bullshit working with an independent strong ass woman'. Now he has had enough. He is ready to check the man's ass, fire him, and get him off his site. Not only will he not talk to Lea like that, Zion won't have him working for him. He clears his throat to announce himself.

Lea jumps, and she and Martin look in the direction of the sound.

Sorry, baby, I didn't mean to scare you.

He wants to go to her and put his arm around her and take over handling this fucking slime ball. Lea curses under her breath, and the guy looks at Neil for help. Neil stares at him, not saying a word.

Lea takes a deep breath and addresses Zion formally, almost, terse with him again. "Mr. Landon, Neil. I'm so sorry. How long have you been standing there?"

"May I be of some assistance? Something I need to be made aware of? I have been here long enough to hear about deliverables not arriving." Zion asks.

Lea blanches, looking as if she wants to pass out. With Zion here, she becomes unsure of herself for a split second. Does she plunge ahead and take care of business as she is supposed to, or does she step back and let the men handle it?

Fuck this, I'll just apologize later, but Martin ain't about to get away with this shit. Not today.

"Mr. Landon, I apologize. This is Martin Jones, the electrician who was working on this project to run the wiring. Martin, this is Mr. Zion Landon, CEO and owner of Landon Enterprises."

Because she used my formal name, something tells me I need to be in business mode. But the whole time I feel a sense of pride in her handling this jerk as I would. Don't worry baby, I got this.

Zion and Martin say at the same time, "Was working?"

Martin glares at her but doesn't allow the emotion's escalating through his body to come out in his words. "Lea, come on. You can't be serious?"

"Not my call," she says balling her hand into a fist, digging her nails into the palm of her hand. She whispers under her breath just loud enough for him to hear her. "Make a scene, and I will bury you."

Lea is bracing herself. Martin did not adhere to the contract. She has to fire him and his crew. A client heard her cussing. All Zion has to do is lodge a complaint with Tom, and they can lose the contract, or heaven forbid, she could get fired for what he saw and heard.

Oh, shit, I'm in for it now. Shit, Shit, Shit. Technically I didn't know Zion was around but still. Shit.

Thinking fast and hoping to make a positive impression, Martin steps to shake Zion's hand, but Zion doesn't move to accept it.

"Was working?" Zion asks again. He didn't catch any of that last bit of what Lea said to Martin but from the reaction in her body, it wasn't anything nice.

"Yes sir. As of five minutes ago, he is no longer the electrical contractor. Neil, would you escort Martin off the premises and inform everyone that neither he nor his crew is allowed back on site. After that, please meet me in your trailer?"

Great, now I gotta explain this to Tom and apologize to Zion for catching me cussing. I could strangle Martin for putting me in this bind. All I wanna do is stomp my feet, punch the wall, and cry like a two-year-old child needing a nap but fighting it.

"Sure Ms. Adams. Martin, this way." Neil directs Martin off the site.

They leave and Zion turns to Lea. She is walking toward him, still in business mode. He wants to engulf her in a hug and tell her he got this, but she halts him in his tracks.

"Can you give me just one moment and come with me and allow me to fix this? I'll answer any questions you have, I promise. Oh, and I'm sorry for my unprofessional behavior. This is not something

I usually display, and please don't think any less of Tom and G-TEE for what you saw. I was wrong and it won't happen again." *Within earshot of you.*

"No apologies needed. Lead the way," I state enjoying the fact I get to see that tight pretty ass in those hip hugging slacks.

They go to the trailer, Zion opening the door for Lea. She strides in and takes a seat at Neil's desk as if she owns the place. He notices she puts her camera down and picks up a large carry tote. She takes out her phone, tablet, pen, and paper. Zion sits back and watches her in action.

First, she calls Tom from the office phone, putting him on speaker. She isn't hiding any of the conversation. Keeping it one hundred even in business.

I want this woman by my side more and more with each passing minute.

"Tom, it's Lea. Plan B is now in effect. Martin is out for this project. He used our prepayment to purchase materials, but he used the materials for another job he was working on and can't meet the deadlines we have for this job."

"Shit, I knew something was up. Is this going to be any disruption that I need to inform Zion about?"

"Actually, Zion is here in the office. I have you on speaker phone. He heard the tail end of my discussion with Martin if you want to call it a discussion. And I have apologized for my, well, you know me. Say hi."

"Zion, man, don't worry we got this covered. Lea will get this on track. And I'm not going to even bother to say I'm sorry for what you may have witnessed. She knows how to handle her business."

Lea shyly smiles and shakes her head.

"Hey, I've been instructed to wait my turn for questions, so I'm just sitting here. Waiting," Zion says not taking his eyes off Lea.

"Instructed to? Oh yeah, right. Lea when you get in the office tomorrow, let's meet to discuss."

"Will do," Lea ignores the heat in Zion's smile.

By this time, Neil is back, he sits down, listens and takes notes.

Next, she is on her smart phone looking at her contacts. She then dials a second number on Neil's phone.

"Hi Brad. Plan B. Are you ready? Can you step in and take over?"

"Sure, Lea. No problem. I have everything you had me order in the warehouse. Get me the details," Brad says.

"Good. I'm sending you the contact information with the address where you need to pick up what supplies are left. You should have just received the contract with deliverable items needed and dates. Have your lawyers review this and get back to me. Have the signed contract couriered over to Crystal so she can get you setup with an account for funds."

"No problem, I'll give Neil a call and let him know about my crew and see how soon we can get onsite."

"He is sitting here listening to this conversation along with the owner of Landon Enterprises. Make sure you are at the wine tasting Saturday and find me or Tom, I wanna introduce you to him. Also let me know the cost changes."

"Will do Lea. Talk to you soon. And Neil, I'll call you tomorrow."

"No problem, Brad."

"Thanks, bye." Lea hangs up the phone.

She then turns to Neil. Before she can even speak, he jumps in.

"Don't worry I got it covered. Security has been informed about Martin not being allowed back on site. His crew hasn't even been here yet."

Lea shakes her head, this time controlling the cuss words she wants to let loose.

"Mr. Landon, did you want to finish your tour?"

"No, Neil. I need to talk with Ms. Adams about this. I'll give you a call if I have any more questions."

"Yes, sir."

"Neil, if this in anyway will adjust any kind of timeframe, please let me know as I have to inform Tom and Mr. Landon about the details."

Lea looks pointedly at me. All I can do is smirk.

"Gotcha." Neil stands up, grabs his phone, and leaves the trailer.

This woman has just fired and hired who knows how many people without breaking a nail or batting an eye. She can give me a run for my money.

Before Lea can say anything, Zion speaks. "First, stop calling me Mr. Landon, I think. Second, I'm impressed with how you handled things. Third, have dinner with me tonight? Fourth, I wanna date you, sex you, fuck you, tame you, feel you under me, kiss you into submission, make you moan, scream, and cry my name over and over and over."

She looks at me not shying away from what I just said. And when she looks down at my crotch, she sees my second head, is rock hard and pressing for some release. Staring at it, she licks her lips then looks up at me.

"In that situation, I had to address you as Mr. Landon. It was imperative Martin understood who he was being introduced to. When working with people, I give them more than enough of what they need to get the job done. When I get a slacker or excuses, I get angry and frustrated. I would love to have dinner with you."

AND ON A SIDE NOTE, CAN YOU LAY US OVER THIS DESK AND SLOWLY GLIDE YOUR DICK IN AND OUT OF US?

"Oh, so you just gonna ignore my fourth point."

Lea brings herself back to the present and away from the Sex Diva's wayward sexual thoughts. "I'm not ignoring it. I'm digesting it, trying to keep my clit from throbbing and rubbing my legs together to set off an orgasm. I'm way past the age of ignoring a sexual come-on. Especially one so bluntly. I'm feeling the wetness and heat between my legs, but a quick masturbation session before I see you for dinner will take care of that, seeing as how we won't be fucking before we do an STD check. Do you have any more questions about what happened here today?" Lea leans over the desk stretching her blouse across her breasts on purpose.

Check out my swollen breasts why don't you.

"I got it. Is this how you get when contractors fuck up this way?"

Nice cleavage Ms. Adams. Ima bury my head in it and inhale.

"Honestly, I think I took out more anger and frustration on him than he deserved."

SEXUAL FRUSTRATION DOES THAT TO A GIRL.

"No, you didn't. I wanted to put my foot up his ass for his last comment. He insulted you, and I hated it."

"You are a savior. How wonderful," Lea says unable to keep the warm protective feeling spreading throughout her body.

"I don't mean to cut this conversation short but I gotta get back to the office. How about I pick you up at seven-thirty?"

Man, I would kill for this woman. Where in the hell that come from?

"No problem. I need to see if I can get into the doctor's office. I need some tests run. Here is my address. Wait, would you rather meet somewhere?"

"No, I'll pick you up."

Good she gave me her real address considering I know it from the background check.

They stand ready to leave. When she gets in front of him, he presses her up against the wall letting her feel how much he is turned on.

Zion stares down into her face.

"We know we won't be sexing tonight." He kisses her neck.

"We will just be having dinner, talking and enjoying each other's company." He nibbles her ear lobe.

"Don't masturbate; I want all your pleasure for myself." He cups her ass and squeezes.

"Now I'm going to pull away, you will give me a few seconds to adjust my dick while you gather your things, and we will walk out of here as if nothing has happened."

She looks up at him with her mouth slightly parted, shudders, steps away and grabs her things. As she walks past him, her arm purposely brushes against his dick sending him hard again. He stops and groans.

Shit, this woman is fucking toying with me, and I thought I was toying with her. I gather myself and walk her to her car, confident that this project will go off much smoother than I expected. After how she handled that Martin guy today, her business demeanor is one to be reckoned with. I wonder how that carries over to her personal and sexual life.

Lea gets in her car saying goodbye with a sly smile staring at his crouch.

I watch her drive off making sure she is aware we're still having dinner tonight by sending her a reminder text. I get in the SUV and Sam drives me to the office. Calling my doctor's office, I schedule an STD checkup. I plan on having nothing get in the way of our sex life. Especially oral sex. Shit, I can't wait to feel her pulsing clit on my tongue.

-19-

Lea watches Zion in her rear-view mirror for as long as she can.

The Sex Diva is talking a mile a minute, WE NEED A NEW DRESS, SHOES, GOTTA SHAVE THE LEGS, UNDER ARMS, AND THE PUSSY. WE HAVIN' SEX WITH ADONIS.

Lea calms herself and the Sex Diva, rewinding and backing up. Okay, she can move in two directions with this. She can continue to put her cards on the table and let the sex hit the sheets, or she can do something to slow it down.

I'm going for broke. I should learn how to play the roulette tables.

She gets home, rushing to shower and shave. She tries on multiple dresses, every pair of shoes she owns, and multiple pieces of sexy underwear.

I haven't been out on a date of this magnitude in like forever.

How does one dress for this? *In three fricking hours.* Then she stops, rehashing their conversation.

He ordered her to do things, and she followed his instructions without giving it a second thought.

Okay, calm down, breathe, and get a hold of yourself. Remember sex is not happening tonight. It's just small talk and dinner. That's it. Yes, he said y'all will be fucking but not until after the STD results come back. I can deal. He is cautious. He isn't the first who wanted those tests before sex.

DAMN, WE HAVE NO CONDOMS. MAYBE HE WILL.

During the drive back to the office, Zion elected to sit in the back seat, something he only does when he is working or making calls.

Glancing in the rearview mirror, Sam notices Zion isn't doing either.

He sure isn't working and he hasn't even taken his phone out of his pocket. His mind must be fully directed toward Lea Adams, Sam thinks smiling. He turns on some jazz music to fill the silence for the drive.

Zion is wracking his brain, thinking of all the other women he has worked with whom he was attracted to as much as he is with Lea. He can't think of one. He has kept his social and working relationships separate. He has worked with some beautiful, smart, intelligent women who could have been Mrs. Landon. Not one of them intrigued him as Lea.

Martin was right about one thing. Lea is a strong ass independent woman. In business. How could she not be, having to work with all the men she works with? But Zion saw a different side of her. During their first meeting, he saw Lea the business woman. He also saw Lea, the woman. In the Central West End, he saw Lea, a woman he wanted to bed. He got introduced to Lea the woman who wants more and is sticking to her guns at the charity ball. Which Lea will he be having dinner with tonight? He can't wait.

He finishes up his afternoon schedule thinking about the night ahead and where he would like to take her.

Should they do dinner and see something at the Fox? Or keep it just the two of them, maybe go for a drive later.

Naw, not the Fox. I want to be alone with her. I'll have Sam do the driving so we can talk. Hell, let's keep this simple. Dinner. Nothing more.

Back at his apartment, Zion showers looking at himself in the mirror. He told Lea not to masturbate, and here he is, third leg wanting some release. He turns on the cold water and drenches himself.

Well, it kinda worked.

Getting down to the garage, Sam is waiting. "Sir, you never said which car to have ready," he mentions to Zion.

Mr. Landon has been distracted since leaving the building site.

"The Cadillac is fine. Why wouldn't we take the Caddy?" Zion asks.

"Sir, no reason at all." Sam strolls to the car, wanting to grin.

"Okay, I get it. Yes, she is different from the others. Am I seriously that transparent?"

"Only to me. And your father. I thought you would have elected to drive yourself. Or selected the Beemer. It's nice to know you want to give her your full undivided attention. Lots of privacy."

"I've given women my undivided attention before."

"No, you haven't. Or at least not since I have known you. Her independent nature doesn't frighten you off. It draws you to her."

"This can go in any direction. It's just dinner. Nothing else."

"Yes, sir. It is just dinner." *At his favorite restaurant which he has never taken a woman to,* Sam thinks and leaves that part unsaid.

They drive to Lea's house, letting the jazz from the stereo feel the car with calm as it did this afternoon.

Lea is ready fifteen minutes before Zion is due to arrive. She settled on a navy and white dress with small blue and white polka dots on top and flows into a pink skirt to mid-thigh. She puts on navy pumps and changes her purse into a simple clutch containing identification, phone, money, keys, and lip gloss. She takes a small shot of Patron with lime juice to calm her nerves. As a light-weight, she avoids drinking unless she is completely comfortable around someone, she is not driving, and she knows she can count on her friends to get her home safely no matter what she says while drinking.

Sitting on her couch all prim and proper, practicing how to cross and fold her legs, she hears a car door close. It's seven twenty-five, he is five minutes early.

Okay, get a grip, Lea. Get a tight grip on yourself. You can do this. Breathe. Deep full breaths.

She stands and waits for the bell. No point in rushing to the door like a love-sick-lustful-in-heat-out-of-control-crazy female. The doorbell rings, and she opens the door to Zion, dressed in a black suit, crisp white shirt, no tie, and shoes she can see her reflection in if she looked hard enough.

Shit and the man smells good, too. I wanna dance a jig all over the room I'm so excited. I just gotta hide it.

"Hello, Zion. Please come in," she says inviting him in.

YOU SOUND NORMAL. GOOD IDEA WITH THE PATRON SHOT.

She moves back out of the way into the foyer as he steps into the house. Suddenly, her small bungalow feels like a card-board box.

"Good evening, Lea. You look fantastic."

"Thanks. Just let me grab my clutch and keys and we can head out."

"Wait. I need to make a call first," he pulls out his phone and hits a speed dial number.

Lea stands there, listening, with her hand on the door ready to close and lock it.

"Hi, this is Zion Landon." He looks her up and down.

We need some privacy. I need to caress them legs.

"I need to change my dinner reservations to a private dining room. Yes, private. Thank you," he hangs up, "I'm not sharing any looks with you in that dress tonight. Shall we go?"

"Sure."

He steps out onto her porch with Lea stepping out behind him closing the door and locking it. She sets the alarm from her key fob as a last thought. Sam is standing by the back door of the car waiting to open it so they can get in.

"Good evening, Sam."

"Good evening, Ms. Adams."

Lea catches on quickly that Sam is in work mode and is here to provide security and transportation.

Okay, this is different.

She slides in and adjusts her dress and legs as she had practiced sitting on her couch, so she isn't showing too much leg. Or trying not to. Zion slides into the car on the other side sitting close for such a spacious back seat. He grabs her free hand and plays with her ring.

Hey, that's my nervous twitch. Sex Diva, he just stole my coping mechanism from me.

WHO CARES, YOU FEEL HOW SOFT HIS HANDS ARE? NOW IMAGINE THEM ON OUR BODY.

Oh okay, you right.

Lea relaxes her hand allowing him to continue, looking at their clasped hands. She then looks up into his eyes.

"A private dining room? What do you have behind those eyes of yours, Mr. Landon?"

"This isn't business, but when you say Mr. Landon that way, with it rolling out of your mouth so sexy, I think I can let it slide. As I stated, I don't want anyone staring at you in that dress other than me. Do you ever wear stockings, thigh highs, or pantyhose?"

"Only when necessary. I don't think I even own a pair. I buy them when I have to wear them. I usually put a run in them when taking them off, so they get trashed. I do wear leggings, tights or thigh highs with designs in them with certain dresses and boots,"

Lea is nervously talking nonsense, but she can't help herself. Anything to avoid an empty silence is her goal tonight.

"Are your legs as soft as they appear?"

She looks at Sam wondering if he can hear this conversation, she has a feeling it could get hot quickly. She notices a privacy glass between them. She turns back to Zion and answers his question. "I do my best to make sure they are."

He looks at her then runs his fingers against her thigh.

"Yes, they are."

It's gonna be nice having these to caress and massage at my discretion.

They arrive at The Enigma Tower. The hotel is in downtown Clayton with its signature restaurant at the top. Zion touches a button on his side of the car to lower the privacy glass, telling Sam he can sit. He will get her door and will call him when it's time to come back. Sam nods. Zion gets out, and Lea sits waiting for him to come and open her door. Seconds later, she feels the night's breeze across her freshly shaven legs and steps out of the car putting her hand in his. He squeezes it and has her step aside to close the door.

Her introvert tendencies are taking over. She wants to turn around and run back home.

This is too much. This is way too much. This man, being picked up and driven in a car, a private dinner, this everything. This is too much.

She wants to squeeze Zion's hand but digs her nails into the palm of her other hand instead.

Zion looks down at her questioning, "Are you okay? Are you cold? You're shaking."

"No, not cold, just nervous."

He looks surprised at that. He puts her hand in his other hand and places his free hand on her back.

"It's okay, relax." This isn't the first time Zion has taken a woman out, a woman who is unsure of how to act. He didn't expect it with Lea after what he witnessed earlier today.

They walk into the hotel and straight to an elevator that leads to the restaurant. Lea feels as if she's in a fish bowl.

People are staring at Zion probably wondering what the hell is he doing with that plain Jane?

The number of women trying to get him to look at them is astounding. Lea has always wanted to do those seductive looks women do, but she always found herself feeling uncoordinated and stupid.

She and Zion get to the elevator, he presses the button, and it opens immediately. Some big tittyed female hops onto the elevator with them. Zion steps in and moves directly behind Lea, placing his hand around her waist and pressing himself up against her behind, effectively putting them in their own bubble of intimacy as much as he can with this woman on the elevator. She reaches over in front of Lea to press the button before either Zion or she can do so and stands back saying "Excuse Me" to Zion. He doesn't acknowledge her. Not with a word or glance. Zion dismisses her.

I wanna poke her in the tit and make it deflate. It will probably make a sound like a deflating balloon slowly loosing air. Lea giggles.

Zion nibbles Lea's ear whispering "What's so funny?" Lea shakes her head.

The woman looks at her like, "What the hell you laughing at"?

They arrive at the top, and Zion allows the lady to walk out before them, having them hang back. He tells Lea he wants the hostess to take care of Big Boob girl before they walk up to the desk. The woman is talking to the hostess, then walks off toward what Lea thinks is the bathroom. They step up to her and are immediately escorted to a private dining room.

They walk into the room and Lea feels as if she has just walked into heaven. The lighting is soft from the corners of the room. A table is sitting in the middle with two chairs around it. On the table are two place settings for dinner, with candles. There is a vase of delicate Japanese irises. R&B instrumental music is playing softly in the background. The view is wide and looks down at the city lights through the full wall of windows. In here, no one can see them.

It's amazing. I was just expecting a simple dinner, some flirty talking and then back home. Never have I experienced anything like this.

Zion allows her to walk around taking in everything. She realizes she keeps forgetting how rich this man is. He is talking with the server and this gives her a chance to get hold of herself while looking out the windows. He comes up and stands behind her.

"I hope you like it. This is my favorite restaurant. I've only had the private dining room for client celebrations. I've never had it for a dinner."

"It's beautiful. The view is breathtaking. I'm glad you invited me."

"Let's sit. I've taken the liberty and ordered for us. I hope you don't mind. I don't want to constantly be disturbed by hovering staff. I want us to enjoy ourselves without having to stop in the middle of a conversation."

"That's fine. What did you order?"

"A small dinner salad, with vinaigrette dressing, sautéed chicken breasts with a Champagne glaze and braised mixed veggies, and Strawberries for dessert with Champagne. Now that I think about, it I should have asked if you are vegan or have a special diet. I can change it."

"No, it all sounds great. I don't have to worry about trying something out of the ordinary, not liking it and having to fake it. What you ordered takes at least one pressure off me tonight. Why Champagne? Are we celebrating?"

The hovering server leaves the room to go have their order placed after the confirmation from Zion with a head nod.

"Yes, we are. It feels like a celebration."

"Is it a work celebration?"

"First rule of tonight, no discussing work."

"Deal."

"Let's sit."

They sit down and Lea notices that instead of the place settings being across from each other, they have been moved and placed next to each other for as much elbow room will allow.

"I can't see you across the table. No fair," she says to him.

"But I can touch you when you are next to me. Very fair."

Lea looks at him and says nothing. Something is off, and he can't figure out what. He helps her into her chair and sits in his. As soon as they sit, the salads are brought out along with wine.

"Why where you laughing on the elevator?"

"I was thinking if I had a pin, I could stick that woman in her boob and the air coming out of it would sound like the air slowly leaving a balloon. She wanted your attention. Didn't you notice that?"

"Yes, I did, and all I cared about was you and having you pressed up against me. Don't look away from me. You seem to be uncomfortable when I compliment you. Why are you feeling any kind of pressure? What can I do to ease that?"

"I'm overwhelmed by all of this. I'm a bundle of nerves around you tonight. The second I stepped out of the car, I got nervous and my introvert tendencies took over. My stomach was in knots; I couldn't stop shaking. I wanted to run back home and say this is not me. I saw the people in the lobby look our way and all I kept thinking in my head was they were saying 'What is that sexy Greek God doing with that frump?' What are you doing with me? Why am I here with you? Is it only because of the sexual tension between us?"

Before he can respond, the server arrives bringing their entrée. He adds the strawberries on a table along with the Champagne in a bucket of ice along with the glasses waiting to be served later. He turns to leave, and they are left alone. Completely. For the remainder of the evening.

"When you say you are an introvert, I hardly see that. You were on your game today with that contractor. That does not say introvert to me. That says you are a confident woman I need to get to know. I was proud of you. Intimidate or overwhelm you is the last thing I want to do. I want you relaxed and smiling and enjoying life around me. With me. You stated you want long term. I'm in. We can take this as slowly or as quickly as you like."

"But all this," I wave my hand at the luxury suite, "It's different from what I have experienced in my past. It's an adjustment for me."

"Lea, outside of work, I want you to see me as a man. A man you are attracted to, a man you want to get to know. Yes, I have money, but I'm still just a man with issues, hang-ups, and problems just like everyone else. As with any relationship, I imagine we will have our ups and downs and things won't go smoothly. But, sweetheart, I'm willing to go through it all. And I hope you are also.

Money allows us to enjoy and do things that you would probably have to save up for. Money allows us to buy things. This here, you and me talking, spending time together is more valuable than anything I have bought or could buy. Let's just go with it. I look forward to getting to know you, introvert quirks, tendencies and all. I have some things in my life that may chase you away. We will never know until we take the time to get to know each other."

"You're right."

"Now let's talk. No topic is off limits. How about it?"

"No topic?"

"Except work and the project. None."

Lea and Zion dive into their dinner, grilling each other.

-20-

Zion is determined to have Lea see him, not his money and not as a client. The best way to accomplish this is to have an open conversation about anything and everything.

"Lea, have you made your appointment with your doctor yet?"

Zion is not going to have sex with her until the STD check is done. Although he has taken all precautions he could during his sexual dalliances, he doesn't want Lea to have any worries on that front and because he is determined to enjoy her as often as he can, it doesn't hurt to be sure.

"Yes, I go Friday. What about you?"

He probably thought I was going to be offended. Nope. I'm honestly going to answer his questions.

"I go tomorrow." Zion caresses her thigh as she crosses her legs. "How often do you masturbate?"

"Every few months. It's safer than a random unsatisfactory dick."

"When was the last time?"

"Friday, the day we met."

"Nice." Zion takes his hand from her thigh and grabs his wine glass, taking a measured sip.

He thinks back to that day. *She made herself cum thinking of me, I just know it.*

"Do you masturbate and when was the last time?" Lea asks him.

"Yes, three months ago. I was out of town and couldn't get to who was my regular."

"Was your regular? Poor girl. All this, she will be missing out on." Lea smiles mischievously.

"I'm currently considering a long-term, monogamous, can't-get-enough-of-her, sexual partner."

"Fascinating. Hope you find her."

"I believe we have found each other. Lea, when was the last time you had sex?"

"Two years ago. I used condoms, always did. Long term, huh?"

Zion almost chokes on the bite of chicken in his mouth.

Lawd, no dick in two years. Well, well, well. She's not sleeping around. Nice.

"And you Zion? When was the last time a woman had the chance to enjoy you?"

"Two months ago. I used a condom, always have."

"Two months. I can't imagine you going two months without a woman. Don't women throw themselves at you?"

"Yes, they do. That's why I had a regular, but about a month ago, you and I met. Geez that just hit me. I haven't wanted another woman since I met you. Even though I had a regular, she knew and understood there was never going to be anything more between us but the occasional sex. The other month was heavy traveling. I don't masturbate that often."

"Should I feel sorry for her? Was she expecting more?" Lea knows too well about wanting and expecting more from a man she wants yet he doesn't.

"We laid out the rules up front between us. She was looking too marry a certain type of man. I didn't fit that type. She wanted sex while looking, and I wanted sex with no headaches. It worked for us."

"Zion, you not being a woman's type. Unbelievable."

"Baby, it happens. More often than you think." Zion skips the reason why. This part of the conversation is moving to close in that direction. He changes course with his next question.

"So, tell me, what kind of B.O.B.s do you use?"

Lea laughs at him using that word. It's strange having a man question her about her B.O.B.s and not be offended.

"What, Lea? Yes, I know they are called battery-operated boyfriends."

Lea responds. "Clitoral stimulation. When I want to be penetrated and filled, I want a flesh and blood, rock hard, throbbing penis, inside of me filling me up."

"Then why has it been two years? You're beautiful. I'm sure you have men who would be happy to sex you anytime you want."

"All dick offered is not all dick that should be accepted. Those men, they wanted no attachments. Don't get it twisted. Once upon a time, temporary dick would have been the route to go, but I got a wake-up call that had nothing to do with sex but with having to do with closely looking at my exact desires, wants, and needs. They don't work well with temporary."

"What was the wake-up call?"

"I'll discuss that later, when we get to the family interview. This seems to be the more personal, sexual interview. I would like to stay on course if you don't mind?"

"I understand."

"You say it has been two months since you last had sex. You have admitted to enjoying the temporary piece of ass. Considering the Big Boob chick at the charity ball you were with, you like them with big tits. Was or shall I say are they giving you what you need? Whatever happened to her by the way? After dinner, she was ghost."

"They fulfilled a moment in time. There was no sexual passion, just in, out, and bye. Hence, the regular. Kelly found a better catch that night. I haven't heard from her since. I thought I was a big titty man, but I'm liking your handful amounts the more I look at them. 'B' cup, right?" he asks staring at her breasts.

"Then why waste your time? Yes, small 'B' cup."

I adjust my bra feeling the heaviness in my tits.

"It has taken more time to find a woman who was agreeable to my terms than it has been to get what I could get out of her and take care of myself the other times. You wear padded bras because of perky nipples, I'm guessing?"

"Oh, I'm on birth control. Yes, padded bras to hide the perky nipples."

"Extremely nice to hear. Both the birth control and maybe the padded bra. I look forward to seeing how perky they get."

Her being on birth control doesn't mean she can't have kids. At forty-four, why is she using birth control anyway? It seems we both avoid the subject of children, and I'm going to keep it that way for now. I need her to get to know me before I drop the bomb about not being able to ever give her any.

"Does my cussing or vulgar talk bother you?" Lea asks.

"No. Not many women I've worked with freely cuss the way you do, but it only seems you let loose when frustrated. I keep wondering if you are that vocal when being made love to. I'm not looking for a quiet docile female in my bed anymore. Does my saying the word 'fuck' bother you? You adjust your body every time I say it."

"No, I like hearing it. I can't stand a quiet man while having sex. I feed off his moans, groans, instructions, and participation. You saying the word 'fuck' makes my clit throb."

She looks down at my dick and sees that it's hard. Has been since we started talking.

"That looks a little uncomfortable. Maybe we need to change the subject."

"Lea, why hasn't this conversation offended you? We have talked about sex. Most women would be upset at thinking I only have a one-track mind. I don't want you thinking I am in this just for the sex."

"Zion, we are not kids. I want to be with someone I can talk freely about anything and everything at any moment. No topic off limits, remember? I've done the coy thing, the avoidance of issues because society says do this or that. I'm tired of that. I've never been down this road before—. This open and honest discussion road. If it bothers you, which I hope it doesn't, maybe we are incompatible. I'm not going back to the coy playing games of my past."

"It doesn't bother me at all. I prefer it. I didn't want to turn you off so soon with all this sex, dick, and pussy talk. Offend your delicate sensibilities with all that shit. This is an adjustment for me."

"I'm not offended. No worries. Now, any more questions? Especially sex questions?"

"How about the strawberries and Champagne?" he suggests.

Lea sees they have finished dinner without even realizing it. She gets up to walk over to the dessert table. Zion joins her, helping to clear dishes off their table. He grabs the glasses and Champagne and Lea grabs the strawberries. They retake their seats, with him turning his chair around and pulling her chair even closer to him, forcing her to slightly part her legs. She tries to do it as lady-like as she can, but he looks at her and shakes his head.

"Open them. It's just us."

GIRL, IF YOU DON'T OPEN YOUR DAMNED LEGS I WILL DO IT FOR YOU.

-21-

HE'S GOING TO TOUCH US, OPEN THEM LEGS.

"Zion, I thought you said we're not fucking tonight."

"We aren't. But I want to kiss you, caress you, and feel you. Two years and no penetration."

"Well, no fake penis penetration. I've used my fingers and Ben Wa balls to strengthen and tighten the inner muscles."

"Ben Wa Balls? What the hell are those? I only know about B.O.B.s," he says.

I reach for my phone and do a search for pictures showing him. "You ever heard of Kegel exercises?"

"Yes, of course," Zion says, continually caressing her outer thighs, moving his hands under her dress, edging closer to her panties.

"Well, I insert these inside of me and do Kegels to keep them in." Lea is attempting to concentrate on the conversation.

He stares at her, amazed at what he just heard and the picture he just saw. Imagining her sitting and contracting her inner walls around these balls.

Oh, my fucking heaven.

"Damn, woman. I bet you are extremely tight; I can smell how wet you are. Yes, baby I can smell your juices. Your underwear is not hiding that precious scent from me. You are extremely fragrant and probably slick. That's why you keep crossing your legs, generating friction trying to calm your clit. You probably thinking, 'damn, I need to get home to my B.O.B'. After tonight, you will only be using B.O.B.s in my presence. Yes, baby, I wanna watch you pleasure yourself with them. I'm not intimidated by them. They just bring a level of eroticism to the playing field."

Lea stares at him with her sexy mouth slightly parted. "You are perceptive, Zion."

Zion pours them glasses of Champagne, covering the strawberries he put in each glass. He hands Lea one and takes the other. He wants to have a toast.

"To getting to know each other and to long term."

"To long term. Are you sure you want long term?"

"Oh yes, I'm very sure."

Zion moves his hands up her inner thigh, edging closer to her womanhood.

"What are you expecting to happen tonight, Zion?" He kisses and caresses her.

Oh, his hands feel so good.

"I wanna make you cum, here and now. We won't be interrupted. I wanna feel you. I wanna feel how swollen you are."

Lea opens her legs all the way inviting him to touch her. He accepts her invitation and rubs her pussy through her panties. He watches her, her breathing picking up, her hips moving in circular movements, wanting his touch.

"Touch me, Zion. I was thinking about you when I was finger fucking myself."

"Tell me about it, talk to me."

"I wanted your lips on my neck, licking my nipples, needing your hands squeezing my tits hard. Fuck, I wanted you inside me. I was imaging your tongue flicking my clit. Over and over, soft and hard. Shit, I was so wet."

"Just like now. Can I feel your pussy, see how smooth it is?"

"Yes, oh yes."

Zion swiftly pulls her underwear down slightly lifting her off the chair and sitting her back down before re-opening her legs as wide as he can get them and placing his legs in between hers. He

Loves Awakening

takes his thumb and finger and presses her pussy lips together squeezing her clit in between them.

Shit, that feeling is rocking my body. Damn. I can cum almost immediately. He's got to slow down.

"Not so fast, I want to enjoy this, I want to remember this forever."

"Don't worry, baby, I'm going to make this unforgettable for the both of us."

He unzips his pants taking his manhood out. They kiss holding nothing back. It's more erotic and harder than the first kiss he gave her.

He opens her pussy lips and slides his fingers up and down the sides of her clit, never touching it. She grabs his penis gently, praying he doesn't jump or push her hand away. He doesn't jump away. He places his hand over hers, encouraging her to stroke him.

"Yes. Feel me. This will all be going inside of you. But tonight, I want you to give me a hand job while I finger fuck you. Do that for me, please do that?"

"Yes, oh hell yes."

Lea moves closer to the edge of the chair so Zion can have deeper access to her pussy, and she can get a nice grip on his dick with both hands. She rubs her thumb around the tip, playing with his pre-cum to get him slick. He moans his pleasure while kissing her neck.

"Damn, your dick is as soft as your hands. So smooth, thick and hard. Oh, I can't wait to taste you, having your veins pulsing on my tongue."

"Lea, squeeze me tight," Zion says, "go up and down on it. Yes, shit yes. Like that. Damn, you keep rubbing the tip. Shit that feels so damn good. Oh, fuck yes, make me feel how tight I think your pussy is. Squeeze my dick hard with your hands."

She squeezes him with every up and down movement, continuingly brushing the tip and caressing the underside of it. Each time she does, he jerks with pleasure. He slides two fingers inside of her at the same time, fingering her clit. She gasps.

Shit, that feels so good. I wanna cum.

"Zion don't stop, keep fingering my clit. Oh, fuck yes. Yes, shit yes. You gonna make me cum. Oh, fuck that feels so damn good."

He slides in another finger and she feels his middle finger caress her g-spot.

Shit he found the g-spot on the first try.

She presses his palm against her pussy, grinding against it wanting to cum. The action is so unreal. He has a finger on her clit, a finger on her g-spot and his palm pressing her pussy for every grind she makes. She makes a noise between a growl and a soft purr, surprising herself.

"Baby you are so tight. Even with three fingers you are squeezing your pussy, gripping them. Cum for me, shit yes, cum for me, that's it. Let me hear you cum. Squeeze my dick, harder. Yes, harder. Fuck yes. Make me cum. MMMhhhmmm. Damn you sound like a purring kitten. I may need to start calling you Kitten."

Lea's hands are working Zion into an explosive orgasm, but he slows her down so he can concentrate on her. She is about to explode and he wants to make sure he doesn't miss any of it.

Her moans are driving me crazy. And her sex talk is off the fucking chain. No way will this be a quiet lady in bed. She will drive me to the ends of the earth with her sex talk.

Lea is getting closer to the mountain top of her climax.

He moves faster on her clit, stroking it with every thrust of her hips.

Yes, maybe I can even get a squirt out of her tonight, shit yes.

"Cum for me, yes that's it, come on baby, yes."

Lea explodes, cumming, squirting.

Geez all over my damn hand. She is so sticky and wet and I'm loving it. Her blissful orgasm. She screams and grips my dick harder, moving up and down feverishly. I bury my face in her neck, begging her to make me cum. Squeeze hard. And she does. She does everything I tell her. Exactly as I tell her, adding the squeeze of the tip of my dick with every movement she makes. Shit, she keeps flicking the under skin of my tip. Damn, I didn't realize I was that sensitive. I grip her thighs and keep bucking, wanting to cum. I grab a napkin off the table, knowing I'll unload all over her if I don't catch it.

"Oh, yes, milk it, damn girl, milk my dick dry."

I kiss her neck, placing my hands over hers along with the napkin over the tip of my dick. Shit, one more squeeze and pump and I shoot my jiz all over our hands and into the napkin jerking in the chair, almost falling out of it. Damn. Best fucking hand job ever. I keep jerking while she strokes me dry, getting all the cum out. As sensitive as I'm feeling, I don't want her to stop caressing me. Not ever.

"Oh, Kitten, you are so good. You feel so good. Watching you cum. Fuck that was nice," Zion breathes into her neck.

"Kitten, huh? I don't think I have ever had such a pet name. I like hearing you call me that," she says, smiling broadly.

"It fits you and the purring sound you made. I hope you cuddle like a baby kitten also. I can't wait to have you in my arms like that."

"You've surprised me tonight," Lea says while still holding his dick. It's getting soft, and she doesn't want to let it go.

They both grip the napkin. She wipes him down as best she can and he sits back basking in the afterglow. She shakily stands, taking her napkin and wiping in between her legs as graciously as she can considering what happened. Zion is sitting in the chair with one hand on the table and one hand in his lap with his pants down to his knees.

Shit, Lea. Ain't nothing gracious about this, just wipe up and put the damned panties back on.

She takes the napkins over to the bucket that contained the bottle of Champagne, putting them in and swishing them around, washing her hands, bringing one back to him. He jumps to attention.

Not a cold ice towel on my dick. Shit woman.

Lea laughs. "Don't worry, I'm not about to wipe your dick off with this. It's for your hands. Here. I'm sure you have a cloth handkerchief you can place in your pants and zip up. We can't be walking out of here with a wet spot on the front of your pants."

He takes the wet napkin from her and looks down at his semi-hard penis. "Woman you had me nervous there for a sec."

Yep, cum still dripping from the tip.

He takes out his handkerchief and wipes up, standing and adjusting himself, zipping up. She is looking around for her panties. He picks them up from under the table, studying them before handing them to her. She sits down and slips back into them. He stares at her.

"Are you okay?" he asks her.

"Yes, my legs are shaky. And I don't think a man has ever looked at my underwear so closely. Kinda weird. What were you looking for?"

"My legs are shaky, too. I've never given a second thought to a woman's underwear before. Yours I wanted, I had an urge to smell."

"Well, all righty then. I don't know how to respond. That was better than I imagine, Zion. You are changing the way I think about foreplay sex. Most people don't see the point in finger fucking or hand jobs if they don't lead to sex. You may enjoy those as much as you may enjoy penetration sex. Am I correct?" she asks him.

Loves Awakening

"How are you so aware like that? I have never met a woman who would think that, let alone say it out loud. Actually, I just wanted to feel my fingers inside of you and to make you cum. I figured we would both be leaving here sexually frustrated. No woman has ever given me such a hand job. And I have never finger fucked a woman the way I just did with you. You're right. Most people say what's the point if we not fucking. With you it would appear finger fucking can be foreplay or sex, as long as we're enjoying ourselves. Right?"

"I enjoyed you finger fucking me. I hope to have you finger fuck me often. I enjoyed giving you a hand job. I hope to give you hand jobs often. In addition to sexing you."

Lea leans in and gives him a kiss on those last two words. He looks at his watch after she pulls away and sees that it is almost eleven o'clock.

"I do believe we will be having a lot of firsts. I look forward to each and every one. Come on, let's get you home. Away from me before I do decide to sex you tonight."

"Oh, so you decide and it's a done deal. Hmpfh. I don't—," he stops her by kissing her neck, "Okay, uh yes, let's get me home before you decide to sex me tonight." They both laugh, knowing they want it.

The Sex Diva is standing in the background with her arms crossed and tapping her foot.

I CAN'T BELIEVE YOU ARE NOT GOING TO HAVE HIM BEND US OVER THIS TABLE AND TAKE US. GIRL, YOU WORKING MY LAST NERVE.

Zion takes out his phone and calls Sam to let him know they will be downstairs in ten minutes. While he is talking to Sam, Lea takes the strawberry out of her Champagne glass and puts it in her mouth biting down on it. Some of the juices are sliding down the side of her mouth. Zion kisses and licks it off, then eats the remaining half from her hand, staring at her the entire time.

"Ten minutes. The elevator is only a thirty-second ride," Lea whispers.

"I know. Come here," he opens his arms, and she moves to sit in his lap.

"I'm going to give you a proper good night kiss here and play with your ass a lil bit more to tide me over until I see you again. I don't want to do that when we get to your house. I'll ONLY walk you to your door and give you a hug and then we'll turn away and end it for the night. If I kiss you at your house, I won't be leaving. We know that."

"Okay. I had a wonderful evening tonight. The finger fucking and hand job were delectable."

"So have I. And the finger fucking and hand job were very delectable."

They kiss, with him rubbing her ass. He finally breaks the kiss, and they leave the dining room. The restaurant is closed. In the elevator, they make out during the ride down.

The man can kiss, that's for sure.

Sam is waiting with the car door open. They sit in the back in silence. Zion has not let her hand go, he keeps squeezing it. She looks over at him, and he gives her a conspiratorial smile. They are thinking the same thing.

Shit, what a night.

When they get to her house, as planned, Zion walks her to her door, gives her a chaste kiss on the side of her mouth, and makes sure she locks the outer door before saying goodnight and leaving. From her window, she watches him get in the car with Sam. The windows on the car are tinted, so she can't tell if he is still looking.

I hope he is. I can't stop smiling.

The Sex Diva is grinning as hard, fanning me saying, WE'RE FINALLY GOING TO HAVE SEX AGAIN. WOO HOO.

-22-

Lea gets to work the next morning on a high from last night with Zion. She wants to tell everyone, but she can only share this with one person right now.

Let's hope he returns my damn text sometime before Saturday before his birthday celebration.

She spends the morning, briefing Tom on the issue with Martin, the now former electrician on the job. He agrees with everything and states he will call Zion to make sure he isn't panicked or upset.

HE SURE AS HECK WASN'T PANICKED OR UPSET LAST NIGHT. OMG.

Sex Diva, hush.

HEEHEEHEEHEEHEE.

Of course, Lea doesn't bother to mention anything about last night's dinner. In all honesty, she has no clue what to say about it, or if she has anything to say at all. They had foreplay sex. They talked about having sex. Yes, Zion stated he is down with the long term but neither of them clarified it further. Are they dating, in a relationship, or just hanging? Lea has no clue. The doubts are sinking in.

She shuts down her wayward thoughts and focuses on the wine tasting event, helping Crystal to ensure all is going well. They make calls checking on deliveries of the food, chairs, and linen, verifying the setup with Linda. Reviewing the guest list of confirmed names, she sees Zion's. She forgot about that plus one.

Shit, wonder who he is bringing? Maybe it's the former fuck buddy. If she truly is a former. Maybe it's a piece of eye candy

She hears her smartphone vibrating and reaches for it looking at the number.

It's him.

She does a silent squeal, takes a deep breath and answers, hoping she sounds calm. "Hi, this is Lea."

"Hi Kitten."

"Hello handsome, how are you today?" Sitting in her desk chair, she twists it back and forth mimicking the gesture, playing with her hair and grinning.

"Hating that I had to wash my hands during my shower." Zion wasn't going to call Lea until he landed, thinking he could get some work done. Instead, he's been sitting staring at his fingers, flexing them thinking about her warm folds.

"It didn't work for you either, holding your hands outside the shower while letting the water rinse you off."

"No. Maybe I need to hire someone to wash me so when I finger you, I can make sure not to wash the scent away."

"Now we can't be walking around smelling like sex all the time. People will notice. That's not cool."

"No, I guess not. How did you sleep?" Zion asks.

Small talk. I am having flirtatious small talk with a woman. What the hell?

"Half awake, half sleep. By the way, I didn't mention our dinner last night to anyone here at work."

"Good idea. What you and I do after business hours is between you and me. It would be a pleasure getting to know you without everyone else's well-meaning advice directing where they think we should be going. Besides, I'm sure they know something is up considering the dance at the charity event."

"It's a Catch twenty-two situation. I want people to know we're dating if that's what we will be or are doing, but I also want to date you and not tell anyone so I can enjoy you. Is that crazy?" Lea asks.

"No, it's not, and yes, we're dating. How about this? If we're asked, we be honest and say we have spent time outside of business and leave it at that? I'm not going to hide you from any part of my life, but my usual standard is to not offer anyone any details of my personal life. We won't be hiding anything. We just won't be inviting the world into it. How does that sound?"

"I like the idea of not inviting others into our lives and unless asked, don't offer. Anyway, you have to get used to my quirks. You may not like my sleep fighting. Or when I talk to myself out loud. Gotta break you in slowly."

"Kitten, you fight in your sleep? I'll just have to pin you down and kiss you awake. Break me in slowly, huh. I can take that in so many directions. Slowly that is," Zion says in a low seductive voice.

Lea giggles.

"I need to go; I'm arriving for my client meeting. I hate the idea of texting in a relationship. It keeps things too impersonal. You don't mind if I text you a miss-you and want-you text whenever I'm thinking about you and can't call?"

"No, I don't mind. As long as you don't mind either."

"I look forward to it. I'm landing and gotta go. Talk to you later."

"Okay, talk to you later Zion."

Landing. He was calling me from his plane. Lea, the man is rich, remember that. No, forget it. He is working, and that is part of the way he works. Plain and simple. Don't let the money cloud your judgment of him.

Lea dances around her office mouthing, "I'm dating. I'm dating Zion Landon. I'm going to be sexing Zion Landon. Me, me, me. Dating Zion Landon. Woo hoo."

She sends him a text wanting to test out this relationship thing.

Lea: *I can't wait to see you again. I'm missing you.*

Zion:*Kitten, I'm missing you. I'll call you later. I hope I can concentrate on my meeting.*

Lea squeals in delight, staring at Zion's picture on her phone.

-23-

Saturday arrives, and Lea gets ready for a day at the winery and an evening out with friends. Tom and his wife purchased a small vineyard in Hermann, Missouri, about ten years ago. He wanted something to dabble in like beer making or woodworking, and his wife, Linda, wanted a small restaurant. They decided to go for a vineyard instead.

How they got to that conclusion I still don't know.

Golden Vineyards is located in the hills of Missouri about an hour outside of St. Louis. Many people might not want to drive that far for a wine tasting event, but every year Tom gets more people interested in attending. The vineyard produces white and red wines. Instead of the restaurant, his wife decided on working with caterers for special events and focus on making the vineyard succeed. And she has gone beyond what anyone could imagine. There are few African-American owned vineyards and to have one in Missouri is an example of their success. This is the Midwest, they have to deal with all four seasons, yet their wines sell in three different wine stores, two grocery stores, and four restaurants.

Today's weather calls for sunny, a high of eighty-five degrees, and no rain. A great day for pictures.

Lea is wearing white jeans, a white and yellow off the shoulder top with white flats. She grabs her yellow heels for tonight's birthday party. She has an oversize white shirt she can throw on over the top and jeans for a change of look for the birthday party. Today's jewelry selection is simple: her blue pendant necklace with a blue ice ring.

She arrives an hour before guests are expected. Crystal, Stanley, Tom, and Linda are here. So are all of the volunteers. They are ready to go. Lea isn't the photographer for this event. G-TEE hired someone for that, but she has her camera and snaps away as usual. One o'clock arrives and so do the guests. The staff walks around greeting guests making sure they are having a good time. Everything is going smoothly as Crystal has planned. They have clients, contractors, and staff mingling together, enjoying the wine, food, and music. Linda is running the sales office so the purchases go smoothly and shipments of cases of wine are set up for delivery. Tom is in his element, relaxed and even dancing a little. He will hate the blackmail pictures Lea has of him.

Lea stands off in a corner taking pictures of the seated guests, chatting at tables, wanting to get names and email addresses, identifying guests in her snapshots. Three hours have passed, and she finally gets to take a break. Spotting a table off to the side, she takes a seat and people watch. Lea feels Zion before she sees him. He is mingling with guests and talking with Tom and Crystal. He can't see her sitting off to the side so she watches him.

Who the hell is his fucking plus one? I see no eye candy on his arm.

Earlier in the day, Lea told Tom that Brad would need to meet Zion. She watches him call Brad over to make the introductions. It's a quick shake of the hands, a short conversation, and Brad and his wife move off. While they are talking Lea snaps pictures of them, zooming in on Zion's face.

DAMN, THAT MAN IS SEXY AS ALL GET OUT.

One of the many single men Tom has tried to hook Lea up with sits down at the table with her. This one is Henry. Forty-three, newly divorced, three kids under the age of ten, and an evil crazy baby mama.

Well not evil and crazy. She just ain't letting him go.

Henry has been interested in dating Lea or so he thinks. Whenever he would ask her out, he would run back and tell the ex-

Loves Awakening

wife. Then she would come up with an excuse about their kids, and he would cancel. Lea doesn't know which is worse; her introvert tendencies causing her to cancel or Henry letting his ex-wife causing him to cancel. Finally, Lea lost interest and moved out of the line of fire. Here he is to say what?

Please not another suggestion for a date.

"Hi. Lea. How's it going?" he asks.

"Pretty good. How are things with you? How are your kids doing? Are they loving the new school?" I ask him.

"Wow, you remember that about us. They're doing fine. Will you go out with me next Friday? A movie maybe?"

"Oh, I don't think so. I'm pretty busy with this new contract. But thanks for asking."

Lea looks for an escape route while Zion is still talking with other guests.

I really don't want to see some plus one coming up to him and linking arms with him.

"Sorry, I gotta go mingle. It was good seeing you. Take care, Henry."

Lea stands up moving off to the side out of view where no one can see her, suddenly feeling shy and unsure of herself. She overhears some of the female guests talking about Zion and mentions how good-looking he is and wanting to know more about him.

And the thirsty ladies display their sharpened claws.

Right as she is about to turn and go sit in another spot, she bumps into Sam.

Geez, where did he come from?

"Hi Sam, how are you?" she says, catching her camera before it dropped.

"I'm good, Ms. Adams. Mr. Landon wanted to be sure I located you. He wants to say hello but got caught up talking with a group of people before he could get over to your table."

Lea looks up at Sam behind her dark shades.

So, he saw me sitting there talking with Henry. Wonderful.

"Oh. Okay. I'll head over his way."

"Please, let me escort you so you don't get detained further."

Lea looks up at Sam again, "Okay. Let's go."

She walks next to Sam trying to make it look as if she isn't being escorted like a child. It's almost funny, but kinda annoying. And extremely heavy handed.

I must re-hash this over and over later tonight.

She walks up to the group that Zion is chatting with and plasters a smile on her face ready to ask if everyone is having a good time and if she can get them anything. Sam falls back into the shadows. Zion looks at her and before she can give her speech, excuses himself saying he needs to speak with Lea in private.

He places his hand on the small of her back, walking them away from the group.

"Hi beautiful, that color looks great on you." *And who the hell was the jerk talking to you,* he wants to ask her but holds his tongue.

This is a business function; he can be anyone.

"Thanks. You sent Sam to cut off my escape. Why?"

"The only reason I'm here is for you. I don't care about meeting these other people. Well, no one other than that Brad guy you told me you were going to introduce me to. When I saw you sitting at that table alone, I couldn't wait to get to you. Then I kept getting stopped and some guy sat down talking to you. I had to send Sam over before I lost you in this crowd when you stood up to leave."

"Oh. Where is your plus one at?" I look around hoping not to see some female staring us down about to interrupt us. "Wait, you noticed all that about me while talking to a group of people? I didn't think you saw me at all."

"Lea, Sam is my plus one. I didn't know how things were set up, so I included him in the number. I always include him when I need to RSVP. I had no plans on bringing a woman here with me today when I told Tom I would come. My goal was to see you. I can't do that with another woman on my arm, now can I? Besides after Wednesday, I don't give a damn about another woman on my arm. I want just you. From the moment I walked in and spotted you, you have not been out of my sight."

"Oh." Lea looks at him and leans into him but catches herself remembering where she is. Standing outside with a large group of people who are probably watching their every move. She won't even look over there.

"I'm glad you didn't bring a woman. I didn't want to have to mess up my white pants getting into a cat fight."

"Oh, you would fight for me. I wish I could see your pretty eyes."

"Well, I may need to slap a heaux for getting out of line with you. Some don't understand, 'no' means no, and I need to stake my claim."

"Kitten, you just did."

She grins at him mischievously, and as she is about to respond, Crystal, Tom, and their spouses join them.

Tom interrupts, a little too jovially. "What are you guys talking about? I hope it isn't work."

Zion jokes with him. "Oh, this isn't a work event? How did I not realize that? I need to get out more and experience what life has to offer."

He moves to Lea's side so they are standing close enough that he keeps brushing up against her every now and then.

Lea attempts to keep up her side of the conversation as best as she can, keeping her thoughts in the here and now. "Nope, no business discussion here. How do you think things are going? Everyone seems to be having a good time."

I play with the strap on my camera feeling bored and distracted. It's another nervous coping skill when I get overwhelmed in a group. Playing with inanimate objects, lint, dust, anything. My hand is getting numb from the twisting and lack of blood circulation, but I don't care.

"You guys don't mind if Lea shows me around, do you?" Zion asks.

"No, sure go ahead. We'll see you two later," Tom responds.

Zion and Lea walk off.

Tom remarks, "Okay everyone did you see how intense that conversation was between the two of them before we walked over here?"

"She was about to lean into him and do something. I hope it was a kiss or at least a hug. Crystal, is she saying anything about him to you? I mean the night at the charity ball, something was between them, right? We noticed it, right?" Linda pipes in eagerly.

"No, we have been so busy these last few days with this wine tasting. I'm so excited. I want to pin her down and give her the third degree, but I'm afraid I'll give myself away. Don't worry, I'll get an update somehow," Crystal says.

Crystal's husband, Stanley, looks at everyone. "I would not ask her anything." The others stare at him wondering if he's lost his mind. "No, hear me out. We have brought them together, and we know they are attracted to each other. We can't do any more than that. They have to make it work. Not us. I have no problem with tweaking, listening, and nudging. But I'm not in for the prodding with a cattle rod. Let's all be patient and see where it goes."

Crystal remarks to her husband. "Oh, all right. Tom, we need to go mingle."

Kia Lui

-24-

As Lea and Zion walk away from the group, she feels some of the stress leaving her body, replaced by a spreading arousal being alone with Zion, "Thanks for the suggestion to show you around. I really wanted to get away."

"I could tell. You were getting increasingly quiet by the minute. I didn't want you to break the strap on your camera or lose any fingers."

Lea looks down and sees the strap wrapped around her hand and how tightly she's twisting it. She has left an impression in her hand. Zion grabs it and loosens her grip. He kisses her hand and rubs it, making the blood circulate.

"Better?"

"Yes." She looks at him and smiles, "Thank you."

"What's wrong? You seemed to be having a good time, and then you drifted away." He is walking behind her with his hands on her waist pulling her into him. They are walking on one of the paved paths outside of the vines where no one can see them. It's their opportunity to get in some make-out time, and they don't pass it up.

"I got a lot on my mind."

"Sweetheart, what's wrong?" Zion asks.

Now that's a switch. Me asking a woman what's wrong and seriously wanting to know. Lea Adams has definitely encroached into my world.

Lea shakes her head, clearing out her mind.

"I'm just a little stressed is all. So, what do you think of the vineyard? Have you been here before, am I wasting my time showing you around?"

Zion is staring at Lea, waiting for her to elaborate, but she doesn't.

I must keep it together. I can't burden him with my issues this early in the game.

He accepts her change in subject wanting to get back to flirting and kissing.

"I've never been here before. My focus is you. I like the privacy." He grins, stealing another kiss. "Now that you have taken so many pictures of me, how about you turn over the camera, so I can get some pictures of you?"

"You really were keeping a close watch on me."

"Yes, I was. Now, camera please."

"But the photographer always stays behind the lens. We are rarely photographed," Lea says handing him the camera.

"Not today. Smile for me Kitten." Zion snaps off about ten images of Lea. Her against the vines, with the sun behind her, with her jumping up and down and with her staring off into the distance.

Returning the camera, he takes her into his arms and they continue walking.

"I have to go out of town for a while, Lea. What are you doing tonight? I would love to spend some time with you."

Lea caresses his palm with her thumb wanting to ease the rejection she is about to give him. "I'm sorry, I can't. My best friend is having a birthday party at a club, and I promised I'd be there. I've been skipping a lot of events, and if I don't show up, he'll hunt me down."

"A club huh. Your *best* friend is a male? Is he gay? Should I be jealous?" Zion kisses her hand looking for any sign she will hide or deny her relationship with another man.

Lea laughs. She always gets asked that question when she tells people her best friend is a guy.

"No, he is not gay. He is straight, married fourteen years. He is madly in love with his wife as she is with him. There is nothing to be jealous about."

"I guess. What club if I may ask?"

I actually care about where my girl is going to be. This relationship stuff is so new to me.

"Why?" she asks.

"Just wondering." He pulls her close.

"I don't know why I'm telling you this. Club Element in the Earth City Casino."

"Hmm, I know that one."

Sometimes, it's great having clients who own entertainment venues.

"When will you be leaving town, and when will you be back? I understand if you don't want to answer."

Zion never had to report his schedule to anyone outside of business, not even his family, but with Lea, he wants to link his calendar to her phone.

"It would seem we have to get used to each other knowing the other's whereabouts. I leave tomorrow evening and will be back in a couple of weeks. I'll be on the West Coast, Washington, Nevada, California, and Arizona."

Lea deflates. Her test results come back next week, and she was hoping to have sex with him the day they arrived.

"Yep, it's weird wanting to report and wanting to know."

Fuccccckkkkk.

"I know what you're thinking, but no, this was an unplanned trip. I need to go but as soon as I get back, I'll have you. Just remember, no masturbating."

"I'm making no guarantees to such a ridiculous request."

"Ridiculous? How is that request ridiculous? Don't you want to wait until you can feel me inside you?" he asks, grinning at her.

"Of course. But see, you just had sex a few months ago. It's been years for me. After the foreplay sex we had, you want me to not think about that and not touch myself. How am I supposed to do that? Are you going to refrain from masturbation?"

"See, we not talking about me. The topic is you, Ms. Lea Adams. I'm calling double standard."

"No fair." Lea walks up to him seductively. "If I do masturbate, I'll call you so you can listen. How about that?"

Zion looks down at her, "Uh, well, I hadn't thought about that. We can negotiate. Maybe."

They head back to the party. Their flirtatious walk has been fun. It's something Zion has never done with a woman. Even for Lea, walking with a man, holding hands, is something new.

She and Zion continue to talk. They unconsciously put distance between them as they approach the party. Checking the time, it's seven o'clock and she still has an hour drive back into St. Louis for the birthday party. Lea forces herself to walk around, saying goodbye to guests and hoping they had a good time, instead of gluing herself to Zion's side. She finds Tom and Linda and lets them know she is leaving. They are staying on the vineyard for the remainder of the weekend, and she'll see Tom in the office Monday.

Zion bids everyone goodbye and tells Tom he will escort Lea to her car.

At her car, Lea stashes her camera in the trunk and takes out a pair of sexy yellow and white, peep toe, high heels.

Dammit, her ass in them jeans. She took off some kinda jacket and the top is showing off her shoulders and arms. Shit, she is going to some club tonight, and I'm not there. Not having that.

"I'll see you before I leave. Have fun tonight," he tells her.

"Thanks. Tomorrow then?" Lea stares at his lips.

"Absolutely; beautiful. Absolutely. And keep staring at my lips, I'll make a scene," he says closing the distance between them slightly.

"I can't help it. Besides, you wouldn't dare?"

They want to kiss but hold back. Too many eyes looking at them.

"Wanna bet? I won't. This time. Don't think ima keep restraining myself when I wanna touch you. This is new to me," Zion admits realizing public affection is new to him.

"I can't recall a time being that way with a man. Rather sad," Lea whispers, "Good night, Zion."

"Talk to you later, Lea."

She gets in her car and drives off.

Zion and Sam get in the SUV. He takes out his phone, making calls.

"Mrs. Vance, are my bags packed and ready to go for tomorrow? Yes, two weeks. Okay great, please have them sitting in the front foyer."

He calls Club Element, "May I speak to Roy please? This is Zion Landon. Roy, what up man? I'm going to need a private booth tonight. Actually, make it two. I have a friend who'll be sitting with a group celebrating a birthday. No, I just want to have a couple of booths. Thanks man."

To Sam: "You have everything in place here for the build site, correct?"

"Yes sir. Saul and I plan on being out there monitoring things."

"Great, keep me posted. When we get back to the city, drive straight to the Earth City Casino and park in the usual spot. I'll call you and let you know if you need to stay."

Zion is thinking to himself, not hearing Sam's response.

Lea is different from the others. Displaying affection as his parents and his sister and her husband do is something he now wants. It's time he gives into that and stop worrying about what others will say or think. At the charity event it felt natural. No back stepping now.

"No problem sir," Sam smiles.

Mr. Landon is finally chasing after a woman worth chasing after instead of one chasing after him whom he shouldn't even have given an ounce of energy to. Love in all its glory is a wonder to see.

-25-

Lea arrives at the casino and parks on the upper level of the garage. She changes into the heels and prepares herself for the night, refreshing her make-up, spritzing on Rihanna's Reb'l Fleur perfume. She is happy because she will get to see Gordon and Lily. Gordon never responded to her text messages about needing to talk to him. Maybe she will get to tell him about Zion tonight.

She strolls into the club looking for him and his group. They are sitting against the wall and hoarding tables.

Guess he waited too late to get that booth.

Lea walks over and greets everyone, giving hugs where hugs are due and takes some teasing about finally getting out. She grabs a vacant seat and gets comfortable to people watch. Looking around tonight, it's going to be pretty entertaining. Something to take her mind off of not seeing Zion.

Gordon sits down next to her.

"Tell me, what's going on with you? You been pretty closed off lately," Gordon yells, because the music is so loud, especially where they are seated.

"Just busy with work and stuff. I texted and called, but you didn't return any of them."

"Still on that forced celibacy gig? How is that going?" Gordon asks, ignoring her comment.

"What's with the ignoring shit. You ignored my calls and now my comment. What up with that? Where you been?" Gordon is about to respond but Lily beats him to it.

"Yes, Gordon. Tell Lea how you dropped your phone in a toilet full of shit and didn't admit to it for a week. I couldn't figure out why he was carrying around the tablet and not his phone. I found out about it when the replacement phone arrived in the mail. To my attention. He figured if he didn't say anything and because I was traveling on business for a couple of days, I wouldn't notice it. I'm not letting him live this one down. Not ever. Right, sweetheart?"

"Damn you woman. Lily, we had a deal. I don't wanna talk about this no mo. I'm done."

Lily and Lea are laughing at him. He takes it in stride and even laughs with them. They have always been able to joke with each other like that from the day Gordon started dating Lily.

Having a man for a best friend can be difficult. Men often accuse Lea right off the bat of lying about her relationship with him. She figures if a man can judge her without even meeting Gordon first, he won't last. And none have so far. She decides to bring up the subject of Gordon to Zion tomorrow when she sees him before he leaves for his business trip.

"My current state of lack of sex is not forced. Well not the way you think. I want more than soft love-making from a man who isn't scared to touch me for fear I may break, and I don't want a man who wants to take things so far I may end up killing him for attempting to abuse me. Is that so wrong?"

"No, seems like it's hard for you to find."

"I can't mention BDSM or submission to a man without him thinking I want to be abused or he wants me to act like I'm supposed to bend to his every command. There has to be an in-between."

"There is, but you have to be willing to trust a man to do that and to find it."

"I know, and I'm working on that. Actually, I may have met someone. Someone who can give me the in-between I want. I think."

SOMEONE? GIRL, TELL GORDON WE GOTS US A MAN. A SEXY-VIRLE-NICE-SIZE-DICK-WE-GONNA-BE-SEXING-BILLIONAIRE MAN.

Hush Sex Diva.

"Really, tell me more."

"Some other time. It's too loud and crazy in here tonight. You couldn't find any seats away from the speakers?"

"Not for the number of people who said they would show up."

"Well, don't think ima sit here all night. I'm not suffering a headache to help you celebrate."

Lea feels her phone vibrating in her back pocket. Pulling it out she sees it's a text from Zion. His name and picture popping up on her phone makes her giddy again.

My man is texting me. Yay.

> Zion: *"Hello Kitten. I told you I'll see you before I left for my trip. Look up and to your right."*

She looks up and sees Zion looking down at her from the top level of the club.

Gordon looks in the same direction she is looking and asks. "What's wrong?"

"The guy I mentioned? He's here," she says smiling up at Zion.

> Lea types: *Hi Zion. What are you doing here? I thought I would see you tomorrow before you left, like at the airport?*
>
> Zion responds: *I couldn't wait that long, come join me.*

When Zion walked into Club Element, he was met by his friend Roy who quickly escorted him upstairs. From his vantage point, he scoped out the club looking for Lea in her white jeans and yellow top. When he sees her, he smiles. Watching her talk to a guy he can only assume is her friend Gordon and mingling, gives him a sense of pride knowing this woman is his. He watches her for another few minutes, then texts her. She looks sexy pulling her phone out of her back pocket.

Geez, Zion man get a grip. You acting like a teenager.

His gaze tracks her, walking to him. The men watching her ass with desire makes him feel like the luckiest man in the club. She is walking to him.

Keep watching all you want fellas. She is mine. All mine. It's time I staked my claim.

Lea and Zion lock gazes, smiling. She tells Gordon she will be right back. Looking around for either some stairs or an elevator, a guy approaches her. "Ms. Adams, if you will follow me."

She follows him to an elevator, and he uses a card to activate it. As she walks in moving to the back of the elevator, he reaches in, slides his card through the panel, presses the button for the top floor, and steps out. Ascending to the top, the doors open and Lea steps out into Zion's stare. He grabs her, moving them to a darkened corner, kissing her passionately. They come up for air after about a minute.

FUCK US NOW. PLEASE.

"What are you doing here, Zion? Don't get me wrong, I'm delighted to see you."

"I won't see you for two weeks when I leave. Didn't want to wait for a kiss until tomorrow. Spending as much time with you as I can is my goal right now. So why not make it here? Let me hold you in my arms before I leave?"

Lea hesitates in responding making him a tad bit nervous. Everything this man is saying is music to her ears.

HOLD US, SPEND TIME WITH US. YES. YES. YES.

With Lea's hesitation, Zion second guesses himself

Maybe it wasn't a great idea to come here after all.
Then he dismisses it instantly.
Fuck that.

Lea teases him, "Additional make-out time. I likey that idea. What do I do? Stay up here and make out with my man or go back to my friends? Decisions. Decisions. Decisions."

"No decision, I have reserved two booths down on the floor. And I'd much rather make out with you in private," Lea looks at him stunned. Those booths are not cheap, "I'm not trying to impress your friends. A business associate owns it and was willing to give them to me. They still have to pay for everything they drink and eat."

Zion followed her to a club, purchased two booths for her friends so he can be with her. If she could jump up and down and do the running man dance, without embarrassing herself, she would. Instead she grins, gloats and hugs him.

"Okay. Let's go. Gordon is going to love this. I don't have time to give you each the lowdown on each other so this will be interesting to watch. A good old-fashioned male pissing contest."

They get in the elevator and descend. Even in that short ride, Zion kisses her then backs away quickly before the doors open. When they get off, she approaches Gordon and the group of ten whom he invited to celebrate with him tonight. Zion stands behind her. He has grabbed the attention of plenty of women trying to grab his attention but he doesn't take his eyes off Lea.

"Gordon. Hey. This is Zion. Zion, this is my best friend Gordon and his wife Lily."

Gordon and Zion shake hands and size each other up.

"We're all being moved to two of the booths behind the ropes. Grab your things, everyone, and let's go," Lea yells.

"What? Hell, Lea I can't pay for that. I waited too late," Gordon whines.

"It's okay, come on. You get to grill Zion. Wait, the replacement phone. That's why no booths?"

"Will you shut up about the phone already." Gordon looks at Zion, at Lea, and shakes his head. "Okay, lead the way. Hey everyone, grab your drinks and follow Lea," he yells and motions to the others.

Behind the ropes are ten plush booths with tables in colors of purple, gray and black. The tables are lit from below casting a soft glow on the people sitting at them. These tables are away from the speakers allowing for patrons to have muted conversations without having to yell. Lea won't be suffering from a headache after all. The booths face the spacious two-level dance floor which is crowded.

Zion, Lea, Gordon, and Lily take one booth and the remainder of the group squeeze into the other booth giving the four some privacy.

Before Lea sits down, she informs them what is free and what isn't. "Listen up, we only received an upgrade in seating. Any food or drink is at your expense. Do we all understand each other? Y'all know I don't have a problem with money collection. Don't make me get in nobody's ass if you try to take advantage of my friend." They all agree, and tell her she has nothing to worry about, thanking Zion with a shout of gratitude.

Lea takes a seat on the inside of the booth next to Zion. He and Gordon are sitting on the outside corner seats across from each other. Four burly men block the entrance to the booth area, and two more stand near their booths.

"Yes, the two extras are because of me," Zion tells her before she even asks.

"How did you know what I was thinking?" she asks him. "And why would you need extra security? Is it because of your sexiness?" She smiles at him.

"They are here because Roy insists. He likes it when people think this is such an elite area. Lots of security says important people. Or maybe it is because of my obvious sexiness." He winks at her.

Gordon catches Zion's attention by interrupting their conversation. "Zion, man, thanks for the upgrade. What do I owe you for this?"

"It's my pleasure. A client is the owner, and he was happy to do so."

Lea is fidgeting. Her leg is shaking like crazy. Zion places his hand on her thigh and gently caresses it, calming her instantly. She places her hand in his. Where it belongs. He looks down at their clasped hands then at her, smiling.

Zion whispers to her. "You okay?"

"Yes, it's just that we haven't had the family and friend discussion yet. Especially this friend. This meeting my best friend may be too soon. I wanted to prepare you first."

"Don't worry, I won't embarrass you," he grins devilishly.

A line dance song comes on, and Lily begs Lea to join her.

"Uh, but, I—." she hesitates, worried about leaving the men alone.

"Kitten, go dance. I wanna see you dance for me. Gordon and I will be fine. No pissing. I promise," he says, teasing her.

"Zion—." He kisses her objection and stands, letting her slide out of the booth and past him.

"Go dance, Lea." Gordon says.

"All right," Lea snaps back at him.

She follows Lily to the dance floor, leaving Zion and Gordon alone giving Gordon an evil look.

Lea puts her hands on her face, looking back at Zion and Gordon sitting at the table before she steps onto the dance floor.

Both men smile at her; Zion, because he likes looking at her and Gordon, because he knows Lea is wondering how much of an ass he is about to make of himself.

I'll probably never see Zion again after Gordon talks to him tonight.

-26-

Gordon knows Lea will be with any man she wants whether he likes the guy or not. His opinion is secondary to her mother, her instincts and her desires. That doesn't keep him from being her voice of sanity and verbalizing his concerns whenever he likes.

"How long have you known Lea?" he asks Zion.

"A couple months. She is the Technology Lead on a project for my company." Zion isn't going to lie to the guy, he's just going to play it down.

Ain't none of his business about what Lea and I are doing anyway.

He turns his head to watch Lea on the dance floor, swaying her ass in them white jeans.

Shit, this woman has me mesmerized dancing.

"Oh, that's great," Gordon says watching him watch Lea. Gordon smiles mischievously.

Zion turns back to Gordon hating having to talk to him and not being able to watch her. "How long have you known each other? She introduced you as her best friend."

"About thirty years. We met when we were seventeen." Now the fun begins. Lea hates when Gordon does this to the men she thinks are the one. But he figures the men should know exactly whom they are dealing with when it comes to being a part of Lea's life.

"Wow, thirty years. That's amazing. Did you guys go to the same high school or live in the same neighborhood?" Zion can tell this guy is baiting him. He wants to drop some knowledge, so he will let him.

"We dated. Teenage sweethearts. I was her first."

Zion shows no visible reaction. He has mastered his emotions against opponents in the business world, and this one could be his biggest.

"Usually, I would've never done this to a guy Lea is dating. She normally briefs me on the men I meet, and she tells him about me, but you seem to want to impress her. These booth upgrades are expensive. Again, I'm grateful. There is extra security in this area. Lea purposely did not give me your last name during the introductions, and I don't want you to tell me who you are. When Lea is ready, she will."

Now that Gordon has Zion's full attention, he continues. "I do want you to understand that I love her dearly. We did a lot of maturing with each other to get to a place of respect. My family loves her, and her family loves me. I'm not going anywhere. Because you're the man she's 'dating', and I use that word loosely because I don't really know what's going on between you two, I'll show you the utmost respect because I respect her. But if you hurt her, I'll hurt you."

Gordon watches Zion move his hand from his leg reaching out for a handshake. Now that is totally unexpected. He figured he was going to get cussed out. Well, he probably will after Lea hears about this conversation.

"Not that your opinion matters but duly noted. I have no plans to hurt her. Ever. I just wanna get to know her and be with her. All I ask is a chance. Whether you give me one or not is irrelevant to my relationship with Lea." Zion doesn't care if Gordon gives him a chance or not. He's dating Lea. Not her best friend/ex-fuck boy.

Gordon reaches out his hand and they shake.

Well, Zion isn't running or showing that he is pissed that the first guy Lea has ever fucked is sitting right here in front of him and not going anywhere. He is staking a claim. The man has balls. Lea may have found the one at last. Hope ole boy can handle her.

Lea and Lily come back, hesitantly approaching the table. Lea stops, looking at them, and is not saying a word. She fiddles with the charm on her necklace.

"What, Lea? I acted as you knew I would. Don't go giving me that evil look. I ain't scared of you Lea Adams. Just don't go telling your mother on me," Gordon says joking with her. He and Lily walk to the dance floor. Zion stands up and allows Lea to sit, caressing her on her ass as she slides into the booth. When she sits down, he pulls her hand away from the necklace before she breaks it.

"What where you two talking about?" Lea asks.

"He's your first? The one who deflowered you, and you two are now best friends?"

"Yes. Have been for years."

"I'm jealous. I don't like him. I hate all your prior lovers, and I want them wiped from your memory." Zion watches Gordon and Lily dancing. The love he displays for his wife is a man truly head over heels in ecstasy. Zion wants that. Maybe Lea is the one.

"I'm sorry, I didn't want you guys to meet like this. I wanted to prepare you. And I never claimed to be a virgin."

"He did mention something about a briefing. Don't worry about it. I'll get over it. We will talk about him some other time. You aren't a virgin but your pussy gripped my fingers like a tight virgin pussy would. I never gave any thought about running into any of your past lovers. Extremely selfish of me I know, but well, there you go," Zion tells her. "I liked watching you dance. Do you move your hips like that while sexing?" Zion has turned his body toward Lea in the booth and has placed a hand on the back of it effectively closing them off from the crowd with his body.

"Yes. Have you ever had a tight virgin pussy?" she asks as she leans into him, wanting to feel close. He leans down and kisses her temple.

"Yes, two. One in college and one ten years later. Nothing to brag or reminisce about, trust me. Did Gordon teach you a lot about fucking?" He whispers in her ear, nibbling her neck a little.

"Yes, only after we stopped having sex. He told me how I should embrace my sexuality and not make excuses. He felt I was denying myself pleasure and happiness, and he was right. It took me a while to really embrace me, but I have."

"How has that worked for you?"

"In my thirties, not so well. In my forties, I take no prisoners. In my fifties, I expect to have the best sex ever."

Zion looks at her heatedly. "You will, you can be sure of that, and you do have a prisoner."

"I wish you could have met Gordon under different circumstances."

"Why? This was perfect. He was being a straight shooter."

Roy, the owner, comes over to speak to Zion. "Mr. Landon, I have an urgent call for you."

"I'll be right back," Zion says as he gets up and walks away.

Lea watches the women watching him. He walks behind the bar into a room. A woman who was eyeing him has decided to stand right at the end of the bar, waiting.

This should be interesting.

When Zion exits the private room, the woman moves quickly and bumps into him. He catches her up quickly and apologizes and steps to move off. She stops him saying something, but he shakes his head, leaving her standing at the end of the bar with a look of disbelief on her face.

Lea laughs and turns her attention away from Zion walking back to her, not wanting to get caught drooling at the sexy specimen that he is, coming her way. Instead, she people watches, especially trying to catch Gordon's eye.

He will be on the dance floor all night long. I'm going to strangle him. He just couldn't keep his damn mouth shut. I wonder what all he said to Zion.

Zion sits down blocking her view from the dance floor, forcing her to focus on him. "Lea, I need to leave. I have to get to the airport. I have to fly out early," he says looking for Roy to pay for the booths.

"Let me drive you," Lea suggests.

"That's too far. It's the Chesterfield Airport. I can have Sam come get me."

"Zion let's go. Just let me tell Gordon. I'm ready to get out of here anyway."

Lea talks to Gordon on the dance floor. "Hey, I'm leaving. I'll get with your ass later. Remember, only the booths are paid for. Got it?"

"Got it. Take care, and I know you'll be calling me. I'll answer this time. I need more details about him. If I can't scare them away, they are keepers. Well, almost keepers."

Lea walks out with Zion. He and Gordon head nod at each other. *Damn men and their pissing contests.*

"Against my better judgment, I'm only allowing you to do this because I can't be away from you yet," he says guiding her toward the exit.

While saying this to her, he is texting on his smartphone. Lea keeps quiet while he handles business, not walking too closely beside him to give him some privacy. When she moves too far away, he brings her back to him with either a hand on her waist or ass or walks up behind her putting his hands around her kissing her on the neck. They arrive at the elevators, and Lea pushes the up button. They step onto an empty elevator alone. She presses the floor button for the top level.

Lea starts to ask him if everything is okay, but before she can finish, he has her pressed against the wall, kissing her. He bends his knees slightly and grinds his dick against her pelvis.

Oh, it feels so enticing.

He abruptly pulls away and steps back from her. She stares at the panel watching the numbers go up.

"Ladies first. Always," he says, smiling at her holding the opened elevator doors at their floor.

"Do you want to drive? You know where we're going?"

"Sure, lead the way. Kitten."

Shit, she struts in heels like no woman I have seen in a looooonnnggg time. Or this woman makes walking in heels look sexy because she is sexy to me.

They get to Lea's car and she presses the button to unlock the doors. He presses her against the passenger door before she can reach to open it.

"Look at me Lea. Why are you so quiet?"

Lea looks up into his eyes and melts. She can't turn away. She rarely stares this deeply into a man's eyes.

She rushes over her sentences saying everything and anything to temper her raging thoughts. "I'm wondering about your conversation with Gordon. Why the kiss in the elevator? What is wrong that you have to fly out earlier than expected? Is not seeing you for two weeks a good or bad thing? Why does your dick feel so good? How can I get one last kiss? Will I ever see you again? Is there any Red Hot Riplet potato chips in my house? Will a cold shower keep me from masturbating? How soon can I get to Gordon and punch him? Should I ask you for a hug? Can I convince you to grind your dick into my pelvis a little bit longer so you can make me cum?"

Zion throws his head back and bursts out laughing. She smiles. That sounds nice. She shakes her head and makes a move to get into the car. He presses her back against the door and gives her that hug she mentioned. A full encompassing full body contact bear hug.

I wanna cry it feels so safe. Now I understand how he got the nickname Bear. I hold onto him for dear life not wanting to let go. Wanting to beg him to please stay, to come home with me, to hold me, but he pulls out of the hug.

"We gotta get going. My plane is waiting, and Sam will be wondering what is taking me so long. Not that I don't want to stand here holding you all night."

Lea releases him and gets into the car. He gets in, adjusts the seat and mirror, starts the car and they're off.

"Nice car."

"Shut up," she laughs and gets comfortable in the passenger seat of her own car.

"Does your mind always race that fast with so many questions?"

"Yes. No. Usually. The hard part is never getting answers."

"Well, let's see. My conversation with Gordon. He told me how he was your first and that he wasn't going anywhere. The kiss in the elevator. Elevators are made for kissing. I'm flying out early to meet with some friends. A personal crisis. Us, not seeing each other for long stretches of time is something we will have to work through. I'm glad you think my dick feels so good. I don't know why it does. You're getting a kiss, and no, it won't be our last. Yes, you'll see me again and again and again. I hope some Red Hot Riplets are in your house so you don't have to come back out and get a bag or pull over and stop this late at night to quench a craving. A lover of spicy food, I like that about you. Cold showers only dull the fire within. Do not masturbate. Trust me, you won't regret it. You will get to Gordon quickly enough. You never have to ask for a hug. I enjoy having you in my arms. And grinding my dick against your pelvis would be a bad idea. I'll drag you onto the plane and steal you away. Let's skip that for now."

"Wow. You have some recall there, mister. You put a woman to shame."

"Goes with the job."

He pulls into an airport hangar next to his SUV. Sam is standing at the steps of a Gulfstream G650ER sitting on the tarmac waiting for Zion so they can take off. Getting out of the car, Lea pops the trunk pulling out a pair of flats for driving. Before she can close it, Zion pulls her into his arms, kissing her again. Nibbling her neck, her ears. She slides her hands down the front of his shirt wanting to touch him.

"I wish I could stay."

"So do I. Have a safe trip."

"Text me when you get home."

"I will."

"And I'll call you after I land. Well, when I get a chance after I land anyway."

He closes the trunk and they walk around to the driver's side of the car. She kisses him one last time, gets in the car, and sits.

Zion leans over into the car window turning her face toward him so he can look into her eyes, "Lea, go home. Don't over think this. Get your chips. And a glass of milk because, if I remember correctly those are extremely spicy."

"Good night, Zion."

"Good night, Kitten."

I drive away watching him in my rearview mirror as he walks to the plane and boards. Two weeks. I'm never gonna see that man again.

-27-

It's been three weeks and Zion and Lea have not seen each other. He has been traveling on business for what was supposed to be two weeks but has extended into three weeks and maybe even beyond. They have texted and talked every other day avoiding any mention of sex. It's as if they are friends keeping in touch.

They have each received their STD results from their doctors and shared them with each other, all clear.

Lea is attempting to not over-think things like she normally does. She focuses on her projects, especially for Landon Enterprises. All is going as expected. Brad did not have any issues with picking up the remaining materials from Martin. He informed Lea after unlocking the warehouse and letting him in, Martin drove off and never even came back to lock up or discuss anything with him. Brad's crew has been onsite sticking to the agreed-upon schedule.

She finally got to talk to Gordon about Zion when he showed up at her job to have lunch.

Gordon and Lea can go weeks without talking or hanging out and spend hours catching up. Today, all he wants to hear about is Mr. Zion Landon and Landon Enterprises and how Lea has managed to land his attention.

Gordon overheard the club owner mention Zion's full name when they were paying for their food and drinks at the club. He did his research. Forever bachelor. No social media accounts. Not one story about the guy in tabloids, gossip columns, or the news other than business. How can a guy as rich as him, hell a black guy, have such a lack of a dirty past and not be found on the Internet? That's not possible. Let's see how much personal and private information Lea knows.

"Okay give me the details on this guy. How in the hell could he get those booths at such short notice? From what I heard at the club when you guys left, they were reserved but the party showed up late and lost them to us."

"His full name is Zion Landon. The owner of Landon Enterprises. We are upgrading the technology for his company. Lord, Gordon, I get wet just thinking about the man. And it has nothing to do with his money. He is sexy, he has a commanding presence, and his lips are so soft."

I reminiscence about our kisses.

"Ohh. So, you done made out with him. Is he a hit-it-and-quit-it or a long-term prospect?"

"I'm hoping a long-term prospect. I did lay out my wants and desires even before our first kiss, and he is still interested. I'm officially in a relationship."

"You sure of that? Landon Enterprises. Billionaire status."

"So. Are you trying to say I can't attract someone like him?"

It's not like I haven't said this to myself numerous times already. To hear this shit from Gordon. Not really interested.

"No. Hell no. I like that you are finally dating. Period. Especially attracting someone like him. It proves my point I keep pounding into your head that you can do better when you stick to your standards. My issue is with him. Billionaire. I'm sure he got ass waiting in every state to be fucked. He's doing the relationship thing with you. Why?"

"Fuck you, Gordon."

"We've been there, done that. Moving on. Don't get stupid and start wearing them rose-colored glasses because you 'bout to get some dick."

"And don't you start looking for every asinine negative quality you can come up with. We've talked. I've told him what I want regarding long-term, and I'm ready to walk away if I don't get it."

"Good. Wait. You've only told him about the long-term part. What about the rest? And where is the man at anyway?"

"Traveling since the night you met him. Don't give me that all-knowing look. You don't know shit. He's traveling for business. I'll see him when he gets back."

"And when is that?"

"Whenever he gets back, a week, two weeks, three weeks, a month. Whenever."

"And all this time he not supposed to be getting some ass? Yeah, okay."

"How about we end lunch? I'm beginning to think not seeing you for an extended period of time was a good thing."

Gordon sighs, "Look, I don't want you moving too fast and getting hurt. If I can't be the ass you expect me to be and look at the shit from the outside, I wouldn't consider myself your best friend and neither could you. Enjoy him. Date him. Hell, for all I know, he may be the one you fall head over heels in love and ride into the future with. Or he may be a stepping-stone to something better. Just enjoy it. Take your time. And fuck his brains out. Get all the dick and orgasms you can. Wear his ass out."

"Thanks. That sounds better."

"And now you are ignoring my other question? What about the rest? Have you told him about the BDSM part?"

"No."

"Why not. Are you scared to?"

"No not scared, but as I said before, that subject is a touchy subject. I'm not doing it over the phone, especially while he is out of town. That would be cowardly. When he gets back, we'll discuss it."

"Don't let this get too far if you want more sexually."

"I'm not."

Zion is in London, sitting in his hotel room, which overlooks Hyde Park. Normally, he would be out enjoying dinner, drinks with clients, trying to set him up with a bevy of women. Tonight, he prefers to sit here, staring at his phone, spinning it in circles on the table, and staring at the busy nightlife happening below outside his hotel window. Thinking about Lea. He never gave any woman this much thought when he was out of town. With Lea, he wishes she was here with him.

Man, just call her. Naw, not gonna do that. Why not? Naw, I'll wait til I get home. Just do it. Naw.

He shakes himself mentally from the argument in his head and gets back to business. He had to let one client go, or the client decided he no longer wanted to be hand-tied with his own money. Landon Enterprises gained four other million-dollar clients, so no loss. Saul informed him that everything was going as scheduled with the new building and that Ms. Adams had met with him again to test the recommended equipment. He informed him she is even looking into training schedules for his staff so they can get familiar with the new technology without missing too much downtime with clients.

Nice work, Lea.

This trip should have only taken two weeks. Normally, being away from home weeks or months at a time never bothered him, but he never had a woman he wanted to get back home to. Now all this fucking traveling is working his last damn nerve. He understands it's sexual frustration. Here, he has been telling Lea not to relieve herself sexually, yet he has been walking around with a semi-hard-on since he met her. He feels like a teenager about to have a wet dream. He just wants to get back home to her.

Amazing. Me, Zion Landon, wants to get back home to a woman.

Zion checks his schedule with his assistant Morgan. Nothing pressing out of town for the next month if he takes one more week away from St. Louis to clear everything. He calls the office.

"Morgan, did you get all my meetings re-arranged for next week?"

"Yes, sir. I'm currently updating your calendar. Everything is set and in place. This will leave you in town for at least the next month. All your other client meetings can be handled via phone, WebEx, or Skype. They're only check-ins."

"Great, thanks. I should be flying in Friday, correct?"

"Yes sir. You are due to leave London at three a.m. Friday and you should be back home and in the office by three p.m. Unless you wanted to go straight home and come in Monday?"

"Actually, that works out better. I'll be back in the office on Monday. Email me with any pressing issues."

"Will do, Sir. Will that be all?"

"Yes. Thank you and have a good weekend."

"You, too, Sir."

Zion ends the call and thinks about how he would like to seduce Lea when he gets home wondering about her plans for this weekend. He would like to have her waiting at his apartment but she hasn't been there yet and that might freak her out. He gives her a call dismissing all arguments against it this time.

"Hi. This is Lea."

On hearing her voice Zion smiles.

"Hello, Kitten. How is your day?"

"Zion, how are you?" *Every time I hear his voice, I feel the silly grin on my face.* "I'm keeping busy and focused."

"And why is that may I ask?"

"If I don't, I'll end up touching myself," Lea gets up and closes the door to her office. This conversation may get a little hot.

"What are you doing? I hear a lot of moving around. Are you driving?"

"No, I'm at the office. I had to close my door."

"Good, now tell me more about not touching yourself."

"Well, I haven't, but that doesn't mean I haven't orgasmed."

"Explain please."

"I can mentally cause myself to orgasm. I'm not always successful in starting or stopping it, and that night I was unsuccessful stopping it. You are haunting my dreams."

"Dammit, baby. You amaze me. Why hasn't some man locked you down before I came along?"

"Hmmm. That's a good question. Maybe we should find a few of the men that attempted to date me and you can ask them. I doubt you will get an honest answer."

"You know what, never mind. Their loss and my gain. I'll be home Friday. What will you be doing?"

"Hanging out with friends while you get some sleep."

"What? Wait? I don't need no stinkin' sleep."

"Zion, you've been traveling four weeks straight. Do you even really rest in hotel rooms when you are away because I sure as heck don't? (Silence). I thought not. When you get home, I'm ordering you to take a shower, eat, climb into bed, and go to sleep. Then call me when you wake up on Saturday. Deal?"

"Yes, mom. I mean Lea."

"So, that is something your mom would tell you also. Good. Great minds think alike."

"All these bossy women in my life. I can't deal, I just can't deal."

"I miss you."

"I miss you, too. And because you know me so well, I guess I'll go do some work."

"You do that. I'll talk to you tomorrow. Maybe. I'll be out of the office visiting clients all day."

"Okay and stop with the orgasms. I'm tired of missing out on them."

"Get out of my dreams then."

"Kitten, never."

They laugh and say good-bye.

Kia Lui

-28-

Lea was right. After Zion got home Friday, he crashed, completely, totally, and didn't wake up until around nine on Saturday. He remembered texting her that he was home and getting a text back saying goodnight and nothing after that. He was tired, but he'll be seeing her tonight. They'll be having dinner here at his place, that way if he crashes again, he can at least hold her.

He goes in search of Mrs. Vance to set up a special evening. He finds her in the laundry room.

"Hi Mrs. Vance. How are you?"

"Hello, Mr. Landon. Doing pretty good. I have unpacked for you. All your suits, shirts, and ties have been sent to the cleaners. Everything else has been washed and ready for you to put away."

Although Zion has Mrs. Vance working for him, for some reason, he prefers to put away his own laundry. He can fully thank his mother for that life lesson.

We came to a compromise, she would wash and fold, but I will put away my stuff.

"Thanks so much. Could you cook something for me tonight? A salad and something light. Oh, I know, how about preparing me some shish-kabobs for two that I can grill."

"I would be happy to, Sir. Any particular meats and what time?"

"Chicken and steak, garden salad, vinaigrette or Italian dressing, fruit tray for dessert. Have everything ready to go about seven. I can take it from there. Thanks."

I hear Mrs. Vance chuckling at me as I walk away to my bedroom to plan out tonight with Lea. I don't care if it is sex or not. We'll be seeing each other. I locate my phone and call her.

"Hey sleepy head, how are you?"

"Wide awake and rested. What are you doing?"

"Grocery shopping and running errands for my mom."

Zion and I haven't discussed anything about parents, siblings, or any personal things like that. I don't think we're ready to go there yet.

"How about dinner tonight, here at my place?"

"Are we really ready for that? I mean are we ready for what could happen?"

"I want to see you. If you feel more comfortable with me taking you out, I will, but I would like to see you."

"Okay, but only on one condition."

"And that is?"

"I drive to your place."

"Lea, I do not want you driving. I can send a car or come pick you up myself."

"Please, I would like to drive. I need to drive." Lea figures if she drives, she will have the option to run if things go poorly. She needs that control.

"Okay then, you drive. I'll text you my address. When you get here, someone will meet you at the garage entrance on the Busch Stadium side and give you instructions on where to park and go from there. How about seven-thirty? Casual dress."

"Okay. See you at seven-thirty. Later," she tells him.

"Later, Kitten."

Mrs. Vance steps into the living room, giving Zion a sly look. He shakes his head.

"Yes ma'am, I'm inviting a lady friend to my home. Just do your thing as a woman who is going to have dinner, would expect to encounter. This is a first for me okay."

"I got you covered. No worries," Mrs. Vance grins walking toward the bedroom upstairs to 'woman it up'.

'Bout time that man got a woman up in this place.

-29-

Lea is on edge, and she wants to cancel her dinner date tonight with Zion. The Sex Diva is stalking her every move.

OH, YOU GOIN'. DON'T GIVE ME THIS BACKING OUT CRAP. YOU GOIN'.

While getting ready, she gets a call from Gordon who skips over the hello, "Well, is it on for tonight or what?"

"Hi, Gordon. How are you this evening? Lily doing all right?" Lea responds back sarcastically.

"Hell. Hello Lea, I'm fine. All's well. Called to ask are you getting fucked tonight?"

"The dinner is on. Fucking, hhmm, don't know. Neither of us have said the words 'we fucking'. Okay, we're going to have dinner and make out a little. Don't keep encouraging me to do more," she tells him.

"I ain't got to encourage yo ass to do nothing. It's been two damn fucking years. You are going to a man's house to have dinner. You didn't even come close to that with Jake. What, two damn dates the whole time y'all was talking and here this man. Shit. Girl, this man has invited you to his house for dinner. He is cooking for you or having a meal prepared for you. Either way, this is so much better than the last one. Fuck him tonight, okay? What are you wearing?"

"I don't know. Jeans, top, and heels. He said to keep it casual."

"Lea, do I need to come over there and dress you? Are you for real? Jeans. Jeans? If you don't put on one of those sundresses, I'll disown you as a friend. And skip the bra and panties while you at it. Easy access. Easy access," he tells her.

"But wouldn't that be advertising being ready to fuck?" she asks him.

"Woman, you been single way too long. This is your man, correct. Or, is that not true? Do you want to get fucked?"

"Yes, I have been single way too long. This month away has me unsure of everything. And yes, he is my man. That just sounds so weird."

"That's because it's been so long. Sundress, heels or sandals. On second thought, put on a sexy bra and pantie set. Y'all been talking all this time, right?"

"Yes, but we kept it casual. Nothing major."

"Well, that shit will get cleared up tonight with the tangle in the sheets."

"Glad you are so sure of that. I gotta go. I'll take all your advice. Bye, Gordon. And don't go telling anybody Lea is finally getting laid. I may not be."

"Oh, you will. Have lots of fun," he says, ending their conversation.

Lea takes out a peach and lavender sundress and sandals. She showers and shaves everything, even checking for hair on the nipples. The older you get, the stranger the places that hair grows. At seven o'clock leaves the house taking the streets downtown instead of the highway to give herself some thinking time. She has driven past the Warehouse Lofts where Zion lives, going to Busch Stadium and barely noticing them. She gets there at seven-twenty and drives directly to the garage entrance. As she arrives, a gentleman is standing at the entrance. He addresses her as Ms. Adams, uses a key card to allow her access, directs her to a private elevator, and hands her the card. He states it will take her to the top floor and Zion's apartment. She parks across from three black vehicles. The Acura NSX, the Cadillac Escalade SUV, and a Cadillac CT6.

Well, at least I made sure my Acura TLX is clean and shiny.

She enters the elevator moving to the back corner. During the ride up, she plays with her necklace.

I'm so scared.

YOU ARE NOT LEAVIN', YOU HEAR ME? STOP BEING A DAMN SCAREDY CAT. WE HERE, WE STAYIN'. AND WE MAY BE FUCKIN'. DEAL WITH IT.

I smile. At least the Sex Diva has a plan.

Lea steps out of the elevator directly into a foyer. She sees soft lighting to the left with shelves that have glass decorative pieces, vases, and bowls in them. To the right, African paintings are arranged erratically of people, animals and some paintings with abstract designs. All colorful.

I feel like I'm in a museum and I take my time walking through. I can't help myself. I wanna study the art. I guess I had been standing there too long because I see a movement out the corner of my eye and turn and see Zion watching me. I smile.

"Sorry, I got hooked on looking at your pictures."

OMG, THIS MAN IS SEXY, SEXY, SEXY. YEP, WE FUCKIN'. QUICK, FAST AND IN A HURRY. WE SO HAVIN' SEX TONIGHT.

"I noticed. I got hooked on looking at you." He walks over and stands next to her. "Welcome to my home. And right on time." He kisses her.

"Thanks."

Shit. That went straight to my clit.

Zion escorts her into his apartment.

Apartment, my ass, Lea thinks.

They walk into a softly lit living room with clean and simple lines but comfortable furnishings. The dining room and kitchen are to the right with couches to the left.

If I sit on the couches, I could watch the view from the wall of windows that meet in the corner from the left and right of the apartment loft.

Jazz is playing in the background. Further into the apartment, a door leads onto a wraparound balcony with a small kitchen, bar, and seating area. One can sit on the balcony and watch a baseball game or watch the fireworks on the riverfront.

AND IT'S SECLUDED ENOUGH FOR HAVING SEX.

Down Sex Diva. Down. I got this. Don't you worry. I have a plan.

DON'T YOU FRICKIN' BLOW THIS.

Back inside the apartment is a flight of stairs that Lea assumes leads up to the bedrooms. Zion is watching her the whole time, not saying a word.

He is nervous, I think.

"Can I take pictures of the fireworks from your balcony? I'll give you a dollar to rent the space from you."

"How about a kiss and you can have it anytime you like."

I put my arms around his neck and lift my head and kiss him. He lifts me up and presses me against him.

"Hi, Zion."

"Hi, Lea. We don't stop, we won't eat." His dick is steadily getting harder and difficult to control.

Maybe some ice down there would help.

"We'll eat. Eventually," Lea says. She has decided to get this first nutt over and done with. She kisses him again, deepening the kiss. Her sundress is flowy enough that all he has to do is grip her ass to hold her up.

"Kitten, you start this, and it'll be difficult to stop."

Give me the word Lea, please say yes.

"Zion stop talking and fuck me. Now," she tells him, soaking wet and clit throbbing for release.

Between kisses on her mouth and neck, Zion assures her of his desire for her, not wanting to scare her with his excited love making. "Uhhhmmm, Lea, I may be a lil rough. It has been a while, and I want inside of you so much."

Green light, yes. Every time I thought about her over this past month, all I wanted to do was jack off but held back. I wanted, hell no, needed my next nutt to be in her and not in my damned hand.

Lea reaches down between them and grips his dick. Hard. "Promise?" she whispers in his ear.

Before she realizes it, Zion has kicked off his shoes and walked over to a wall. He is kissing her neck and face and lips so feverishly, she can't almost keep up. She gives him a kiss for every kiss he gives her. He is grinding his crotch into her pelvis needing to feel her.

"Oh Lea. You feel so good. Pull the top of your dress down. Let me see them titties."

Lea pulls her sundress down off her shoulders. She exposes her breasts and Zion latches on, suckling, biting, and sucking each one alternately. She whimpers from the pleasure of it. She keeps grinding against his dick wanting to feel it. Needing to feel it. She hears and feels her underwear rip. Zion has torn them off and thrown them across the room. He unzips his pants and takes out his dick. He lifts her up against the wall, digging his fingers into her ass to get a tight grip.

"Lea, grab me. Squeeze me. Feel me."

Damn his words. Shit. A man that likes to talk during sex.
FINALLY, YES, YES, YES.
Sex Diva is screaming in my head.

Lea grabs his dick with one hand squeezing it and stroking it up and down, feeling the pre-cum on the tip. His pants and underwear have slipped down to his ankles.

"Baby, you know I'm completely clean but if you want me to wear a condom I will. Tell me now, hurry up," he says pulling back getting ready to stop.

"Zion, you know I'm completely clean, too. Fuck me," she tells him, "so good. Feels so good," she moans.

"Lea, I wanna slam my cock inside of you. I can't wait any longer. I can't go easy. I want you so much. Please tell me to stop now if you can't handle that."

Why the hell am I talking so much? Shit. I've never been this talkative during sex. What the hell is wrong with me? Man, just fuck her. Damn.

"Fuck me, Zion. Fuck me as hard as you can. Make me cum. Fuck me now."

He gently presses the tip of his penis to the opening of her pussy to make sure she is ready and wet enough.

Geezus, the woman is soaking. Lord, don't let me be too quick.

Zion slides in and fucks her with a vengeance unable to hold back. She is fucking him back just as hard with her face buried in his neck wanting not to scream.

"Don't hold back. Let me hear you," Zion tells her pumping inside of her enjoying the feel of her pussy.

She lifts her head and kisses him, moaning in ecstasy.

Damn, she sounds so good. A woman enjoying sex. Not that fake ooh, aah, yes, nice, crap. Shit, I'm in fucking pussy heaven.

"Yes Zion, yes. Slide it all the way in. Come on give me all that dick," she begs him.

Finally, I get to feel, this man's dick. I can cry from the force of pleasure coursing through me.

Zion knows he is slightly oversized and tends to hold back until a woman gets comfortable and adjusts. But Lea is instantly relaxed and swallows him inside of her. He feels how tight a grip she has. With every thrust up, she squeezes it with her inner wall muscles. He is on the brink of cumming.

"Lea, you gonna make me cum too soon. Stop squeezing me."

She is contracting the walls of her vagina squeezing him. He braces one hand against the wall concentrating on not coming and holding her up.

"No, feel me, feel how tight I am. Cum for me. Let me feel your hot cum inside me. Feel how wet I am. See how much I have wanted you. Feel it."

Zion pumps faster. Harder. She grips him, feeling like a suction cup, and he cums. It takes him over the edge, and he explodes, growling with pleasure continually slamming her against the wall.

Oh, shit. She feels so damn good. Sooooo damn fucking good. God. It's been so long since I have let go like this. Shit, yes. This fucking. Off the chain.

Lea keeps moving up and down on his dick grinding against his pelvis. He came before her but he doesn't stop, wanting to feel, watch, experience her pleasure. She clenches her muscles and cums.

"Fuck, yes. Lea cum for me."

He encourages her, watching her, listening to her, feeling her fuck his dick.

Oh, so damn good.

She screams her pleasure into his neck and jerks with the force of her orgasm. He holds her up without any effort waiting for her to calm down. Holding her. Soothing her. Comforting her.

They come down off their sexual high breathing deeply. He pulls out of her and gently lowers her legs to the floor, bending down to pull up his underwear and pants and zipping himself closed. He pins Lea to the wall and kisses her.

"I thought I was going to have to ease you into the idea of having sex tonight, getting you a little tipsy to loosen you up or end up falling asleep with you doing nothing and me being left frustrated. You little vixen you. Where is my shy, quiet introvert?"

"I'm only quiet and shy in large groups and with people I don't know or am uncomfortable with. When it comes to sex, we know from being finger fucked, there is no way in hell I could be shy with you. It was only a matter of getting that first orgasm out the way. Now we can relax and not be on edge all night long," she says with a long sigh.

Lea looks down at him, sees his underwear peaking from his pants, and looks over at hers across the room on the floor. "Zion, I'm going to need some underwear. Can I borrow a pair of your boxers? If I unclench, your cum will slide down my leg which will make for a sticky situation."

Zion cracks up laughing.

She continues to floor me.

He goes to the laundry room, grabs a pair of his, what he thinks are the smallest comfortable pair of boxer briefs he has, a wet towel and goes back to the living room. She has not moved from that spot, holding her sundress up, loosely from her waist. He has her open her legs and places the towel in between them to catch wayward cum, wiping her gently. He hands her the briefs and watches her put them on.

She is actually putting on my underwear. She doesn't even ask for a shower; she daintily slips on my underwear. My boxer briefs being daintily slipped on by my girlfriend. Funny.

"I'm not trying to be nasty or dirty but walking with a wet towel between my legs looks stupid and would be uncomfortable, and my

Loves Awakening

underwear is, torn in half. Over there." They look at her lace undies on the floor peaking from under his dining room table, split down both sides.

"If you want me to go take a shower, point me in that direction. Although taking a shower after every nutt tends to dry out my skin. I'm good with a warm wet towel as you can see. How about you?"

"Let's have dinner. I'm starving," he says, holding out his hand for hers.

"Wait, you didn't answer me," she says as she allows him to lead her to the balcony.

"You're not nasty, and I don't shower after each nutt. We will flip the coin for who gets the wet towel. Next time. Let's eat, drink, talk, and enjoy the night."

Zion picks up her underwear and puts them in his pants pocket.
OOOOOO NO HE DIDN'T. KEEP HIS BRIEFS.

Kia Lui

-30-

I've just had the best orgasm I've had in a decade.
I can't believe I let go like that.
Zion and Lea are thinking.

They go out to the balcony. It is the length of the apartment and more. Walking out from the main doors to the left from what Lea can see in the muted lighting, there is a small kitchen area with a grill. The dark green wicker dining table has seating for six. Place settings for two with candles are set up at one end of the table. To the right of the dining area are two lounge settees with a small table in between them.

Zion pulls out a chair for Lea to sit at the table. He moves to the grill and fires it up for the shish-kabobs. Lea serves up salads from the glass salad bowl sitting on the table. He has wine chilled and two glasses waiting. She pours them each a glass. They dive into the salads.

"I'm still amazed. I'll always walk past that wall and think of you."

"You must have a number of places in your home like that. From sexcapade memories I mean."

"Nope, not true. I have never brought a woman here, especially to have sex. It was always at her place or a hotel. Usually the casino hotels."

"Why hotels?"

"Dinner and sexing after. Lea, I can admit I haven't been a decent guy when it came to women. I have kept them at arm's length. It worked out for me."

"Why did you invite me here?"

"I want you here. Within the short time we have known each other, I want you in my home. And I'm glad you're here."

"I'd like to say I haven't had men in my home for sexing, but I can't."

"I plan on erasing all memories of them, believe me."

"You are confident."

Zion pats the pocket where he put her torn panties. "Confident and determined."

"Well, I won't be wearing yours home. They're way too big for me, but they have soaked up the juices well enough." Lea strokes her hips drawing their attention to the bulge of underwear under her dress.

Zion shakes his head, laughing at her. "Woman, you are hilarious." He takes the food off the grill and places them on plates. Two shish-kabobs each, one of chicken and veggies and one of steak and veggies.

"May I ask you a question?" Lea says.

"Sure, ask me anything."

"It may seem like all we talk about or focus on is sex when we get together. I don't mean for it to be that way. But at our age, I see no point in beating around the bush or having assumptions. I would rather be up front, get some things out of the way, and move on to getting to know each other. Without the awkwardness."

"Lea, what's your question? I don't mind the sex talk or the flirtatious path we have been on. It's fun. And relaxing."

"Good, glad you like it, too. You stated you didn't want to be rough with me or hurt me. Have you ever had rough sex or hurt someone doing sex?"

"I was involved with a woman who liked it rough. We were young, so I don't believe either of us had a clue what rough meant. She wanted to be beaten, called names, degraded, and treated like shit. In good conscience, I couldn't do that. I love my black queens, and the last thing they deserve is to be treated the way she wanted to. I haven't fully allowed myself to let go as I did with us, in years. What we did in there, I can't remember a time of fucking a woman that hard, pounding into her like that, and being focused on her pleasure as well as mine. Usually, it was all about me getting mine."

"Lea, I plan on making slow passionate love to you. But when I use the word fucking with you, it is not to put down what we do."

"I understand."

"Tell me, have you ever been roughed up doing sex?" The thought of any man roughing up Lea for any reason makes him see red and want to become violent.

"No. The men I have been with have been 'gentle' and didn't want to hurt me. Over the last five years, I discovered what I mean by rough sex and what I want."

Good. No one I need to hunt down and hurt. "And what exactly is that, Lea?"

Lea takes a gulp of wine.

Here goes. Let's see if I can say this without having him think I want to be beaten.

"What do the words submission, man-handle, or BDSM mean to you? What images do they conjure in your mind?"

Zion hesitates before answering. "Man-handle. I would say is what I did with you up against the wall. Submission, a woman allowing a man to make all the decisions, bowing to his will. BDSM. Whips. Chains. Pain. Where are you going with this Lea? Are you into BDSM?"

What kinda freaky ass woman am I dealing with here? And will I continue to deal with?

"Before you go crazy with your thoughts, calm down and listen to me okay?"

"Okay. But let me re-fill our wine glasses again. I may need something stronger after this."

"While Gordon and I were doing our off and on thing, we got a little freaky with each other. What we did back then would be tame compared to what people are doing now. When I was in my first adult long-term relationship, I wanted freaky sex but that didn't happen. Hell, in my twenties and thirties, I was having sex like I was married and in my sixties or seventies. I did learn what I didn't want when I decided to embrace what I did or do want. Then I started listening to couples, happy couples in relationships. I realized relationships are based on what both people want and need and not about what outsiders say is right and wrong. You still with me?"

"Yes, go on," Zion encourages her.

"First off, I don't want a man to abuse, beat, or misuse me. I would never allow a man to use me as a punching bag and beat on me for what his low self-esteem is telling him about how I should be acting. That's not ever gonna happen. Full BDSM is not what I'm talking about here."

Lea takes a sip of wine, *he's still with me.*

KEEP GOING.

"To me, submission is about two adults consenting to power exchanges in their relationship. They equally have their strengths and weaknesses but, they trust the other will take care of them and things are done for the betterment of their relationship," she says as she looks at him. He is calm and watching intently. Lea plunges on.

"I completely agree with you about the man-handling. What happened in your living room is definitely being man-handled. You didn't hesitate in your love making. I mean, fucking me and fucking me hard. You heard me, understood me, gave it to me and took back what I gave to you. If you would have halted what was going on, to have us slow down or heaven forbid stop and wait, I believe this night would have been a complete letdown because we would have been nervous, hesitant and unsure of every move we made and every word we said. Do you agree?"

Zion is stunned but intrigued. "Yes, you got a point. But what are you getting at?"

"I want to make love to you and you to me. I want you to fuck me and me fuck you. I want you to man-handled me, take me, spank me. I want to try blindfolds with you, and I want you to use a whip on me. I want to seduce you knowing you are receptive to my advances. I want to try freaky, sexy, passionate, man-handling and BDSM. I feel the heat between us, and you have it in you to man-handle me the way I want to be man-handled. But, I absolutely do not want you to physically, mentally, or emotionally abuse me. I want to learn how to submit to you, to trust you and your judgment for us. That's why I need long-term because for what I'm describing, a man can't do this and walk away after a few weeks or keep it casual. My strength doesn't seem to threaten you, especially after seeing me handle Martin. Most men would have stepped in, took over and kept me from doing my job, and would have thought he has to protect the little lady from the big bad man. If I'm asking too much or if any of what I said is something you are not willing to try, then say so now, I can go home, and we can have this one night and end it. But I'm not settling for less than what I just described to you. I want that and more."

WHEW. *Whew.*

Lea sits there after saying what she had to say, allowing Zion to adjust to what he has heard. She has taken a major step and chance in saying this to him. If he hadn't fucked her like he did when she first got here, she would have waited to say anything about her desires.

It's in him, he has to decide what he wants to do about it.

"I did want to step in and handle Martin. If you hadn't fired him, I would've. My protective instincts roared to life. Wow, Lea. Why the hell didn't you bring up any of this while I was out of town? As much as we have talked and texted, you never let on this was something you wanted to talk about," Zion says, wanting to erase the awkwardness he is feeling.

"Because that would have been an easy way out, Zion. I wanted, no, I needed to say this in person, so I could gauge your reaction. I didn't want you mulling this over for weeks with me sitting here in St. Louis wondering. If I had told you this while you were out of town, by the time you got back, we would not be talking to each other."

"What? Why do you say that?"

"Overthinking instead of talking. Distance and time. The human mind can make something basic and simple, a killer of relationships."

"You may be right about the time and distance thing."

"What are you thinking, Zion? Have I freaked you out?" she asks him.

"Hell yeah, you've freaked me out. Dammit Lea. A woman is not supposed to be this upfront with her sexual desires like this. A man is supposed to lead her into getting to know herself sexually. That is the type of woman I have been with. If I left it as an every now and then fuck, in and out sex, they accepted it and asked nothing of me. You want me to forget all that and, shit, let myself completely go sexually. I haven't done that since college. Your introvert personality has jumped off this fricking balcony, you know that, right? An introvert would never say these kinda things. I see why you are not settling for temporary. I could never have allowed myself to be free and completely enjoy any of the temporary ass I have had over the years."

Zion stands up and turns his back on her attempting to get control of his emotions looking out over the balcony. She has taken him back to an angry time. He's remembering when 'she' introduced him to BDSM or what 'she' thought was BDSM. He hated it and he hated 'her'. He had to lay off sex for years trying to get his mind straight and back on track and out of that world. 'She' needed domination and degradation. Years later after therapy, he discovered what 'she' was into. Sadomasochism. 'She' loved the aspects of pain and humiliation for sexual pleasure. It was the only way 'she' could be happy. The only way 'she' eventually could be sexually aroused.

Once he allowed himself to have sex again after his self-imposed celibacy, he made sure to avoid any and all women that needed degradation.

But damn, it has been some boring ass sex. When Lea told me I could be rough with her, I didn't want to scare her but shit I wanted to pound that pussy into next week. My dick is hard now thinking about it. Can I step back into that emotion and do this and not lose control or hurt her?

He goes back and sits down pouring the rest of the wine in his glass.

"Zion, I'm taking a big chance in saying this. I figure I got nothing to lose and a lot to gain. I need and want more than what I had in my past."

Lea looks at him waiting, thinking maybe she should back off. She now gets quiet and sits staring into the night sky. They sit there saying nothing. After a few minutes of pained silence, Lea gets up, clearing away the dishes. It gives her something to do and to get away from him staring at his wine glass. Zion allows her to clean up and take the dishes over to the outdoor sink and, geez, even a dishwasher.

An outdoor dishwasher.
She laughs.
This man really is fucking rich.
"What are you laughing about over there?" he asks, enjoying her laughter.

"Your outdoor dishwasher. It made me laugh because I don't even have an indoor dishwasher. Except these two hands. Zion, how about I go home? No hard feelings. Okay? I understand if this doesn't interest you." She moves to leave attempting to walk past him, but he grabs her hand and makes her sit.

"No, I don't want you to leave. I'm figuring out where to go with this information. I'm never this stunned in business, and you have completely stunned me silent. I decided I wanted to get to know you better that Friday in the Central West End. I'm not going to go back on that. I still want to get to know you. Now, my mind is firing off in many directions. I have dabbled in the world of BDSM."

Dabbled. That's a fucking joke, Zion thinks.

"Am I agreeable to what you said? Shit, some of it yes. Submission has come to my mind a number of times since I have met you. But hearing you talk about the kind of submission you want, hell my thoughts were way off. For someone who has had a tight rein on his emotions since the age of twenty-five, you are asking a lot of me to let that go. And after our session in the living room, woman, I am so looking forward to letting go and enjoying love making and not just sex or fucking. Especially a sex life where neither of us have to hold back. I just needed a moment to think about what you're asking. It seems we're going to be exploring ourselves sexually more than I imagined."

Lord thank you for bringing this woman into my life.

"I don't want either of us assuming anything about this relationship," Lea says. "I want to be able to give into what I'm feeling without a lot of overthinking and second-guessing. I'm good at that by the way. Overthinking and second-guessing. When I leave here tonight, I'm sure I'll rehash every word we said, thinking how I should have done things differently. Was the sex good because you wanted me or were you just trying to get off."

"You're not leaving here tonight. Maybe all weekend. Relax. No need to overthink. Never hold back on me. Never." He leans over, kissing her on her neck. "Never. Okay? Lea, the sex was extremely gratifying and satisfying. I'm glad we waited and you took the lead in getting that first nutt out of the way."

"Okay."

"Because we are having this open discussion, let's talk about the subject of masturbation," Zion says.

"All right, talk."

"The woman I was with in college, enjoyed watching me masturbate. She liked pain. Add the two together, and let your imagination run wild."

"Ouch."

"That's putting it mildly."

"I'm not into pain of any kind. Well, abusive pain. Spankings would be nice." I grin at him, bringing some calm back into this conversation. "Zion, we'll have limits. We'll respect each other's limits."

"Well, you have mentioned BDSM. Just curious how much pain you into. Spankings, huh? Are you going to be a bad girl?"

She looks at him somberly. "Maybe. Sometimes. And not that kinda pain for sure. You'll be watching and thinking about me. And watching me will only result in pleasure."

"Well, that's pretty damn confident of you, missy."

"My underwear, ya plan on keeping it to trash or smell my scent when I'm not around? Grinning like a school boy whose gotten his first toy."

"Smell your scent. And stop being so damn smart and perceptive. That kinda unnerves me. And what will you have to help you masturbate about me."

"I'm sure we will come up with something fitting."

"What about oral? For or against it?" he asks her. *Please be for it.*

"I'm all for it. Having you at my mercy. Yep, can't wait."

"Oh really? Me at your mercy? Come here." Zion motions her to stand in front of him.

He lifts her dress and pulls down his underwear she is wearing. She steps out of them. He is staring at her womanhood. Very intently.

"Zion, why are you staring at me like that? Now, that is unnerving."

"Thinking about who will be at whose mercy. I want you Lea. I want to make love to you and I'm going to make love to you. All night long. But first, we dance."

Joe's, 'Don't Wanna Be a Playa' is playing in the background.

They walk into his living room, and Zion takes her in his arms. They slow dance. Lea reaches up and kisses him. He grips her behind pressing her into him.

Man, why don't people slow dance anymore? This is heaven. Will it always feel good being in his arms like this?

"You dance well, Ms. Adams."

"So, do you, Mr. Landon. And such a telling song to dance to. Are you giving up your playa status?"

"Absolutely. I'm glad you waited to have this discussion in person and not while I was traveling."

They dance through a couple more songs, then the music stops. Zion stands behind her, pressing her into his body. His dick is getting hard. He moves his hands to cup her breasts and squeezes hard, pulling her into his chest.

Shit, that feels nice.

He inches his hand up to her neck and clutches it, pushing her head to one side nibbling and kissing her.

This is heaven. Total heaven.

He moves his hand down to the juncture between her legs and grips her through her sundress.

WHERE HE HEADED WITH THIS?

Lea grinds against his hand.

Sex Diva, that's where he headed with this.

OKAY, LET'S RIDE. OH SHITTT.

Zion decides he is going to see how far he can step back into the world Lea wants and still keep things safe for them. A little domination and submission should show him. He continues playing with her pussy making sure she gets as wet as possible. He needs her slick like the first time. He can tell she wants to cum, and he abruptly stops and pull his hand away, standing behind her not touching her.

He takes Lea's hand, and they walk up the steps to his bedroom. They walk to a darkened room lit by a soft light on a bedside table. He has a California King bed. There is furniture to Lea's left and right, but she can't tell what is or isn't a dresser. A wall is in front of her, but it looks like a bare wall. To the right of it is a door that she assumes leads to a bathroom, with balcony doors to the right. Zion has her standing in the middle of the room, not touching her. She reaches out to touch him and he stands back. She drops her hands.

He has me unsure of myself now.

"That's it, stand right there."

He approaches her and kisses her long and hard without touching anywhere but their lips. Lea leans into him but he steps back breaking the kiss staring at her. Then he leans in and kisses her again. She takes a step toward him to close the distance and he steps back.

"Zion. Stop that. I want to be in your arms."

"No."

They kiss three more times before Lea realizes she should stand still and accept the kiss.

And she does, their tongues dancing around each other, nibbling each other's lips, moaning and groaning and enjoying it.

With a kiss, I could orgasm from this man.

He finally reaches for her.

"Feel how hard you make my dick," he whispers.

Zion grips her ass with both hands and pushes her against him. She holds onto his shoulders in an attempt to keep from falling. He bites into her neck, making her whimper. He stills as if to stop, but she goes limp, giving him the okay to continue and he does so. He proceeds with kissing and licking her neck.

"Zion, I need you inside me."

"Sshhhh baby, you will have me inside of you soon enough."

Zion pulls down her sundress, leaving Lea naked standing in front of him. He looks her up and down while circling her. She keeps clenching and unclenching her hands wanting to cover herself.

This is so unnerving. I'm forty-four years old and even though I have been working out, I'm certainly not that proud of my body and having him look at me like this. The girls are small in my opinion, the ass is definitely no longer rock hard and neither are my abs. The legs are getting back to what they were. My best feature are my legs if you ask me.

She reaches up to cover herself and he stops her.

"Don't. Don't ever cover yourself in front of me. Not ever, do you understand? Put your hands back to your side."

Lea does as he instructs and stands there. He stops behind her. She can hear him unzipping his pants. He throws his clothes on the floor in front of her, close to the wall. She knows he is fully naked and wants to turn around and look. He doesn't move. She gets agitated.

"Zion, what are you doing?"

"Waiting to see how much patience you have. Not much I see. We're going to have to work on that."

He moves to stand in front of Lea.

"Look at me, Lea. Look me up and down. Look at the man you are getting. Flesh and blood with issues like any other man. The money means nothing. It's you and I standing here naked with our vulnerabilities for each other to see."

She looks him up and down. He has no excess fat; he is built. Most would describe him as thick. Muscular arms, down to large hands. His chest has enough hair that it would tickle her nipples into perkiness. She licks her lips when her eyes land on those nipples.

I want to bite and nibble them.

He flexes his chest, probably on purpose.

I giggle.

"Woman, are you laughing at what you see?"

"No, you flexed your pecs. Did you do that on purpose or was that a reflex?"

"I have no idea. I've never allowed a woman to stare at me so intently before. Usually, it's get undressed, walk across the room, and get in bed. With you, I want you to admire the man you are getting as I admire the woman I'm getting."

Lea continues her admiration of Zion's body. She looks down at his penis.

Oh god, it's thick, long, and fat. The feel of it inside me was amazing and to now see it, to gaze upon it, not hidden by my hands or his pants, is even better. How the hell am I going to get that in my mouth?

PRACTICE. WE FIGURE OUT SOMETHING 'CAUSE WE LICKING AND SUCKING THAT POPSICLE. YOU NEED TO BUY SOME GREAT HEAD ORAL GEL WHEN WE GET HOME. AIN'T NO SHAME WITH HELP IN RELAXING OUR THROAT MUSCLES. NO MA'AM. NO SHAME AT ALL.

Muscular thighs down to powerful calves. She walks around him to view his ass. Nice round and perfect and firm. His shoulders are in that perfect 't' that travels down into his waist.

I wanna hug and grip him.

She comes back around to stand in front of him. He is looking down at her with a confident look in his eyes. She looks up at him with a look, hoping it says, "I want you and this".

He steps closer to her kissing her again, taking her in his arms allowing her to finally touch him. She slides her leg up his waist wanting to have his penis slip inside her but he stops her. He pushes her back onto the bed, forcing her to lie on her back. He stands over her, spreading her legs. He slips two fingers in her pussy teasing her g-spot but not touching her clit. She slides her hands down to touch herself and he shakes his head telling her no, not to do it.

"Zion, I want to touch my clit."

"No, Lea. Not until I say so."

Lea arches her back, hoping his thumb will slide across it, but it doesn't. She begs him to touch her and he keeps saying no.

Dammit.

Instead, Zion takes his fingers out and flips her over onto her stomach and pulls her to the edge of the bed. He opens her legs and places them on either side of his waist. He slowly slides into her and she whimpers with the pleasure and pain of the feel of his dick being enveloped by her warm folds. He didn't even say he was going to do it, he just slid right in to the hilt.

"Oh, fuck Lea, damn, you feel so good."

"Oh yes, fuck me," she pleads.

Instead of pounding into her hard and fast this time, he moves excruciatingly slow.

And I hate it. I need it fast, and he wants to go slow.

She lifts her body and presses into him. He grips her waist and pins her in position. She tries to reach for her clit, but he grips her hands pinning them above her head with one of his hands and holding her waist with the other one, slowly fucking her.

"Baby, this feels so damn good. Oh yes, squeeze it baby. Squeeze my dick. Yes. That's it. Harder, squeeze it. Shit. You feel so damn tight."

Lea turns her head to the side so she can catch her breath. With every thrust, she concentrates on squeezing his dick as hard as she can. She can feel the veins of his penis pulsing inside her.

Shit, it's too damn good.

He moves faster, pounding harder, and she can tell he is about to cum. He lets go of her hands to play with her clit.

Shit, that feels so good. I'm about to go over the fucking edge.

With every thrust in her, he stops and pauses and flexes his dick and pulls back, then slams it back in.

Damn, it's so good.

He stops and flips her over onto her back without breaking contact.

How in the hell did he manage to do that?

Zion continues sliding in and out of her pussy slowly, again. He pins her hands above her head and leans over and sucks on a nipple. Her legs are wrapped around his waist to keep them from breaking contact.

His movements are barely noticeable; but feel so damned amazing.

He is going in and out and grinding his pelvis against her clit with every thrust.

Lea attempts to pump, moving to increase the friction.

I want to cum so damned bad. I can feel it building and building.

Zion pumps into her harder and harder with each thrust up to the hilt.

"Oh, Zion. Yes. Make me cum. Cum with me."

Zion picks up the pace squeezing her nipples. He moans and Lea cums. He shoots, slamming away at her pussy, one, two, three, four, five pumps into her, cumming, filling her with his seed.

Shit, I'm shaking all over.

On his final push in, he lets his penis sit inside her and flexes it.

I cum again, feeling him grazin' my g-spot.

"Yes, baby give me those orgasms. They are mine. Shit, give them to me." Zion's body shudders through the course of his orgasm. He emits a low growl, gripping Lea's legs.

Lea rides the waves of her orgasm sliding down into reality.

Zion pulls out of her gently, pushing her farther onto the bed. He gets on top of her, kissing her.

"Be careful what you ask for." He stretches out next to her, wanting to yell, YES, YES, YES, SEX, GOOD SEX, HOT SEX. OOO BABY. He mentally fist pumps the air but doesn't move an inch, smiling.

Shit, this man is fantastic.

"Closed mouths don't get fed, Zion."

They lay catching their respective breaths, languishing in their own worlds. Lea doesn't want the sex to end, but she knows she needs a break. Two years with no sex and now multiple orgasms in one night. She has never experienced this before.

WOOOOOOOOOOOOOOOO HOOOOOOOOOOOOOOO.

The Sex Diva is running around, screaming, jumping up and down, sliding across the floor. Lea smiles, agreeing with her happy display.

-31-

Zion finally got to let himself go and Lea wasn't scared or didn't cringe away. She reveled in the pleasure. She came alive. She submitted.

They lay thinking, *Now what*?

He turns on his side and looks at her naked silhouette, one leg bent up swaying back and forth, her hand next to her side, her fingers drumming lightly. She is humming a tune. He is limp after that last go round.

"Lea, are you okay? What are you humming?" Zion asks in a hesitant whisper. He strokes her body, wanting to touch her.

Lea looks over at Zion and smiles. "Barry White's, 'Practice What You Preach'," she says. "I don't know why, it popped into my head."

"Did I hurt you or scare you?" He asks.

"No, Zion, I'm not hurt nor was I scared. I was and probably will be giddy for some time. I enjoyed everything you did. Did I disappoint you?"

"No baby, no disappointment here. None what-so-ever, but we're going to have to discuss our limits, our safe words, and other things. First, we shower."

Zion gets up, pulls Lea with him, to the wall, and he presses on a door. They step into a bathroom the width of her bedroom in her house. The bathroom is the length of the other side of his bedroom's wall. As she walks in, she sees a vanity to her left with two sinks and open shelves beneath with baskets of towels. Two separate mirrors are above the vanity. There is a steam shower with waterfall and massaging shower heads. Behind the shower on the same wall is a tub that looks like it has whirlpool or sauna spigots. After the tub is a door which leads to the toilet and a bidet with an additional sink. Looking to her right is a door leading to a walk-in closet.

They walk into his closet. Lea stares in awe at the cleanest, most well-organized, collection of men's apparel she has seen outside a men's department store. Dress shirts, shoes, suits, ties, even jeans and casual pants and shirts are hung and neatly spaced out. In the middle of the closet is a long bench one can sit on. Under the hanging clothes are plenty of drawers.

Zion walks over to a set of drawers and opens them.

"Lea, what do you sleep in if anything at all?"

Lea looks at Zion, mesmerized by his nakedness, not saying a word. She is standing, fidgeting and wanting to cover herself with her hands.

"Lea, baby, what do you sleep in or do you sleep in the nude?"

"Oh, sorry," Lea shakes herself to respond, "T-shirts, tank tops, whatever's light and comfortable." She finally folds her arms under her breasts and hopes he doesn't mention the movement.

"Not silk lingerie, gowns, or things like that? You should be in silks." He walks up to her and unfolds her arms. "Don't hide from me. Your body is beautiful." He caresses her lightly on her hips pulling her toward him.

"Okay," she whispers. "If it goes beyond my thighs or elbows, I feel constricted."

Lea concentrates on his caress. She wants to cover up. *Really unnerving.*

"Well, let's see. A workout tank for you and nothing for me. I want you nude, your skin next to my skin. We'll work up to that. Let's shower. Sorry, I don't have any shower caps, so your hair will get wet. We can make it a quick shower, and I can keep you from the flow."

"No worries. It's just hair. A towel or old t-shirt will dry it fine."

"You use a t-shirt to dry your hair? Fascinating. I must adjust. Dating a woman with natural hair will be different for me."

"Yes, for natural hair, it's better. T-shirt drying is better than a towel, but a towel will do."

Lea rambles trying to keep her mind from focusing on them walking around in the nude. Something new for her. Usually, it's have sex, get up, clean up, and leave. Well, not with Zion. This man is completely relaxed walking in front of Lea with dick on full display. She is not that relaxed walking in front of him. She keeps shifting from foot to foot, turning her head away from being caught staring.

DON'T WORRY, I'LL STARE ENOUGH FOR BOTH OF US. WOW, CHECK OUT THAT POLE. OOOOOOOOOWEEEE.

Yes, ooooowwwweee indeed.

Zion lightly tugs on one of the spiral curls in her hair. It stretches and snaps back into place.

He kisses her on the nose. "Kitten, stop covering yourself. I like what I see. All of it. Come on, let's shower."

They return to the bathroom, and he turns on the shower, pulling her inside with him. The water is warm, hitting them from different angles.

She feels they could be standing under an island waterfall.

"You don't mind smelling like a man, do you? That is the only body wash I have."

"Liar. I see Avon Skin-So-Soft shower gel and bath oil over there on the ledge."

Zion looks over and yep, Avon's Skin-So-Soft products. He laughs, for he did tell Mrs. Vance to do what needed to be done for inviting a woman over and making her feel welcomed.

"I must thank my housekeeper for that. I did tell you, you were the first and only woman who has been here, didn't I? Other than family that is."

"Yes, you did."

They lather and clean each other. Lea dries off, putting on his gym workout tank and he wraps himself in a towel. She would like a barrier between them so she can overthink as usual.

"Are you hungry?" Zion asks. "I have a fruit tray in the fridge."

"No, I'm fine," she says, walking back into the bedroom, picking up their clothes. He takes her dress and hangs it up, along with his clothes in the bathroom.

"Lea, what are you thinking? You're awfully quiet," Zion whispers, hugging her from behind.

"How this is the best night I have ever had in my life. Well, so far," she says.

"No man has ever made dinner for you, fucked you into sexual oblivion, showered with you, and slept with you, which I'm about to do, holding you close to him?" he asks.

"Of course not. If they had their own place, they rarely invited me over. Why cook for me when they could take me out. Some expected me to cook for them. Shower with me? Sleep with me? Ha, no overnight stays. As a former playa, you know how it went."

"Hey, I slept and kinda showered. Hotels are great. Know what, let me shut up pathetically defending the playas of the world. Let's go to sleep, I wanna hold you."

He picks her up, gripping her behind and carrying her to bed. She kisses him on the neck.

"Keep it up, we won't be sleeping tonight."

"I like that I can kiss and hug you without second-guessing myself."

"Baby, never with me." He pulls back the covers, and they fall into bed.

"Excellent," she says liking the feel of him on top of her.

"You gonna unwrap your legs so I can hold you?"

"I guess." Lea unwraps her legs, and they stretch out next to each other. Zion holds out his arms and she puts her head on his chest cuddling up next to him.

After about fifteen minutes, Zion is asleep. Lea lays there, enjoying his breathing, having him hold her and staring at the print of his dick under the sheet.

This is heaven. Hopefully no night terrors. I can lay here and stay awake.

But after about thirty minutes, she drifts off to sleep. And then the dream starts.

-32-

I'm alone in a room full of happy couples. Everyone is smiling, enjoying themselves. I'm sitting on the outer fringes. Watching. Waiting, Wanting. Needing. Jealous. Always on the outside. The outsider looking in. Then HE comes along. We're a couple. In my mind, we're happy. In my mind, he wants me, he loves me, and he has chosen me. But no. This isn't reality. This isn't real. He hasn't chosen me. He doesn't love me. We aren't a couple. He pulls away. He gets cold. Distant. Why? What did I do? Why is he leaving? Where is he going? Why didn't he choose me? What did I do that was so wrong? What didn't I do? No, don't leave me. Don't go. Please. I don't want to be alone. Please. I don't wanna die never being loved. Please. Why do men always leave me? Why? I hate you. I hate you all. Hate. Hate. Hate.

Zion wakes up to Lea talking. No, pleading in her sleep for someone not to leave. She is crawled into a ball with one hand reaching out, begging not to die alone and unloved, hating someone.

God what do I do? How do I bring her out of this?

He reaches for her hand, latching onto it gently. She instantly wakes up, straightens, and looks around focusing on him. The look in her eyes is so lost and lonely. Hurting.

"You okay? You were dreaming," he whispers reaching over to wipe a tear from her cheek.

Focusing on me, she says she is fine. She looks around frantically. I watch the rising panic take over her body. She hops out of the bed and bolts out the door.

"Lea. Stop! Where are you going?"

"My phone. I need to check my phone. It's been too long. I need to check it."

Zion jumps out of bed, grabbing a pair of shorts following her, hopping one leg and running, putting them on. When he gets down stairs, she is looking at her phone.

"Lea. What's wrong? You were having a dream, then you bolted for your phone. What's up?"

Lea looks up at him. Shit. She doesn't want to remember the dream, waking up feeling that extremely lonely feeling, which is killing her.

She needed to see if her mom had called or left her a message. The dream threw her into a panic. Always the same panic of never being loved.

"I wanted to see if my mom had left a message needing me, that's all. I'm sorry. Go back to sleep, I'll be right up." She needs to pace and regroup.

Dammit, I hate waking up and feeling alone. I wanna cry. If he will go back to bed, I can get this cry out and my emotions under control, and everything will be fine. Then I can sneak out and go home.

Zion walks over to her, taking the phone out of her hand and putting it on the table.

"What makes you think you are going to die alone, never being loved? Lea look at me."

She shakes her head no.

He heard me. Dammit no. He witnessed my terror. No. Dammit no.

"Lea, don't hide from me. Look at me. Now," he says firmly.

Lea jerks her head up with tears in her eyes, rolling down her cheeks.

"Oh, baby. What's wrong? Come here. It's okay."

Zion holds her and lets her silently cry. He says nothing, comforting her. She calms down and takes deep breaths. He picks her up and carries her back to bed.

"I'm sorry Zion. You must think I'm nuts. I've been so stressed out lately. I guess it all caught up to me. I don't remember the dream, I just needed to check my phone to make sure I hadn't missed any emergencies."

Please, she tells herself, *don't let him ask me about the dream. I always remember the damn dream because I always end up alone.*

"Okay sweetheart, I won't press you. Let's watch some TV."

Zion lays her back in bed, getting in beside her. He hits a button on the night stand. Black out shades cover the windows and patio doors and what she initially thought was a simple blank wall lights up and a TV comes on. He finds a movie and they lay watching in silence. He has a leg thrown across hers, linking his fingers with hers, laying them close to his pubic hairs. He tries to stay awake, but his jet lag is still affecting him. She is determined not to fall back to sleep.

I gotta figure out a sleep mechanism so I don't wake up like that again with him. If there is an again with him.

Lea lays awake the rest of the night watching him breathing, his chest rising under the sheet. His penis flaccid but still looking strong and powerful. She studies every bit of him, etching him into her subconscious. This will be their one and only night together. He won't want a woman dreaming about being left alone. He wants simple, uncomplicated. That is not her.

When dawn arrives, Lea slips out of bed, puts on her bra and sundress, smiling at the thought of her torn missing panties, then goes downstairs. She doesn't leave, but sits on his balcony enjoying the morning sun rise over downtown St. Louis, thinking about what happened before they fell asleep.

I could seriously get used to those kinda dates. But will he wanna still date me after—. Well after. Stop this Lea. Be happy you got this much.

She busies herself cleaning the balcony and gathering the dirty dishes from the balcony dishwasher taking them to his kitchen sink to wash them. To kill time before he wakes, to keep herself busy while he sleeps or to give herself reason to stick around longer, she looks for ingredients in his fridge to make breakfast. Veggie omelets, toast, fruit, coffee and juice. At least they can have one last meal together. Then she can get a hug before she has to say goodbye. Forever.

-33-

Sunday morning, Zion wakes up alone in bed. That's not unusual, but the flowery scent hits him. The memories from yesterday and last night flood back.

Where is Lea? Did she leave?

He looks over at the bedside clock and sees it's seven-thirty.

Seven-thirty on a Sunday. I smell food. Mrs. Vance doesn't work on Sunday morning. Especially this early and not cooking. Lea.

He gets out of bed and goes downstairs. Lea is in his kitchen making them breakfast. She is back in her sundress and watches him as he approaches. She looks nervous. Twirling and tugging on the charm of her necklace.

"Good morning Lea," Zion says calmly not wanting to agitate her further, wanting to seduce her.

"Good morning Zion. Would you like some breakfast?"

"I would love breakfast."

I know she is bare bottomed in that dress and as she moves with the light behind her I can see the mounds of her nice ass. Damn, I wish she would have stayed in bed with me and I could've woken up with my dick pressed against her.

Lea places plates with omelets and toast, on the dining room table with the fruit tray, orange juice and cups of coffee.

We sit down to eat in silence. Half-way through our meal, I decide to break the tension.

"I had planned on waking you up with sex this morning, and my plan was foiled because of jet lag and extremely intense orgasms that wore me out the night before."

She smiles. Yes, keep her smiling.

"Did you fall back to sleep at all?" Zion pulls her hand away from her necklace placing it on the table.

Lea stops, smiling. "No, I'm a morning person. I—."

"Don't apologize. It's okay. Tell me about your mom."

Lea looks away then back at Zion.

If he runs after hearing about this, they will always have this one night.

"A couple of years ago she was diagnosed with cancer. We have been through chemo, surgeries, and doctor's appointments, with me being there for it all. This was the first time I hated being an only child."

She plays with her spoon. Zion takes it from her and puts it on the table.

"Before she was diagnosed, I was attempting to be with someone who I thought was interested in me, on his terms. Turns out he didn't want me at all. I've been alone, not having anyone to burden my troubles with regarding my mom. Friends try to be there for me, but they don't want to be bothered by something like this."

"Sweetheart, your true friends will always be there for you, and nothing should ever be a bother for them. I'm sure Gordon would agree."

"Yes, he was or is a great sounding board. But sometimes I really wanted my own. If that makes any sense."

"It does. So, just you and your mom surviving this daily for two years? What about a cancer support group for care-givers?"

"Zion, remember? I'm an introvert. It didn't work out. When the guy I was interested in chose someone else, that's when I decided no more temporary. I wanted my own monogamous relationship. Someone I could depend on for emotional support, to vent, to fuck anytime I wanted, when he was available to fuck, or wanted to fuck or desired to fuck."

Loves Awakening

"Okay stop with the fuck, my dick is twitching. I get it. You been wanting to fuck," Zion laughs. "Well, that explains the no sex. And you haven't wanted any man since?"

"I tried, but they were on the temporary road, and I wouldn't allow anyone into my life who wanted that. It's easy to walk away before starting something that may not be going anywhere. That's why I'm going home now. Give you your space and mind back."

"The hell you are," he quietly states.

"Zion."

"Lea."

"Dammit, Zion."

"Dammit, Lea. We can go back and forth like this all you want. I got all day," Zion says.

"Zion, do you really want to be a part of this? Of me waking up from crazy dreams?"

"Yes, I do. Especially the sexual ones. I'm looking forward to those. You all wet begging me to slide inside you and I gently kiss you awake so I can have you riding my dick. Oh baby, we have a lot to look forward to and you recall me telling you we have issues and drama in our past we gotta get through to make this work? We will."

"Okay. Other than being a playa and leaving broken hearts everywhere, what could your issues or drama be?"

Zion braces himself for the rejection. But she has to know and it might as well be now.

"I'm sterile. Shooting blanks. If you want kids outta me, it's not going to happen. Ever. No science can fix that."

I rush out, feeling the anger boil inside me. I would love to see my child growing inside her.

"I'm sorry Zion. You know you are not any less of a man because you can't give a woman a child. You believe that, don't you? I'm forty-four years old. I don't see myself having kids at my age. The only reason I'm on birth control is to control my menstrual cycle. I gave up on being a mom a long time ago. I've accepted that me not being a mother doesn't make me less of a woman who can love, and you not being a father doesn't make you less of a man who can love."

"Baby, again, you amaze me. All my life, every woman I've met has looked down on me for being sterile, and you, in one sentence, have made me feel more of a man than anyone outside my family ever has. You are a woman to love, cherish, pamper, adore, make love to, and to marry. I'm not proposing, Ms. Lea Adams, so don't panic, but so you know, you won't die alone, be unloved, or feel like you were never loved."

Zion kisses Lea passionately. They put all their emotions and feelings into that kiss. Zion pulls away and looks down at his plate, then back up, masking his emotions from her. He isn't sure what they may show. Every time he tells a woman he is sterile, he closes up immediately. He doesn't want Lea to see that from him.

"We need to get out of this apartment. Spend the day with me," he says, standing up and taking dishes into the kitchen.

"Uh, sure, but I'd like to go home and change first." Lea quickly accepts wanting to have some fun with Zion instead of going home alone to overthink their confessions. And cry about what could have been.

"I'll change then I'll follow you home. Don't even think about it," he says, knowing she is about to object. "I'm driving us, we're dropping your car off, and I get to see your place. I'm excited."

Zion takes her hand, and they go to the bedroom. While he changes, Lea straightens the bed needing something to keep her busy.

"Kitten, thanks for making the bed but that wasn't necessary. I may want to mess it back up."

"Are you always this playful?" Lea asks, smiling. She is still a little unsure of herself after the dream he witnessed and telling him about her mom. She has held back the most humiliating part of chasing after a man, only giving him the basics.

"Actually, no. I've been all business as long as I can remember. Now that I've told you about me being unable to give you kids and you didn't make me feel low, I feel a happiness I haven't felt in, well, forever."

"Some women can be shitty. I'm glad I made you feel better."

Lea makes sure the kitchen and dining areas are clean before they leave. She gets her clutch and Zion grabs his keys and phone. He checks his; nothing urgent from anyone. They head to the elevator, and the second the door closes, he pounces on her.

"Remember, elevators are made for kissing."

Zion presses his body against hers, grinding into her while kissing her neck.

OH. MY. YES. LET'S DO IT IN THE ELEVATOR.

Lea pushes back wanting more, wanting him to fuck her right here. Abruptly, he stops and moves to the other side.

"Why are you over there? Why did you stop, Zion?" she asks him, tilting her head to one side and smiling.

"Because I'm not fucking you in this elevator. Not today."

She raises her dress, displaying her bare womanhood. "One day, you will lick my clit in this elevator, and one day I'll suck your dick in this elevator, right?"

Zion reaches for his dick and squeezes it hard. "Lea, you can count on it."

"Where is my underwear by the way? My torn underwear."

"Don't worry. In a safe place. And before you go wandering into some deep thoughts, yours are the first and will be the only ones I will EVER snatch and hide. I'm not some nut crazed panty freak."

Lea cracks up laughing. "I'm glad you cleared that up. I don't need my panties to come up missing."

The elevator reaches the garage and they walk off, in a light and playful mood. He walks Lea to her car, giving her a key card that gets her out of the garage. "Keep and use this. I'll follow you to your place."

He follows her, and twenty minutes later, they arrive at her house. As Lea gets out of her car, a breeze gently blows her sundress up. She barely catches it before her vagina is exposed to Zion.

"Hey, don't go hiding all that goodness. Mother Nature is helping me to get a look. I likey. A lot." Zion has stepped out of his Acura, parked behind her in the driveway.

Lea raises her dress and flashes him. He laughs shaking his head. "Woman, you are so much fun."

"Gotta keep you smiling." She disarms the house alarm with her key fob as they approach her door.

"It's quiet over here. How long have you lived here?"

"Eight years."

"Eight. Is this your first house? Most people sell after the first five years."

"The only reason I would sell is if I were getting married. And even then, I would keep it for rental income. I like my house."

Lea unlocks the door and they walk in, Zion closing the door behind him.

"What? Why are you grinning at me like that?" she asks him.

"I'm waiting for my tour; you do those so well."

"Ugh," Lea grumbles.

"Okay, living room, dining room, bedrooms one and two, bathroom, kitchen," she says as she stands in one spot pointing out all the rooms. She knows if she walks toward a bedroom with Zion in tow, they sexing. She is horny. Again.

Zion pouts. "May I see your bedroom?"

She escorts him to the bedroom turning on the light to her left. Lea has a queen. Cozy sleeping. Her bed has red sateen sheets with a red comforter. He turns to her and says, "I was expecting blue. Cobalt blue seems to be your favorite color."

"How did you know that?"

"The necklace you're wearing has a dark blue stone, the ring on your right hand has a dark blue stone, and you wore a cobalt blue dress to the charity ball."

"How perceptive of you. Yes, it's my favorite color. Back here is the deck leading to the back-yard, and down here is the basement."

Lea leads him downstairs, showing him the finished basement.

"So, what's behind all the closed doors?"

"You are rather nosey, aren't you? Bathroom, laundry room, storage room, walk-in closet. So, where are we going? I need to know what to wear."

"Jeans and flats will be okay. Grab a light jacket."

She walks to the closet with him close on her heels.

I was hoping to go in here without him.

Lea has an aversion to people seeing the inside of her closet. One man she dated wanted to see the inside of them. For the four weeks, they "dated", all she constantly heard was how much stuff she had, she didn't have a place for a man in her home or life, all her material shit was proof she didn't need or was ready for a man. Now Zion is looking at all her stuff. She braces herself for the snide comments.

"Well, you are as organized as I am. Color coded. Love the shoe and boot collection. I need to take you out more so I can see those legs in these shoes," he picks up a pair of platform peep toe tan heels.

Lea says nothing.

The insults will probably come later. Best to get the hell out of here now.

"Come on let's go." Lea grabs a top from the closet, some gray flats and a pair of jeans. They walk back toward the stairs. She stands at the bottom motioning Zion to go before her.

"Ladies first," he says with a smart ass look on his face.

"Nope."

"Why, Lea?"

"You know why, Zion."

"Are you wet, Lea?"

"Yes, Zion."

He places his hand around her neck, caressing and gripping it.

His hands are so big, yet so soft and gentle.

"I know, Lea, 'cause I can smell you," he bends down kissing her.

"Well, then from this point on, I'll wear underwear around you and I'll take a shower before we leave."

"You can wear underwear; I can always rip them off. Maybe I should lick you clean and dry, then you can change clothes and we can get going. Which do you want, Lea? Want me to lick your throbbing clit or do you want to shower?" He walks her toward the wall pressing her against it, placing his hands on the sides of her face.

"Lick me," she tells him.

"Say it again," he braces his hands on each side of her face against the wall.

"Lick me," she pleads.

"Say my name, baby," he whispers in her ear, lightly nibbling her earlobe.

"Zion. Lick me," she whispers.

"Hmm baby, are you sure?" He moves back and looks down at her lips.

"Yes. Zion, please lick me. Lick my clit."

He kisses her, pulling down her sundress. The clothes she was holding drop to the floor, ignored. He kisses her shoulders, her breasts, her stomach, on his way to kneeling before she spreads her legs open, exposing air to her womanhood. Her nipples are hard, standing at attention. He again kisses her stomach, lifting a leg onto his shoulder, slowly moving to the folds of her pussy, licking up and down the sides.

Lea holds onto his other shoulder and the back of his head. He caresses her back and squeezes her tits.

"Zion. Oh baby. Please. Lick it."

He goes after her clit, tonguing it. French kissing it like he was kissing her mouth.

"Oh yes. That feels so good."

Lea moves and moans, fucking his mouth as if she was fucking his dick. He latches onto her clit and she screams instinctively trying to pull away and push his head away, but he tightens his grip and keeps sucking her, alternating between hard and soft licks, flicks and sucks. She grinds against his mouth more, wanting, needing that release. He moans into her pussy as if he is devouring her, giving her open-mouthed kisses. He alternates his tongue flicking her clit and sticking it in her, then licking his way back up.

Zion is thinking, *Oh yes, this woman's taste is intoxicating.*

He hasn't eaten a pussy since college over thirty years ago. Smelling her, tasting her is more than heaven. He knew he had mad pussy-eating skills but gave up on ever eating another one. Ever.

With Lea, he could not fucking wait. He made sure she was introduced to the dick before the lick.

She wants to experience man handling. Submission. BDSM. Shit it's on.

She is fucking his face wanting to cum. His mustache is tickling her as he expected it would, which is why he didn't shave it off this morning.

Oh god. Her moans are driving me wild. Yes, baby. Cum for me. I keep sucking and licking.

He latches onto her clit, sucks hard and she screams, her orgasm racking her whole body.

Lawd, this woman is so sexy when she cums.

After she finishes her orgasm, he stands up to go to the bathroom to wash. She pulls his head down and licks and kiss all her pussy juices off his face.

Shit, I hadn't expected that. Fuck shit, I need to fuck her.

He presses against her, unzipping his pants, taking out his dick and pressing into her. She is still dripping wet.

"Oh Lea. I never expected you to kiss me. Do it again, kiss more of your pussy juices off me while I fuck you."

She kisses him, licking his lips. He pounds into her feeling as if he's banging the hell out of her pussy, almost hurting her, being unable to hold back and then he explodes, moaning into her mouth.

This woman is going to wear my dick out.

They stand there up against another wall with him throbbing inside her. Again. They look at each other and laugh.

"It's nice that we can see the irony and humor in our sex life, don't you think?"

"Yes, I do. Shower, then we're out of here," Lea says.

"We don't have to go anywhere," Zion suggests while kissing her neck.

"Yes, we do. We need to be in a place where we can't easily fuck."

"I guess so. Remember, my car does have dark tinted windows, if you ever feel a need to, well, you know," Zion says.

"Maybe, someday. Don't tempt me like that."

He undresses and they carry their clothes to the bathroom and shower. After the shower, he dresses in the bedroom, and Lea dresses in the bathroom.

His presence engulfs her house. She likes that. Lea freshens her face with tinted moisturizer, a lil eyeliner, mascara, and lip gloss. He has seen the raccoon eyes, so there isn't much to hide anymore. He stands in the doorway, watching her.

"Do you skip makeup often?"

"Nope. I enjoy wearing makeup. I stopped wearing the heavy face about ten years ago. Too long to do and left too much on my clothes. I must put on moisturizer and lip gloss. Can't stand a dry face or dry lips. I do my eyes a few days a week, depending on what I'm doing that day. Setting up computer equipment does not require make-up. When I go out, I like to glamour it up. All the color options are fun."

"Makeup isn't a crutch for you or something you hide behind?"

"No, it allows me to play dress up. You will either see me with or without it and accept me as such. The same with the body. I'm never going to be a size two again, nor do I want to be. I'll have to get used to walking around in front of you naked though. I envy how relaxed you are with your nakedness. Anyway, I like my minimal curves."

Zion walks up behind her. "Lea, I like all your curves. They're real. And I will do what I can to ensure you are always comfortable being in the nude around me. I promise. You are for my viewing, touching, licking, caressing, nibbling, and sucking."

"Okay let's get out of here. Now."

"Spoil sport. Grab your camera. You may need it."

I grab my smaller pocket camera. He's driving. Of course.

-34-

Zion and Lea spent the rest of Sunday hanging out and having fun. They had lunch at the Forest Park Boat House restaurant and rode a paddle boat. They walked around the zoo and rode the train. They visited the Art Museum and rested on Art Hill.

He tells Lea about his sister Star, her husband Garett, and their twin girls. He loves his sister and nieces and spends as much time with them as he can now that he is back in St. Louis. His parents are currently traveling in Europe as an anniversary gift from him and Star.

Zion explains that, up until a few years ago, he lived in California, building his business and making his billions. When he realized he was doing more traveling to meet clients outside of California than clients coming to his office to see him, he decided he could move back home and base his work out of St. Louis. The relocation of business and home have been a success. Fifty percent of his staff followed him to St. Louis, and he hired the rest after moving back.

They kiss, hug, and show plenty of affection, keeping things classy in public. Lea can't remember a time she's been with a man this way, out in public enjoying themselves without him being cautious about who is going to see him.

Zion doesn't care who sees him. He's enjoying a Sunday doing something as simple as going to the zoo. At forty-nine, he is walking around the zoo, riding a paddle boat as a date. He can't believe this. Any other woman he knows would want to be flown off somewhere. He'd be spending who knows how many thousands of dollars on her to get some ass and here he is with Lea spending much less. The best cheap fun he has had in years.

"Ms. Lea, you have made this one great Sunday. The most relaxing one I have had in a long time."

"How do you normally spend your Sundays?"

"Working, flying some place for meetings for the coming week. If I'm in St. Louis, maybe watching sports."

"No female company?"

"Not on a Sunday. If I was flying to see one or flying her back, that was about it."

"Really. So some woman got your attention enough that she got to fly away with you. I don't like that."

"Hey, I have Gordon to deal with. Cut a former playa some slack. I'll fly you anywhere you wanna go for the weekend and beyond. Any-place, any-time," he says looking at her, thinking about how he would like to travel with Lea.

"I guess. Will I ever run into any of your exes?"

"Yes, possibly," Zion says, "Will I ever run into any of your exes?"

"Maybe. I have completely changed the type of guy I've dated. You know that 'if you keep making the same mistake then it's time to try something new' rule? Well, I changed. I can't imagine us running into any of my exes, but anything is possible," Lea says.

"I guess we'll cross those bridges when we come to them," Zion states.

They end their Sunday at Lea's house, eating dinner and watching re-runs of Strange Sex on the Discovery channel, heatedly discussing the different things people are into. How they have managed to keep their hands off each other neither of them knows, but they have, as if an unspoken agreement is between the two of them to chill out on the sex for a moment.

Lea asks Zion, "Will I see you at all this week? Outside of work that is. We do have a meeting scheduled for Thursday to go over details of the project."

"Of course, you will. I'm in town all week, but I'm having dinner with my sister and her family tomorrow night."

"Okay, let's play it by ear then. I have a meeting with a client Tuesday night."

Zion caresses her leg. "An evening meeting. Probably dinner. I'm not asking if male or female."

Before Lea can say anything, his phone vibrates.

Zion looks at it ready to silence it before even answering but he see's Saul calling from his office phone.

Shit at eight-thirty. From his office phone? What the hell could be going on?

"Sorry, Lea, I need to take this."

"Go ahead."

Lea moves to the kitchen and dining room to clear away the dishes. She doesn't want to be nosey, so she gives him privacy to take care of whatever is going on. After he finishes his call, she returns. He is standing, getting ready to leave.

Total disappointment.

WHERE THE HELL HE GOING?

"Everything okay?"

"Yeah, as good as can be expected. I need to take off. Let's get together Wednesday for dinner. I'll give you a call," Zion says distractedly.

Lea can sense his mind is someplace else already. He has checked out and is in business mode.

"Okay, no problem."

She walks with him outside to his car, wanting to be near him as long as possible. He turns around and looks her in the eye.

Something is not right, she can sense it, but doesn't ask. He kisses her, pressing her into him, and she kisses him back, passionately, wanting to bring him back to their fun weekend. When he ends the kiss, she feels cold and it's about ninety degrees outside.

"I miss you already. I'll call you, Kitten."

"Talk to you later, Bear."

He smiles. "Call me Bear anytime you like because all my bear hugs are yours for the taking. Now go inside before I take you up against my car."

She kisses him once more, then turns to walk back into the house. He gets into his car, and backs out of the driveway. He looks back at her one last time and smiles before driving off.

This has been a great weekend.

-35-

During the drive home Zion calls Saul back to finish their conversation.

"Saul, now tell me what the hell is going on?"

"Sir, I have a program that runs on our email servers to catch viruses, spam, and abnormal heavy activity. About an hour ago, your email account was flagged for an unusual amount of incoming emails. The first email from this individual came in about four hours ago, then two more three hours ago, and in the last hour there has been a total of sixty emails from this same person to your email account. I set up a rule which moved these emails to a different hold location on a separate server from our daily business and am scanning for any malicious code, but there isn't any. It's just a lot of emails from this one individual," Saul reports.

"And tell me this individual's name again?" Zion asks, running his hand across his face while sitting at a stop light, hoping when he heard the name the first time it was a mispronunciation.

"Addison, Addison Raymond, Sir."

Zion curses. Fuck, not HER. Please, not HER.

"Saul, do a background check on that name. Full background checks back to thirty years ago. I don't have much information after I graduated from college, but you can start with school and work your way up to now. Send me a copy of those emails or the location link to the server hold. I'm on my way home and should be there in about ten minutes. Keep them going to the separate server until I say otherwise. Make sure I have access to that server."

"Will do, sir," Saul responds and Zion ends the call.

Addison. I never thought I would hear that name or have that period of my life return. Mentioning 'she' to Lea was more than enough. But I have spoken her into existence and here she is. What the hell could she want? Sixty damn emails, you gotta be kidding me.

I get home and go directly to my office, turning on my computer. There is the access to the server where the emails are being directed. I open the first one.

> *From: Addison Raymond*
> *To: Zion Landon*
> *Subject: What's Up*
> *Hello from an old friend. I can't believe after all these years I have found you, Zion. You remember an old love, don't you? Just wanted to say hey.*
> *Addison*
>
> *From: Addison Raymond*
> *To: Zion Landon*
> *Subject: Waiting*
> *Hey what's up you can't respond back and say Hi.*
> *Addison*

Zion reads a few more of the emails with subject lines that escalate in hatred and anger. From throwing in his face about their sex life, to loving how she enjoyed being beaten, to wanting to rehash a relationship.

> *From: Addison Raymond*
> *To: Zion Landon*
> *Subject: Mutherfucker Answer me*
> *Dammit you respond back to me now.*

Addison

From: Addison Raymond
To: Zion Landon
Subject: Rich Bitch Ain't Bout Shit
Oh, so now you too fucking good to respond to a fucking email.
Addison

From: Addison Raymond
To: Zion Landon
Subject: Fuck Me
Give me the dick Rich Bitch.
Addison

From: Addison Raymond
To: Zion Landon
Subject: Pain Mutherfucker Pain
You get any pussy as good as my pussy bitch ass. I bet not. We had the best. Come fuck me. Come beat me Mutherfucker. Now.
Addison

From: Addison Raymond
To: Zion Landon
Subject: Drill ME Bitch
Attachments: 3
See Mutherfucker. This how you gonna fuck me. Drill my ass and open it wide.
Addison

Shit. She is sick. What the holly fucking hell is this woman into?

Zion clicks on the attachments. One is a video of a woman being fucked in the ass and there is blood. The pictures are images of an asshole right after the man pulls out and he is covered in blood, sperm and shit. He closes his laptop and pushes his chair back from his desk, flicking his fingers in repulsion as if his keyboard was diseased.

Damned nasty ass. Fuckin' hell.

After a couple of shots of Patron to calm his nerves, Zion returns to his computer and opens the last email, skipping all the others with attachments. The subject line draws his curiosity and his mouth drops open in confusion reading it.

> *From: Addison Raymond*
> *To: Zion Landon*
> *Subject: I'm So Sorry*
> *Zion, I'm so sorry about the emails I sent you earlier. Please delete them. There is no excuse for me to talk to you that way. I'm truly not that person anymore. I'm sorry to have intruded on your life. Please forgive me.*
> *Addison.*

What the fuck is wrong with this woman?

When they broke up, he swore he would never be a flashy billionaire, to keep her from finding him.

How did she find me?

He has avoided college reunions, opening personal social media accounts, and limiting past relationships with people he went to school with. All to avoid ever having her re-enter his life. He can't have this. He can't have her anywhere near him or his family, or heaven forbid, Lea. He has to keep this away from Lea.

Zion calls Sam and briefs him on Addison, her background, and how she can be a danger to him, his family and the business. Sam informs him he will hire additional security, familiarize himself with what Saul finds out and be there tomorrow to pick him up in the morning.

He prowls the apartment all night long. He can't sleep. His bed is empty without Lea after one night. He stares at the products in the shower through the mirror while brushing his teeth. He keeps picking up his phone to call her but doesn't. He knows his voice will betray the anger and distance he is feeling right now. He doesn't want to distance himself from her, but he doesn't know Addison's state of mind. Zion texts Lea good night. She texts him back the same, even sending him a picture of him leaning on the bear statue, at the zoo, laughing.

Dammit, how am I going to handle this and still see her?

In the email from Saul, he discovers Addison didn't return to any college after they broke up. She drifted around, staying with friends and family not settling anywhere for more than six months. Each time she got on her feet and would seem stable, she would mess it up, by moving in with some guy. She had been in the hospital multiple times with injuries reminiscent of being beaten. No drug addiction is listed, but she seems to have had several stints in hospital psyche wards for sex addiction and anger management.

That explains all the angry emails.

The information provides details of a few run-ins with the police regarding domestic violence issues.

I don't need this woman back in my life.

He meets Sam down in the garage early Monday morning. On the way to the office, they discuss the extra security that has been ordered and ready to be put in place when Zion gives him the go-ahead. He has to call his sister and brother-in-law, let them know what is going on, and why they will now have a security detail on hand. His parents are out of the country, so they are safe and are not due back for another month.

Getting to the office, Zion informs Morgan not to interrupt him and to cancel and/or reschedule any meetings he has today. He reads the folder of information from Saul and fires up his computer to see if there are any additional emails from Addison. A few more apology emails appear.

From: Addison Raymond
To: Zion Landon
Subject: My Heart, My Love
Again, I apologize for my crazy emails. You
are my everything. I've always loved you
and have never gotten over you. Please
don't hate me.
Addison

From: Addison Raymond
To: Zion Landon
Subject: No Pain Ever
I would never hurt you or cause you pain.
I'm sorry. Goodbye my love.
Addison

Zion is repulsed by the tone of these emails.
My love, my heart. This chick has flipped her ever lovin' mind.
Saul arrives and lets him know that no additional emails have come in under a different name and he hasn't noticed any other

strange activity. He also checked the video cameras and hasn't found her image on any of their surveillance over the last couple of months, but because he only has an old yearbook picture, that may be the reason why.

"Do you guys think we can accelerate the construction on the new office? I don't have as much control over this building as I would like. She could show up any moment creating trouble."

Saul informs Zion, "They are ahead by about thirty days. We have experienced some great weather. With the pre-prep Ms. Adams had all the contractors do, things have been moving along at a fast pace."

"Sam, make sure you can do something about additional security issues with that building. Go above and beyond what is normally expected, even if you already have."

"Sir, we have had all the best equipment being purchased, delivered, and installed, and I have personally selected the security detail. We're good to go," Sam assures Zion.

"Good. We're going to need eyes and ears everywhere. I don't trust this woman at all. I could be completely blowing this out of proportion, but I don't want to be stupid and underestimate her."

Sam asks, "What about Ms. Adams. You have given her full access to you at all times, but you haven't mentioned anything about security for her. Do I need to add her as part of those you want protected?"

"Not yet. I'll keep it business with her. Hopefully, Addison hasn't found the connection between us. That's all for now. Let's get on this before it blows up any further. Don't tell the staff, but keep an eye on what they are doing. Addison could have contacted one of them trying to get to me. Thanks, gentlemen."

Sam and Saul get up to leave. Zion has Morgan come into the office to review his schedule.

"Sir, I have rescheduled all your meetings today. A number of voicemail messages were on the main line this morning from an Addison Raymond. She left this number for you to return her call."

Zion wants to scream in anger, but he controls himself. "Great. How many and did you delete any?"

"I counted a total of ten. All have been saved."

"Good. Don't delete them until I say so. Did you listen to any of them?" Zion watches for a reaction from Morgan to see if he can gain an idea of the tone of the voicemails before he listens to them.

"Only the first two. I decided not to listen to anymore or transcribe them as they seem rather, personal. Sir." Morgan does not look away from Zion's intense gaze.

Shit. Now what kinda crap I gotta listen to?

"Thank you, Morgan. This Addison Raymond is not to have access to me, is that understood? Notify building security if this person ever arrives and makes a scene. They are to escort her off the premises right away. Here is a picture of her although it's not current. Cancel my appointment with Ms. Adams on Thursday. Only say that things are hectic with my schedule, and she can email any updates on the project."

"Yes sir. Will that be all?" Morgan asks.

"No, extra security has been hired for the office. If this Raymond person does manage to get up to our floors, call security. Sam will have a list of the ones you can call. Do you understand me? This Raymond person is not someone to be entertained."

"Yes sir. I understand."

"Thank you, Morgan."

"Sir, would you like to have lunch ordered in? You cancelled your lunch appointment also."

"No, I may leave and go home for lunch. Thank you. That will be all for now."

"Yes sir," Morgan says and leaves his office.

Zion dials into the main voicemail box and listens to the messages left. They are similar to the emails. Nice, filled with hate, then apologetic.

This woman is really nuts. And that voice is grating on my eardrums. Wish I can flush out my hearing.

He leans back in his chair, thinking about his next steps. And Lea. Six hours into his day and he hasn't texted, called, or emailed her. He see's that he has one missed call and two text messages from her. He wants to see her, but he can't. After another hour of staring at his phone, wanting to hear her voice, he calls her. When she answers, he feels calm. After only such a short time of knowing her, she has become a safe place for him. *WTH.*

"Hello you, good afternoon. How are you today?" she says with a smile in her voice.

"Good. How's your day going?" he asks.

"It was going pretty good until I received a call from your assistant informing me you want all updates on the project via email. Are you sure that's what you want because that's not how I do business with a project of this magnitude?"

"Yes, for now. Some things are going on here, and it would be easiest on the both of us. I need to cancel our dinner Wednesday. I'm sorry, Lea, but I got slammed with an issue that is going to be a pain for me to handle."

"No problem. Maybe we will get to see each other one day this week. Later in the evening?"

"I'll try, sweetheart. I gotta go. I'll talk to you later."

"Later, Bear."

"Hmm, you know it baby. Sending you a hug. Bye Lea."

"Bye, Zion."

Shit, that was rough. I wanna see her. But I can't yet. Figuring out this Addison shit is priority, so Lea and I can get back to us. Damned evil witch.

Lea hangs up the phone, knowing that something is wrong. She can feel it in her gut.
He fucks me then turns cold. Shit. Not this bull crap again.
But what is she to do? Beg him to tell her what is going on.
Aawww naw baby, not this time. Not chasing down a man, begging for attention, and explanation. Hell, we not kids. He can open his damned mouth and tell me what's up. If not, deuces.

She doesn't pester Zion into opening up to her or spending time with her the rest of the week. They do text each other hi, bye, good morning and miss you's, but nothing on the level of what it could be and they know this. Lea hates this tip-toeing around the edges of an issue but what is she supposed to do? Go to his office and demand to know what is going on? Nope, that is not her style. Well, it's not her style any longer. Pestering a man to talk only makes him clam up and close off even more. Right now, she will let him deal with what he has to deal with. It could be a business issue.

Thursday morning, she emails him the updates she would have discussed in the meeting they had scheduled, keeping everything business. His assistant responds back, thanking her for the information and that after Mr. Landon reviews it he will be in touch.

Wow. Just fucking, oh wow. After Mr. Landon reviews it. Sure Zion, fucking sure.

Not going to overthink this, she tells herself. *Or over react.*

Her days stretch along, and she returns to her normal routine of what she was doing before she met Zion. Work, mom, trainer, home, and walks, and does it all over again. It's now Friday three in the afternoon and she hasn't heard from Zion all day. It's obvious she won't be seeing him anytime soon or maybe ever again, so she sees what's up for the weekend with friends. One of her social media groups is getting together at the Moonrise Hotel for drinks. She had RSVP'd she would be there so she might as well go as planned.

She arrives at seven-thirty, finding the group in full swing, having fun, greeting each other and catching up on what's been happening lately. With this group, she is totally relaxed and comfortable and plans to enjoy herself allowing thoughts of Zion and why she hasn't heard from him fade away. For now, at least.

She tries to have a good time putting on a brave face, but she is not feeling this. After a few hours, she makes her escape, giving hugs and telling everyone how she missed them and can't wait to see them next time.

Ethan, one of the group members offers to walk her to her car.

"Ethan, thanks, you don't need to do that. I'll be okay."

"I can't let you go down to your car alone. Anyway, maybe I can convince you to have a drink with me downstairs before you leave. How bout it?" he suggests as they walk toward the elevators.

"Thanks. Maybe some other time. I'm just gonna head home."

"Lea, someday, any day, I'm going to convince you to go out with me."

"Why did you wait so long to ask? I've seen you pounce on other women in the group and me nothing. Why now?"

"Don't know. You seem kinda different tonight. I can't put my finger on it, so I figured I would ask."

DIFFERENT AS IN WE FINALLY HAD SOME GREAT SEX AND NOW HE HAS GONE GHOST ON US.

"I'm the same old Lea."

NO WE ARE NOTTTTTT.

"No. You are not the same old Lea. That's okay. Keep your secret. When we have our first date, you'll tell me. I can wait."

Lea smiles as she and Ethan step off the elevator. When they get to the lobby, walking toward the exit, Lea sees Sam. He is standing next to an SUV. Zion's SUV. He displays no visible reaction to seeing her, as if she is a perfect stranger and not the woman his boss had a date with. Or the fact she is walking toward him with another man.

Bitchassness. We might as well keep walking, we have to walk past him anyway.

As she gets closer, she looks him in the eye and speaks. "Hi Sam."

"Hello Ms. Adams," Sam doesn't even crack a smile.

Stone-faced mute. Oh well.

"Good night, Sam."

"Good night, Ms. Adams."

"You know that guy?" Ethan asks.

"Yes, he works for one of my company's clients."

Ethan looks back at Sam watching him walk Lea to her car. He decides to leave instead of walking back into the hotel to cross paths with him. When a man can stake a claim on a woman with a look, that's a man not to cross.

"Lea, you take care. Drive safely."

"Thanks, Ethan, for walking me to my car. Guess I'll see you at the next group get-together."

"Sure will."

Ethan walks off toward his car and drives off before Lea. She sits in her car, feeling dejected. Zion is in there somewhere. Probably having dinner with some big-boobed arm candy.

Arm candy evil witch.

Move on Lea, move on. It was good while it lasted.

ONE WEEKEND OF FUCKING, THEN HE GOES OFF DATING SOME SKANK AS HEAUX. OH THIS SOME BULLSHIT.

-36-

Zion finally received another call from Addison. He had decided he wasn't going to seek her out, hoping the emails and voicemails would be the end of it. His plan of action is to address her if she makes physical contact and until then, to have security in place.

That phone call. He hated having to take it. She wants to meet him at his place, either his office or his home. He suggests someplace open Friday night. Delmar Loop is open. Not the Central West End where he may run into Lea. He arrives at the Moonrise Hotel and walks into the lobby. Addison is sitting, waiting. She is so made up and over done, she looks like a clown.

What in the world has she done to herself, she was a 'C' cup. Now she's a fake overblown 'F'? I need to get this over with and fast.

I approach her and she stands up. "Hello Addison."

"Hello Zion. Aren't you going to say how good it is to see me and give me a kiss?"

"Why would I lie to you like that? What is this all about anyway? What's with the emails and blowing up my office phone?"

I just want to get this over with.

"Can we at least go in and have a drink at the bar? I want to talk with you."

"Sure, lead the way," I motion to Sam to park and that I'll call him. He nods. Zion and Addison take a seat at the bar. He orders two sparkling waters with lemon.

No way in hell am I drinking liquor around this woman.

"What, no alcohol? We used to always have a drink when we went out."

"Addison, that was thirty years ago. What do you want?" Zion is getting impatient and trying not to show it.

"Well, I saw you in the paper and thought I would reach out to you and say hi to an old friend."

"What paper?"

Paper, what paper? I'm never in the paper?

"Oh, some local rag about a wine tasting party."

She takes out a folded piece of paper. It's a picture of Lea and Zion talking at Tom's wine tasting event. Neither of their names is even mentioned. A small blurb saying "Guests enjoying wine and food at Golden Vineyard's annual wine-tasting event". Zion almost smiles, seeing Lea in those white jeans again. He catches himself before Addison notices.

Okay, maybe she doesn't know about Lea.

Zion folds the paper and puts it in his pocket. He figures without this she will forget about Lea and make him her focus. Addison doesn't even notice it. She is too busy trying to be noticed.

"So why are you contacting me? We don't and never will have anything between us. So, what's up?"

She looks at me, and I can see her getting aroused with my anger. Calm down man, you want to get away from this woman.

"Zion, are you saying you are not happy to see me? Geez, Zion, we had it good back then. The sex was off the chain between us. You can't tell me you can't want to hit this again," she points to her body.

Well I'm pretty much turned off right now.

Zion looks her up and down. "Not only do I not want to hit it, but there is no way I want you back in my life. What's with all the anger and then the apologies?"

"I was having a bad day that day, and I hadn't gotten my prescription refilled, so I kinda freaked out."

Loves Awakening

"Oh, you on medication now? What kind?"

"Something to balance out my moods. When I'm off them, I have great sex like we used to have. When I'm on them, well, not so much. I thought maybe we could hookup when I'm off them sometime. You know for old times' sake. It's not like you're married or anything. Hell, you're not even dating. Hey, are you gay 'cause I couldn't find any pictures of you and a woman online? Don't be offended if you are."

Zion hasn't heard that one in a while. He refocuses his attention back to Addison and what she is saying.

"I couldn't find much of anything about you. Anyway, look, my husband won't mind. He knows about my fooling around when I'm off my meds. He even pushes me to do it. So, what do you say? We can go upstairs, and you can test out my 'Fs,'" she says as she puts her hand on his leg caressing his thigh. He moves her hand away.

"No. Not now, not ever. No way in hell. Look, don't call me, don't contact me. I'm not doing this with you, understand? When we broke up, it was the best thing to happen to me. You go about living your life with your husband, stay out of mine. Do you understand? I don't care to be with you anymore, Addison. Go home to your husband." Zion calls over the bartender and gives him a hundred-dollar bill for the water and for taking up precious space from drinking customers.

"How did you get here, you need a taxi?" The faster he can get her into a cab and out of his life the better.

Addison looks at him, wondering how much of a scene she should or could make and get away with to get Zion to fuck her. Right as she is about to start, Zion looks at her and she freezes. There is nothing there. No emotion. She is nothing to him. No, she is never 'nothing' to any man. All men want her. All men desire her, even Zion.

We'll see. "A cab will be fine," she says, thinking about how she can get him to want her.

Zion stands up and takes a step away from her. He feels dirty as it is, being here. He follows her out the door and, looking down, he sees there is something wrong with her ass.

Dammit, she got market-grade butt injections. No, oh hell no. I have got to get away from this woman.

He flags down the taxi Sam had waiting. She gets in, giving the driver her address, making sure Zion heard it. He asks the driver how much that would be and pays him, giving him double in fare as a tip plus the extra for him waiting. Where she goes from here is not his problem.

The taxi drives off, and Sam approaches him from the other side of the hotel. "Well, did you get all that?"

"Yes sir. Audio, video, and pictures of everything. Especially the address."

"Good. Put it in the file with everything else. If she creates any trouble, I need to be ready," Zion says.

"Sir, I'm not sure I should be mentioning this, but I saw Ms. Adams this evening."

"What, when, where? Did she see me or Addison?" Zion turns to him, wanting to know.

"No sir, she was coming off the elevators as you were walking into the restaurant. With another man. She didn't look left or right. She spoke to me, and I spoke back. Then they walked off toward the back of the hotel alone, I'm assuming to her car. I didn't have a chance to follow them."

"With another man? Could you tell if she was on a date? Are you sure she didn't see me with Addison? Did you see them drive off?"

"No, she didn't see you. She looked directly at me. You were already seated beyond her view."

"Did she introduce the guy?"

"No, Sir. I did get a picture of him. I can delete it if you like."

"Thanks, Sam. You wouldn't be the security expert I hired if you deleted it. Let's get out of here. I need a strong drink and a really hot shower to sterilize my mind and thigh. Addison touched me. I could amputate my leg about now. I wanna know who the hell is my Lea out with? This shit gotta be done and over with."

Zion and Sam walk to the SUV. He gets in the back and takes out his phone to see if he has any messages from Lea. Nothing. He expected as much, considering he has been dodging her for a week.

Just hold on baby, give me time to take care of this. Who the fucking hell you out with tonight?

-37-

Lea can't believe she ran into Sam.

A simple fucking hello and good evening and that was it. Yeah, okay, your boss is out with another piece of ass and I was a hit-it-and-quit-it moment in time. Will I ever fucking learn? Guess not. At least I got memories to last me 'til the next fuck. Am I really gonna go back to random-no-attachment fucking? Hell, why not, it works for others.

This weekend can be considered hellish compared to the weekend with Zion. She hasn't heard from him at all. Not even a response to her Happy Sunday text.

The hell if I risk calling and being rejected by being pushed to voicemail. Oh, no, I'm not going through that humiliation again.

This next week Lea forces herself to stay as busy as possible. Monday her mom has multiple doctor appointments. They spend the day at the hospital and have a late lunch at Cathy's Kitchen.

Tom needs someone to travel out of town to visit two clients that moved to New Orleans and Texas and do some follow-up with clients in Arkansas. Lea hops at the chance quickly. She leaves Tuesday morning and flies home Saturday. The Landon Enterprises project has nothing pressing. Yes, she's now referring to it by its project name and not the owner's name. Tom and Crystal notice but say nothing.

"Don't even mess with me", is the look I give them. I'm not in the mood.

Gordon has agreed to check in on Mom for her. "Thanks Gordon, I appreciate it."

"You gonna tell me what is up with the trip?" he asks.

"It's a business trip. I do take business trips."

"Lea, you haven't been out of town since your mom was diagnosed and you are now going on a four day trip. I know you need a break, but come on. What is going on? Whatever happened with you and Zion?"

Lea turns to look at him. "He finger-fucked me, I gave him a hand job. We had dinner at his house and fucked twice. We talked about man-handling, BDSM, and long-term relationships. He was all for it. Agreeable. Then nothing. He pulled away. I haven't seen him in weeks. I don't know what's going on between us, but I do know I'm not going to sit home and cry about it. I would love to hear from him again, he knows what I want, and the ball is in his court. He may have changed his mind. Because I'm the lead on his company project, I'll see him again. Until then, it's back to business as usual. Got it?"

Gordon stares at Lea, waiting for the emotional breakdown, but she doesn't give it to him.

"Got it. Do you need to be picked up from the airport Saturday?"

"Nope, I'm leaving my car there. It's all good. Thanks for asking."

"Anytime. You know I'm here for you. And if you gave Zion the kinda hand job I know you can give, he'll be back. And giving you exactly what you want," he says as he runs out of the house before the shoe can hit him.

Lea spends her first two days in Texas shopping for electronics with a client and setting up their home office. The Spoede's moved here from St. Louis on the agreement Mrs. Spoede could still do her sales job and that G-TEE would still provide computer support. They have fun looking at computers, printers, and even ways to make their surveillance equipment work with their home network.

Lea checks in with Crystal after she gets the client setup and ready to go.

Another client happy with G-TEE. I love my job.

"Hi Crystal, calling to make sure you got the electronic deposit information from Mrs. Spoede?"

"Hold on. Let me check." Crystal puts Lea on hold. "Yep, everything is here. How you doing? Everything going okay?"

"Sure, why wouldn't it be?"

"Zion came into the office today, strangely looking for you. Why would he specifically come here looking for you, specifically?" Crystal asks.

Dang nosey ass woman. Okay keep it business Lea.

"I'm not sure. We don't have any meeting updates to provide on the Landon Enterprise project. He has requested everything be sent to him via email. I don't have any emails from him. Maybe he got lost on the way to someone else. You know where the files are, so give him what he wants to know."

"He wants you. He wants to know where you're at, when you will be back, and why wasn't he told you would be traveling, because he feels he needs to know this information. Just in case anything came up. And you said 'someone else'. Don't you mean 'somewhere else'?"

"Did I stutter? I said what I meant to say. Oh, fuck him. For heaven's sake, he's a client and nothing more. He doesn't report his comings and goings to me, and I sure as hell am not about to report mine to him. Who the fuck does he thinks he is? Sure as hell not my man. Obviously. Everything on his project is on schedule."

This here shit is pissing me off. He gonna fuck me, ignore me, then expect me to be waiting around for him, or report my whereabouts to him. Fuck that shit.

"Well. That's a mouthful. Is there something you aren't telling me Lea?"

"No. There is nothing to tell. There will never be anything to tell. Anything Mr. Landon needs to know about the Landon Enterprises project, please provide it. As a matter of fact, we may need to switch some things around and assign him a different Project Manager."

Crystal hits the mute button before Lea can hear Zion explode. "Bullshit!" he yells.

"Look, I gotta go. I'll call you when I get to New Orleans tomorrow. Bye," and she disconnects the call.

Fuck you, Zion Landon.

Crystal disconnects the dial tone. Zion looks pissed. "Uh, fuck you, huh?" she asks. "Who is this someone else you are on your way to see? Please do tell? And why would she be reporting her movements to you, you being just a client and nothing more than a client?"

"You even think about reassigning her and I will cancel this whole fucking project, understand me? I don't give a shit about how much it costs me. I will shut the whole thing down," he says to Crystal in a deadly calm voice.

"I'm not stupid Zion. And you not cancelling a thing, even if we needed to do a reassignment. I be damned. When that girl gets pissed she gets on a cussing roll. Her favorite word is 'fuck' by the way. So, tell me, why is Lea pissed at you? Why do we have a client wanting to know her whereabouts? A client who is willing to lose money if we take his Project Lead off his project."

Zion understood he would not be able to get away with only asking about Lea and then leaving. He can't even answer why he had Sam bring him here. All he knew was that he wanted to be here.

I'll fuck her all right. Fuck her into an orgasmic coma. Nothing more than a client. She's outta her damned mind if she expects me to go back to being nothing more than a client. Naw, baby, ima fix this and we getting back on track.

"Zion, I'm waiting," Crystal says.

They are sitting in the conference room with the door closed. She made him sit down because she thought he was gonna tear the place up wanting to see Lea.

"Lea will kill me if I tell you anything."

"I'll risk it. Talk."

"We have been seeing each other or had started seeing each other. Up until about two weeks ago it was great. Then Addison found me," Zion tells her.

"Addison? How the hell did she find you?"

"A picture of me at the wine tasting in the St. Louis Business Journal. I wasn't mentioned by name." Zion takes out the clipping and shows Crystal. She reads it then tears it into pieces. Zion says nothing and doesn't stop her. He no longer needs it anyway, there's a copy in the file he is keeping on Addison.

"She wants to pick up fucking again. She's married, but claims her husband understands her fucking on the side. Oh, and she is on medication that if she skips dosages, which it seems she likes to do, she gets angry and horny and wants to be beaten. When she saw my picture, she tracked me down, emailed, phoned, and asked me to meet with her. I did."

Crystal stares at Zion like he is out of his idiot mind. *Why in the hell would he meet with this crazy chick. Like he can't remember the hell she put him through. Men and their thought processes boggle me.*

"Don't look at me like that, I kept it all public, and recorded it. I rejected her flatly. But I couldn't have Lea in the middle of this.

So, I stopped talking to her until I took care of it. And now I want to see my Lea. Hell, I wanted to send her flowers, candy, a card, jewelry, furs, cars, whatever, but all those things seemed cheap and cheesy. I came to apologize in person and tell her what is going on. I never expected her to be out of town. Dammit. Crystal, where is she?"

Crystal looks at him now, grinning. "My Lea? 'Bout time you fell in love."

"Love, who the hell is talking about love? I wanna see her and tell her—."

"Furs, jewelry, cars. Zion, you love her and you are sorry for being such an ass. But you gonna have to wait. Where she is going next is to see a high-end client. She needs to focus on him and get this taken care of."

"Him, what the hell you mean him? Why are there so many men around her?"

"Him. That's what I said. You can see her next weekend. Men around her? She works in a male-dominated field. What do you expect?"

"Crystal, call her back, get us on the phone. Do something. I don't need another man getting close to her."

"Nope, but I'll give you this," Crystal hands Zion Lea's schedule for the next two weeks. "What other man are you talking about?"

"This says she will be back Saturday. The night I met up with Addison, Sam saw Lea walking out of the hotel with another man. I've had him checked out, and he is not a threat. But I can't risk another one."

"You are checking out other men Lea could probably be involved with? Zion, you are so far gone. When she gets back to town, she has a wedding she will be in. She is being picked up from the airport by a member of the wedding party and is going straight to the hotel, the Cheshire Inn. She had plans to leave after the wedding the same day but things got switched around. Car troubles at the park-and-go lot where she left her car. Anyway, she leaves for Chicago, Atlanta and then Miami next week. You can't see her. Oh flowers, don't do roses, Calla Lillie's. Be creative. Go for extremely vibrant colors. No candy. Cars, furs, jewelry? Get to know her tastes first. I don't think she's into furs. Begging, groveling, and pleading are good ideas. Now about Addison. Is she truly out of the picture? Could she really get ignorant and cause problems?"

"I honestly don't know. I'm being proactive. Doing my due diligence. Cheshire Inn. Crystal, what time is the reception scheduled to start and is it formal?"

"Seven-thirty. Wear a tux. I'm sure you own several."

Bitch. Traveling again. Always using the same Park-N-Go. Bitch. Both of you bitches. Drugged up fucked up as bitch. One coulda stayed away and the other thinks she about to ruin me. Not likely.

The individual circles the car, slashing the tires. Air seeps out slowly. Bitch. I'll fix you.

-38-

Lea sits on the end of the bed wiping away tears, talking out loud to the empty hotel room.

I wanted Zion. I really did. I had dreams of us marrying, having kids. It felt so good being in his arms. Having a man make love to me and really be into making love to me.

But no. He showed me his true colors. He talked a good game. All the way into my gut. All the way into my head.

How is it fucking possible I keep letting this happen? I was up front with my wants and desires. I kept it fully one-hundred. He could have walked away at the first sign of the mention of BDSM or monogamy.

Fucking Jack-Ass.

I don't need this bull shit.

She reaches for her phone, changing Zion's contact information to her standard business contact. Looking at her emails and texts, it hits her hard that she has nothing from him.

I'm not going to chase after him. No Sir. Not going to do that. Can't make a man want me that doesn't want me. And Zion Landon does not want me.

She flops back on the bed, grabbing a pillow and screams into it.

Sex Diva is silent, unable to come up with any words to fix this.

Zion gets home and sits at his dining room table, staring at Lea's schedule.

Love her? There is no way I can love this woman. Yeah, the sex was good, but love? This ain't it.

But damn, I want her. I hate this being without Lea. After such a short time, I hate being without her. And it's all my fucking fault.

He picks up his phone to call her then puts it back down.

No, I can't say this on the phone. I can't. I want to see her. To gauge her reaction. She can easily reject me on the phone but in person. No way in hell can she reject me. I've never been vulnerable with a woman, but to get my Lea back I will do what I need to do.

He walks to his closet and takes out his tuxedo. He leaves it in the living room with a note for Mrs. Vance to have it cleaned and ready for Saturday.

Next, he calls Morgan with Lea's schedule. Hotel rooms in Chicago, Atlanta and Miami will be reserved and Landon Enterprises plane will be ready to depart.

Zion is getting his Lea back.

Love's Awakening II
-Evolving-
The continuing Story of Zion and Lea
Coming Summer 2020

On Thursday Lea is all packed and ready to go for their weekend trip to Charleston. She has never been to South Carolina. Zion says it's a weekend for them to get away, to have some dating time, getting out, and enjoying a city without worrying about attracting stalker attention. They will be traveling again with Sam and Ryan. Ryan picks her up from her house.

Geez, will I ever get to travel out of town alone with this man?

They go directly to the airport and will leave as soon as Zion arrives. He had a last-minute unexpected business meeting. Lea gives her mom a call while awaiting Zions arrival.

"What up my child?" she answers.

"I'm sitting on the plane waiting for Zion. What up with you?" Lea asks her.

"Not a gosh darn thing. Well, have fun and enjoy. Bring me back a souvenir. By the way, you still in love with him? You want to marry him? You see a future with him? Will I be referring to him as my son-in-law? Please not too soon."

"Uh okay, yes to the first three questions, and I don't have a clue to the last question. Humans are fickle and no one has control over them. But I would like for you to. Very much so," Lea admits. Zion is walking onto the plane while she is talking, looking at her and smiling. "Mom, he's here, I think we're taking off soon. I'll call you when we land."

"Okay, like I said have fun and don't worry about me, I'll be going to the movies and dinner. 'Bye my child."

Lea hangs up and stares at Zion.

"Hi Bear. Why are we leaving a day early?"

He sits down next to her and buckles in. Ryan and Sam do the same for take-off. They were scheduled to leave Friday morning.

"Some property has become available for sale on the beach. It's something I've had a realtor keeping an eye out for me. A fire destroyed two beach homes, the owners want to sell instead of re-build. I like the location and I can get them both for a good price. I need to get there as soon as I can to see them. If things work out I'll tear down the remains of both and build a new beach house with enough privacy on either side," he tells her.

"Oh okay. Are we staying in a hotel in Charleston?"

I'm getting excited about this trip.

"Nope, I currently have a house. We'll be staying there. If everything works out, I'll be putting it up for sale and getting these properties. How's your mom? Everything okay?"

"Yep, checking in."

"Lea, stop looking at me like that. I thought I was supposed to be the sex fiend in this relationship," he whispers kissing her.

"But don't you want to take me into the bedroom and ravish me?" she asks him caressing his leg. He takes a blanket and throws it over his lap hiding his erection.

"Yes, you know damned well I do."

"But."

"But I want to make you wait. I want to make you anxious. I want you soaking wet so by the time we get to Charleston you can't stand it and want to attack me. I want to have you ride me, baby. And I know you will. When you have been deprived of the opportunity," he says.

"See you wrong for that, just wrong."

I laugh 'cause he has pegged me right.

For the entire plane ride, Zion blocks her attempts at convincing him to go to the sleeping quarters. They joke and tease each other. Lea cajoles, pleads, and begs.

UGH THIS MAN, THIS MAN. HE KEEPS SAYING NO.

"You are not nice. Remember this. I'll get you back."

"Oh, I can't wait to be punished by you. Not at all," he says unfazed and with a smirk.

They arrive in South Carolina, departing the plane and taking a limo to Zion's beach house. *Hell freaking beach mansion.* Sam and Ryan leave, bidding them a good night and telling Zion they will see him Monday morning.

"Monday morning. Aren't they here to protect you? Securely, from me?" she asks him.

"No sweetheart, Sam is here to see his son, and Ryan is here to see his girlfriend. They are available if I need them but they are off duty. We're on our own. How about a late dinner and a walk?"

"Wonderful. Sounds like fun."

They dine out at the Paradise Shark Seafood restaurant. "Lea, may I ask you a question?" Zion says looking serious.

Shit scaring the hell outta me. "Sure, go ahead."

"Why haven't you had any kids?" Zion has been wondering about this since they became official. As he got to know her, it became an odd circumstance that she doesn't have any.

"I always thought there would be time. In my twenties and thirties, I was around plenty of friends having kids and all they did was complain about the fathers, never having any time to themselves, wishing they could start over. Many of them got pregnant in high school that by the age of thirty, they looked old and haggard. In my thirties, I decided it was time. I had a plan. Find a man, settle down, have a baby or two and be done with it. I failed. By then, the men my age were done having babies, the younger ones were dropping seed all over the city, and the older ones would only date women who had kids or were fixed. I thought about adoption for a hot minute then discovered I didn't want to do it alone. Eventually, I gave up the plan and accepted it was never gonna happen. The strange thing is all those friends that bitched and complained back in their twenties and thirties with multiple babies are so happy and proud of their kids now. Baby daddies or no baby daddies. Guess it wasn't meant to happen for me."

"Do you honestly think you can't conceive now, or do you think it's just too late?" he asks.

"Hhhhhmm, not too late, but a fear. I still don't want to do it alone. Who knows what kind of medical procedure I would have to go through to do it at my age. Will I have a healthy baby? I think that scares me the most. Why do you ask?"

"You are great with the girls, kids are drawn to you. I'm wondering if that is something you would miss with a future with me?"

"I accepted a long time ago it wasn't going to happen. And no I would not miss it with a future with you. Not at all. In a way, a selfish part of me doesn't want kids. I want to be the center of a man's world. I want to be his focus. At my age I was looking to be with a man whose kids were grown, with grandbabies who was done with popping out babies. Zion, if we end up married—."

He gives her a look of 'oh we gettin married'.

Scoffing at the look, Lea says, "Oh don't give me that look. If we end up married, us not having kids won't bother me, break me, or keep us from being happy. I hope you feel the same way."

"Kitten, I want to give you everything. I don't want you regretting anything about us. Ever," he says not taking his eyes off her.

"Zion, I have no regrets. The only regret I could have is not being with you anymore."

The server approaches their table with the check. Lea mouths to Zion she loves him. He winks at her and mouths "I love you" back. They leave the restaurant and go for a walk on the pier.

After the talk, sex is the last thing on Lea's desired. She wants to overthink and rehash their conversation. Zion has to take some calls from Europe and handle some business. Lea showers and climbs into bed.

He cuddles up to her smelling fresh and clean. They drift off to sleep.

The next day they meet with his realtor at the burned-out beach houses. Lea keeps quiet listening to him. He loves the location. His excitement is contagious. Lea thinks about living in a beach house with Zion loving life.

Girl you need to stop. He hasn't even proposed. You have no clue what your future is with this man. Enjoy today.

Based on the asking price for both, Zion makes a full offer for them. As stated, he will tear down both and build one, ensuring privacy. Once the new one is built, he will put the other one on the market, so he informs the realtor to be on the lookout for a buyer who is looking to purchase in the next year or so. From there, they go sightseeing and shopping. Lea doesn't see much that she wants but Zion sees plenty he wants to buy for her. Clothes, shoes, jewelry, purses. It's tough reining him in. Since they didn't have sex last night and she owes him a punishment, she takes him into a store that sells accessories. She spots the scarf rack. Looking at the scarfs, trying them on, selecting which colors are best, she settles for six silk scarves.

"Lea, that's it? Don't you want more?"

"Nope, I'm good."

He looks crestfallen.

"Okay I wasn't going to say anything, but I need a few sundresses."

He drags her off to a store and once there he has her model numerous dresses, selecting the ones he likes with little disagreement from her. When he pays for them she stands there in silence.

Shit, he spent that kinda money on me on fricking sundresses.

"No objection?" he says daring her to do just that.

"Nope, I'm not crazy."

"That's my Lea. Let's head back to the house. We're having dinner in tonight."

"Wonderful."

"Why do you say it like that?"

"Someone has a punishment coming to them, and it sure as hell ain't me."

"Uh okay, see, what happened was, I was, you know, expecting this last night, but you know we can forget about that. I mean, we don't need to punish anyone," he says, grinning and looking forward to what this woman could be coming up with.

"I don't want to hear it. Just remember, silk feels so good on a body and scarfs can be used in so many ways."

When they get back to the beach house, Lea and Zion prepare dinner. He keeps asking her what she has planned for him but she doesn't respond.

"Bear, why so many questions. Don't you trust me?"

He turns her face toward his, ensuring they are looking at each other. "Lea, all kidding aside, of course I trust you. Always and fully. But the gleam in your eyes say I'm in for a world of I don't even know the hell what, and it makes me slightly nervous."

Lea leans across the table to him. "Bear, I promise you, this will be a night you'll remember and a memory that will forever be seared deep in your memory. I promise to keep you safe, but I also promise to drive you mad with pleasure. Now, why don't you go take a shower and I'll bring you a drink. What would you like?"

"A brandy would be wonderful. You have me intrigued. Shall I meet you in the bedroom?"

"Of course."

About The Author
Kia Lui

Is a graduate of University Missouri-St. Louis and Webster University with degrees in the field of Information Technology.

Kia Lui enjoys photography and museum strolling. She started writing erotic fantasies in 1994 never thinking about writing a book. When she started writing this, her first novel, the idea was to expand on those old fantasies. What started as a small idea to generate travel money, has evolved into a book, a series, an expression of love, laughter and happiness. Her motto is, write the opposite of what is normal, typical and expected.

Kia Lui is the owner of Kia Lui Media, LLC. Currently resides in Missouri.

Made in the USA
Middletown, DE
12 November 2019